City Wolf Trilogy

City Wolf
City Wolf 2
City Wolf 3

Tressie Lockwood

Sugar and Spice Press

City Wolf Trilogy
Tressie Lockwood

Publisher:
Sugar and Spice Press
North Carolina, USA
www.sugarandspicepress.net

DEDICATION

To my readers...

City Wolf

Chapter One

Zandrea heaved another sigh and shifted her weight from one foot to the other as she ran a finger around the edge of her cash register. She scanned the cafeteria just beyond the kitchen door and noted how few customers they had tonight. A Friday night meant everyone who could get off had done so, and those like her were stuck working. Then again it was after nine. Night shift staff had come and gone long ago. She imagined that the emergency room would be jumping with activity. It always was all weekend long, like people didn't have anything better to do than to get themselves injured. If it had been her, she would have been in a club with her girlfriends by now. She blew out another breath and tried not to fall through the floor with boredom.

"Girl, you better stop that sighing and go take your break," her supervisor said as she bustled past. "It's quiet around here. When you get back, you can help Lisa in the pantry."

Zandrea's eyes widened. "Oh you're serious? Thanks! Be back soon."

Before her boss could change her mind, Zendrea closed out her register and practically ran to her locker, freshened her makeup and headed down to the emergency room, her favorite place to troll during break.

"Hmm," she mused on the way, "I should have become a nurse." At that thought, she rolled her eyes. She couldn't stand the sight of blood, probably had a phobia about it. When she saw it, even just a little, all motor function froze in her entire body. She couldn't move or speak. "Yet, I hang in ER. I have serious issues."

The moment she rounded the corner and passed through the automatic doors, chaos seemed to jump out at her. Nurses rushed to and fro, and machines in various places beeped. One of the doctors called out instructions for the patient arriving in less than two minutes with a gunshot wound to the abdomen. According to the paramedic calling in, he had lost a lot of blood, and it didn't look good.

Zandrea's heart beat kicked up a notch. She considered going back to the cafeteria with that news, but if she stayed near the grouping of desks where the staff wrote up their reports, there shouldn't be any problem. As long as she kept her eyes averted if any patients were wheeled by.

"Hey, Bev," she called as she sidled up to the older nurse she'd made friends with in order to avoid being kicked out of the area. "Things are hot tonight, huh?"

Bev frowned. "Oh, hey, Zandrea. Yes, it's a madhouse in here." She wiped a hand over her brow and clutched a clipboard in the other. "The only thing making it worthwhile this time around is our mystery man."

Zandrea's interest perked up. She leaned a hip on the end of the desk and crossed her arms, thought of the gunshot victim having fled her mind. "Mystery man? Do tell."

Bev let go of a laugh too loud given nothing was funny. "I thought that would get your interest up." She hooked a thumb over her shoulder. "Got a guy in a short bit ago. Doesn't remember what happened to him and won't give up a name. But damn if he isn't the hottest thing I've ever seen."

"Where at?" Zandrea was about to search for this Adonis, but Bev grabbed her arm. "What? I was only going to say hi," she complained.

"Yeah right. Zan, you're desperate for a man, and if I didn't say this guy was hot, you'd be trolling for the new doctor."

"New...?" Zandrea frowned, resisting the urge to scan the nearby staff. "I am not desperate for a man. I just come here for a chat once and a while, and—"

"Hello, beautiful."

She glanced up to the sexy Dr. Evans strolling by. His big brown eyes and dark brown skin made her heart skip a beat. In fact, she might need medical treatment if he continued to call her beautiful. But Dr. Evans didn't slow down. He winked and walked on. The man didn't take her seriously, and why would he? She was nothing but a cashier. Another heavy sigh escaped her.

A hand waved in front of her face. "I think I've just been proven right," Bev told her before dropping a hand on Zandrea's shoulder. "Sorry, kiddo. It'll come."

"Whatever." Zandrea spun away and marched back the way she had come. Now she was feeling like crap, and it was all Bev's fault. Sure, she had pegged Zandrea right, but damn, a girl couldn't want a man in her life for a freakin' change? It had been how long since her last boyfriend—a year and a half? She had needs, and her girlfriends were great, but she couldn't curl up with them at night. Besides, she knew for a fact that both her best friends felt exactly the same way.

Zandrea's mind was so focused on her silent justification for being man crazy that she didn't at first see the man lurking around the corner she turned. Instead, she barreled right into him, and sent them both to the floor. His grunt of obvious pain made her rush to apologize.

"I am so sorry. I didn't see you there." From her position of being splayed out on top of him, Zandrea glanced up into electric green eyes. Or were they fevered? Either way, the man was hot. Really hot. She scrambled to get off of him. "You're burning up. Are you okay? Let me help you."

"Nurse," he muttered while he submitted to her assistance to stand, although she felt weak herself at the tight muscle beneath her hand on his arm. She was in no rush to correct his assumption that she was a nurse.

Now that they were standing, she realized he stretched a good head taller than she was, and with him looking down at her, his blond locks tumbled over onto his forehead, blocking one eye. She resisted reaching up to brush it back.

That quick the atmosphere changed. Instead of the man being apologetic, without making a move, he seemed about to attack. She couldn't put her finger on why she felt that way, but Zandrea tried to step back from him. One of his hands settled on her hip, and he drew her closer. His lips parted, and she could have sworn she saw his canine teeth lengthening and the rest of his teeth becoming sharper. *What the hell?*

"Food," he muttered.

"Wha-?" She blinked and shook her head. Maybe she hadn't heard right.

He lowered his head and gently thumped her chin higher with his nose. His deep inhale of her scent took the strength from her legs. She would have crumpled to the floor, but he held her in place.

"I smell food on you," he told her.

Can he be anymore unsexy with that statement? she complained silently. "I think you need treatment. Let me go get someone to help you." He didn't let go, and Zandrea was torn between wanting to run and wanting to just remain wedged against his hard body. She went with her usual boldness. "What's your name?"

He leaned up from her neck and snapped his lips together. This must be the patient who wouldn't admit who he was or what happened to him that Bev had been talking about. Zandrea was about to ask him, when she saw it. Blood. Seeping through the white shirt he wore. On some level, she wondered where he had gotten the clothing and why he wasn't in the unfashionable hospital gown, but she stood quietly in his arms.

The man tipped her chin up. "I have to go. Don't tell."

Zandrea didn't respond.

"Are you okay?" He glanced down at his shoulder. "Damn! Don't worry. I'll heal. Hey, did you hear me?"

His voice came from far away now.

He pressed his mouth against her ear. "You're afraid of the blood. Don't be. I guess it's natural for me. I'm used to it. I have to go. Don't fall."

From the corner of her eyes, Zandrea spotted another man, this one all in black. His hair and even his eyes were dark. His eyebrows were low over his eyes, and his jaw was set in an angry expression. "We have to go," he commanded.

The mystery patient propped Zandrea against the wall, began to walk away and then came back. He caught her under the chin a second time and then kissed her full on the lips. As he and his friend disappeared out an emergency exit, setting off the alarm, Zandrea's one thought was why did her first kiss from a white man, which she'd fantasized about in secret, come when she couldn't even kiss him back.

Chapter Two

"Girl, are you serious?" Nita shrieked.

Zandrea nodded and bit into her apple, savoring the delicious sweetness. "Yes, I lie not. He was so fine—*weird*—but fine. He was losing a lot of blood, and I wouldn't be surprised if Bev doesn't tell me he was brought back in either dead or close to it."

"Try not to be so flip about it," Stacy told her irritably. "Besides, you were no help to the poor man with your phobia."

Zandrea rolled her eyes. "I can't help it. If I could have I would. And on top of that he kissed me." She sighed, her vision blurring with the memory. "I didn't enjoy it like I wanted to because I was so scared. Then again, I'm not sure what he was."

Stacy stood up and peeled off her dress for the fourth time. She hadn't yet decided on what to wear to the club that night. Zandrea had a habit of mentally choosing what she would wear, and Nita couldn't care less as long as it was comfortable. They always ended up waiting for at least an hour for Stacy.

"What do you mean by '*what* he was'?" Stacy questioned her.

A chill ran down Zandrea's back, and along her arms goose bumps popped out. "He said he was used to blood, that it was natural for him. What the hell could that mean?"

"Maybe he's a vampire," Nita suggested.

Zandrea rolled her eyes. She stood, marched over to Stacy's bed and twitched a skimpy aqua green mini-dress from the pile of clothing. Stacy had the best body of the three of them, and she might as well show it off. Zandrea pressed the garment into her friend's hands. "Here, wear this, and let's get out of here. I have a desire to shake my ass on the dance floor so I can forget my troubles."

Stacy smiled her thanks and slipped the dress on. While she sat applying her makeup, Zandrea arranged her hair. Stacy's thick long hair that extended down her back was another feature Zandrea admired. She kept her own hair cut short in a simple style that complimented her face. She'd been told her rich cocoa brown skin tone looked great with her large brown eyes. While she knew she wasn't ugly, she didn't think she was all that either. If she looked like Stacy, the men would be crawling over each other to get to her. Then again, Stacy wasn't beating them off. Not one of them had luck with the opposite sex lately.

"So, Stacy." Nita interrupted Zandrea's thoughts. "Did you meet anybody interesting on the road today?"

Stacy grunted. "Nope, I only drove with Kevin down to Norfolk, and the customer was this old guy, but he did grab my butt on the way out the door. I resisted slapping him, and that dumbass Kevin made fun of me the whole way back."

Zandrea laughed. No matter how many times Stacy dropped off or picked up a car in her job of working for Circle Rent a Car, she did not meet any available and interesting men. Yet, Stacy never gave up hope. Zandrea thought the girl should open her eyes to how much her co-worker, Kevin, liked her. If she dated him, at least she could get some, unlike Zandrea and Nita.

"Did you kick his ass?" Nita asked.

Both Zandrea and Stacy stared at Nita in the mirror above Stacy's bedroom dresser and then burst out laughing. After clutching her stomach on the floor for a while, Zandrea fought to catch her breath.

"Oh no she didn't just say that." She glanced at Nita again. Nita's face, which they called 'high-yella' was almost beet red. Zandrea jumped to her feet and pulled her friend into a hug. "Aw, sorry, girl. You know you don't speak that way. It just sounds funny when you try to get all ghetto on us."

"Yeah," Stacy echoed. She stood up. "Okay, girls, I'm ready to go shake my thing on the dance floor."

* * * *

Half hour later, they pulled up to their favorite club in Nita's smokin' red Shelby GT500. Zandrea had to struggle to unfurl her legs without showing the long line of club goers at the front door all her goods because her short skirt rode up. Nita tossed the car keys to a valet, and the three of them strolled toward the front of the line.

Zandrea hooked her arm through Nita's, and Stacy took the other one.

"It's so great to have a friend with family connections, huh, Stacy?" Zandrea asked.

"You know it." Before they reached the front of the line, Stacy pulled them to a stop. "Hey, y'all, look at that." She nodded toward the corner of the building where a sexy man in black slacks, covering an ass that should be illegal, was escorting a woman around the corner.

They sighed in unison, knowing what was about to happen. With unspoken agreement, they followed the couple into the alley. There was lots of sex going on inside the club these days. Everyone knew that, but sometimes, people liked to really be dirty about it, like fucking outside.

Zandrea shuffled along the best she could in her high heels so close to Nita while trying to move in silence. Not too far down the narrow opening, they found the couple engrossed in each other to the point that they were attempting to swallow each other's tongues. Zandrea and her friends watched.

Nita speculated, "Do you two think we don't get any because we're too immature for our age?"

"Too wild," Zandrea piped up.

"Too stupid," Stacy concluded. "We always run behind these guys who either already have a woman they're devoted to or—"

"We won't be home wreckers even if they aren't married," Zandrea interjected.

"—or we try for men who are too far out of our league. Well out of Zandrea and my league. Everybody can't live off a trust fund like you, Nita. I remember that guy I went after in Jersey."

"You mean the one with the Porshe? Girl, you know damn well you wasn't getting any of that." Zandrea shook her head. "The problem is that we can't find the right combination."

They all commiserated as the couple finished up. With no shame, Zandrea and her friends stayed where they were as the two people moved by. Zandrea had the nerve to toss the guy a look of approval. He winked and wrapped an arm around his girlfriend's waist before they disappeared back around front.

Zandrea sighed. "To find a guy like we like, who is hot, not a loser and doesn't mind a little too much junk in the trunk..."

Nita winced. "Give me a break, Zan. Your butt isn't that big. You shouldn't put yourself down."

Zandrea rolled her eyes and slapped her ass. It jiggled, and she gritted her teeth. "Whatever."

They headed back around front and were soon in the midst of the pounding beat of the music. Near the door, they paused to take in the scene. Zandrea was satisfied to note that there were plenty of people packing the small club, and there was a nice range of social statuses so she didn't feel like she was in the midst of people with money and didn't fit in. That's what she liked about the club. It was higher class but not so high that it was exclusive.

With two dances down and a drink in her hand, Zandrea was able to breathe out the stresses of the week and just relax. With an elbow on the bar behind her and her friends lost in discussion about which guy looked approachable, Zandrea scanned the dim interior of the club. Just because of her experience the night before, she was starkly aware of all the good-looking white men. In fact, the group to the right of where she and her friends were standing looked especially fine. They were all in dark slacks and white or light colored collared shirts. Stretching at least a half head taller than every man in the place and with well-toned muscled bodies to match, they stood out from everyone else.

Zandrea drifted a few steps in the men's direction, a feeling a familiarity coming over her at the closest man with his back to her. She leaned out a little to her left trying to see his face and hoping no one would notice. The guys threw their heads back and laughed at something funny one of them had said. Zandrea caught her breath.

She backpedaled to her friends, hooked their arms and dragged them along in the opposite direction. When they had almost completely circled the place, Zandrea bothered to respond to her friends' continued complaints of being dragged around.

"Girls, over there." Zandrea nodded with her head. Stacy and Nita turned in the direction that Zandrea pointed. "That guy, the one on the right end facing the others. The blond. See him?"

Stacy let out a low moan. "Yummy. They're all hot. Didn't know you wanted a white boy though, Zan. Guess after last night though, who could blame you. You've chosen the blond?"

Zandrea shook her head. "No, that's *him*!"

Nita frowned. "Him who?"

"The guy from the hospital. The guy who was bleeding all over himself. The blond is him!"

Chapter Three

"Don't look now, Brant, but you've got three pairs of sexy chocolate eyes all over you," Lucas quipped.

Brant turned, ignoring the warning. He spotted the three women in the corner right away. All three lovely faces were frozen in shock, mouths hanging open and eyes wide. When they caught him looking, they grabbed each other and spun away, whispering furiously.

He had a hard time filtering out the noise around him to pinpoint what the ladies were saying, but he did catch one sentence from the biggest, sweetest eyes he'd ever seen. His groin tightening and his attention arrested by the curve of her ass facing him, he almost didn't process what he had heard. Then it hit him. *"I'm not mistaken. That is the guy I met at the hospital, and he was for damn sure bleeding too much to be here tonight!"*

"Fuck!" He grunted.

His brother sidled up close to him. "So, I didn't get there in time."

Brant frowned. "It's not like she was the only one who saw me. There was the whole staff too. I wouldn't let them look at the wound. Only the paramedics saw how bad it was, and you took care of them."

Lucas nodded. "I did, which was why I was late getting to you. They won't remember a thing, and like you said the other staff didn't get a close look at the wound. That girl could be a problem." Brant's half brother rotated his shoulders and flicked another button on his shirt open. He glanced back to one of the other men and snapped his fingers. "Brant, dance with her, see what she remembers. If she remembers too much, take her and bring her to my place later. I'll straighten it out. I'll take the studious one, and Nash can take the other one."

Brant fought not to grind his teeth. He hated when Lucas got it into his head like he was the leader of their little group. They didn't run in packs, damn it, and he didn't need his half brother who was the same age as he was bossing him around. Yet he did see the wisdom in following Lucas' plan. To deny it was pointless. They were always careful to cover what they were from those on the outside. There was no other choice but to find out what the women knew and to erase their memory of any events that would threaten the secret of the city wolves' existence.

"Fine," he conceded. "I'll dance with her."

Brant took a deep breath and strolled over to the ladies. He planted himself in front of the woman who had crashed into him at the hospital, knowing he stood too close, but liking the way she smelled and the fear and excitement mingled in her eyes when she looked up at him.

"Dance with me," he commanded.

Her lips parted. Brant had been feverish from loss of so much blood, but he remembered the taste of those lips. He wanted to taste them again and crush her body to his. The short skirt she wore coupled with the high heels made her legs seem to go on forever, and her blouse was cut so low, it was indecent. Did she want a date or to give it up to whomever asked? No, there was still innocence in those eyes of hers, and she looked like she was no older than twenty-two or twenty-three.

Brant turned, placed a hand at her waist and guided her to the dance floor. As if on cue, the music slowed, and he swayed with her, never taking his eyes off her face. "What's your name?" he asked.

"Zandrea." Her voice came out in a breathy whisper, and Brant grinned.

"Nice." He lowered his head enough to make her think he would kiss her, and then he drew back. The disappointment in her expression pleased him. "So, you think you know me?"

She frowned, pulled back a little from him. He ignored the sense of loss and waited for her to speak.

"I don't think I know you. I saw you at the hospital last night. I'm sure of it, and I know you couldn't have come in here without a medical miracle or something, because the blood that stained your shirt was—"

She swayed. He caught her close to his chest and waited. A memory came back to him, of how she had gone still, neither speaking nor seeming to know what was going on around her. This reaction was different, but he knew she was remembering the sight of his blood. He'd met one or two people like her in his long life, those that had an excessive fear of blood. If she only knew the truth, that he hunted with his brother and their friends who were also wolf shape shifter. They didn't do it often, preferring a more civilized lifestyle, but it could get bloody upon occasion. Someone like Zandrea wouldn't be able to stand it.

That his brother would have to wipe Brant's memory from this little beauty's mind didn't sit right with him. He considered lying, but didn't dare. Their family was more important than getting into her panties. And boy did he ever want to get a taste of her. Some of the other wolves ached for a mate, but Brant liked his freedom. All he had ever wanted was a woman to share his bed and to move on when it got boring. A woman's scent was what attracted him first. Of course that was only natural given what he was. So, it must be his imagination that he craved more than to just be intimate with her.

"You're mistaken," he said after realizing he had let his mind wonder without responding to her. "I've never seen you before. I would remember such sweetness."

Her eyelids lowered. She rested her soft breasts against his chest, and he grew hard. The small gasp escaping her lips let him know she had felt it. No matter. There wasn't a reason to hide how attracted he was to her.

"Have you ever been with a white man?" he asked boldly.

She rolled her eyes. "So you've got a fantasy, huh? Of checking out the other side, see what it's like? It's not like I haven't met your kind before. Although I don't normally indulge those kind of fantasies."

"Oh?" He smirked. "And here I was drawing the conclusion that you shared my fantasies by how hard your nipples have gone and how you're panting. I had the impression that you wanted me like I want you."

She tried pulling away from him, but he held on.

"Don't deny us both pleasure." He knew his words sounded like a command. He hadn't meant them to come out like that.

"You're used to bossing people around aren't you?" she demanded. "What do you snap your fingers and women just fall in your lap, eager to please you? Sorry, I'm not the one. There are plenty of girls in here willing and able. I don't jump into bed with any man I first meet. And you haven't even told me your name."

She broke from his hold at last and spun away to stomp off the dance floor. Brant darted forward, caught her arm and swung her around to face him. With little effort, he bent her body over his arm and pressed tight against her. Even with all the noise around them, he didn't miss her moan of pleasure.

Brant pulled her tighter still and pressed his lips to her ear. "My name is Brant, and if you don't want to jump in my bed right away, how about going out on a date with me?"

Her expression was one of shock at his boldness. "You're not even going to deny that you only want to sleep with me."

He shrugged. "Why lie? I'm not looking for a girlfriend or a potential mate. I want to lie between soft legs, to please as I am pleased. Does that not interest you at all? You're not attracted to me?"

"Being attracted to someone is not all there is to a relationship."

When he had them moving again, still at a slow rock despite the fast beat of the music, she didn't complain. Brant was enjoying the feel of her body on his. "As I said, I'm not looking for a relationship. In fact, since you don't want to go back to my place now, then I'm not sure we will eventually be lovers."

She blinked up at him. "What's the rush?"

He waved a hand. "Never mind that. Do you want to leave here and let me buy you dinner? I promise I won't try to seduce you."

"Yes, you will."

He chuckled. "Okay, I will try, but I would never force a woman. I don't need to." Brant let his hand around her waist slide lower until he cupped her ass. He waited for her to push him away, but she didn't. She tilted her head back boldly and stared into his eyes. For a second, he lost focus, drowned in her sweetness. It took some effort to gather control of his emotions, and he blinked a few times to break whatever spell she had attempted to weave around him.

He glared down at her innocent face, wondering if there was more to Ms. Zandrea, but she seemed open enough. Besides, he could sense and even pick up the unusual scent of those who were not fully human, whatever they were. Zandrea had no special ability. She was an ordinary woman. Still, there was something about her that drew him.

In the emergency room, he had been half out of his mind for a while when his fever had reached a certain level. He had thought only of escape, and then he had bumped into Zandrea. The sensation was of... Well, he wasn't going to think too hard on it. She was a woman, and the same with all of his kind, women were a weakness.

Zandrea was just like every other woman, and there were a hundred more who could share his bed since she had denied him that much. After Lucas erased him from her memory, Brant would find one of those women and take her back to his place. He would spend the rest of the evening working out his sexual frustrations.

"Okay, Brant." She grinned at him. A flutter tickled the inside of his chest. He ignored it.

He raised his eyebrows in question.

"Okay, we can get a cup of coffee or something. I've eaten for the night."

Brant didn't even bother informing Lucas of where he was going. They knew the drill. Besides, Lucas had said for Brant to bring her to his place later tonight. He must have figured Brant would get Zandrea into his bed, and his brother never brought women home. It was either the woman's place or a motel or wherever. In fact, Lucas had happily fucked a woman in the alley earlier and been fine with it. If he knew his brother, Brant figured Lucas would now take one of Zandrea's friends and get her as well. His brother's appetite was insatiable.

Just the thought of all the sex took Brant's strength. While he guided Zandrea out of the building, he took another look at her cleavage and licked his lips. She might not sleep with him, but he was going to taste and feel those beautiful mounds if it killed him.

Chapter Four

Zandrea figured she should tell her friends that she was leaving and with who. They liked to be safe. Stacy had gone so far as to demand a man show her his ID so she could write down his name and address should anything happen, and they had always complied. Somehow, Zandrea didn't want to go find them. She wanted to escape the noise and find somewhere to chat with Brant. A text to Nita and Stacy should be enough.

When Brant led her by the elbow through the crowd and out the door, she wasn't surprised to find he drove a sporty car that looked more expensive than Nita's, but she wasn't that into cars to know what it was. The vehicle was sleek and built low to the ground. Only a two-seater, the black body shimmered despite the dark night. Thick tires with deep treads looked ready to tear up the road, and Zandrea shivered. She'd bet anything, Brant had a heavy foot and would care nothing about doing ninety or more on the road.

He helped her inside and they were soon off. Brant's hands gripped the steering wheel with almost a reverence. Zandrea rolled her eyes. "So where are we going?" she asked him.

"Coffee shop. You said you weren't hungry."

She glanced out the window. "There are like five coffee shops within a block or two of the club."

He laughed. "Where's the fun in that? Let's open it up and stop where the mood strikes."

"You mean after you've worn the tread off your tires." She crossed her arms. "Are you kidnapping me, because I'm going to tell you right now, Nita's people are connected. They can find anyone, anywhere, and they have the money to make anything happen."

"Is that right?" He had the nerve to wink at her, and when he placed his hand on the handle between them to shift gears, Zandrea caught her breath. For some odd reason, she had been thinking of him reaching across to rest that hand between her legs. She shook the thought away. No way in hell was she letting this stranger get between her legs. Not on the first night at least.

Then again, technically, this was the second night.

"What's going on in that head of yours?" He asked the question but seemed to know the answer already. Zandrea resisted slapping the knowing look off his face.

"I just remembered what we were discussing earlier. You are the man from the hospital last night. You tried to blow me off, but I'm not stupid, and I would never forget a face like yours."

"I'll take that as a compliment. Thanks."

"And!" She almost shouted to hide the fact that it *was* a compliment. "I want the truth. What happened? You were bleeding bad. I've spent enough time in the emergency room and talking to nurses that I know what's life-threatening."

"Which proves my theory."

She gritted her teeth. The man was infuriating. "What theory?"

"That you're not a nurse as I thought at first when I was feverish."

"So you admit it!"

He shifted gears, pressed harder on the gas and took a ramp to the highway. Soon they were flying along to God knows where. Despite that, Zandrea wasn't afraid. She wondered if it was her intense attraction to the man, but didn't really feel like analyzing it. Just for tonight, she wanted to enjoy it. Men didn't hang around long in her life, and it had been awhile. She could pretend a man as obviously established and hot as Brant was, was into her for the time being.

He had paused at her declaration and seemed to be considering what to admit to her. At last, he nodded his head and reached out to caress her cheek. "Yes, it was me. I heal quickly. There wasn't really any threat to my life, just to my secret, and that cannot be tolerated under any circumstances."

Zandrea stilled. His secret. She wanted to ask him more about that, but courage failed her. She should tell him to let her out of the car, admit that he was out of her league and go back to the club. Her life wasn't so bad. After all, a little action with her vibrator did the trick more often than not.

A glance at his powerful arm muscles flexing while he gripped the steering wheel, the matching sculpted thigh muscles filling his pants oh so right, not to mention the bulging package between his legs, made her sigh. No way a vibrator could replace that. And conversation wasn't anything to discount either. Damn it all, she was lonely for male companionship!

Brant seemed to pick up on her fear of pursuing his secret and continued on. "I suspected you were not a nurse by your scent."

She grumbled. "Oh yeah, the most unromantic thing a man could say to a woman. You smell like chicken."

He burst out laughing. "I didn't say that."

"You might as well have."

He grinned at her, flashing beautiful white teeth that had probably never needed braces. In her mouth, she ran her tongue along a tooth that was slightly crooked. She'd never minded the imperfection and she didn't now. Just looking at Brant was pleasure. He winked, the second time seeming to know her thoughts. It could be her imagination.

"I thought you must work around a lot of food. That coupled with the fact that you are terrified of blood means there's no way you can be a nurse." He cast her a look of curiosity. "So why would a woman with such a problem hang out in the ER?"

"None of your business." She glanced away from his smirking face to the area where he was slowing down. He had exited the highway in a more middle class area. Zandrea blinked. Not quite what she had in mind, she thought as she surveyed the townhouses they passed, more like humble, simple, not the playboy with money Brant seemed to be. "Where are we?"

"Near my favorite coffeehouse."

"Huh? Are you nuts? This area looks to be all residential. There's no way there's a coffeehouse around here. Besides, a man like you wouldn't hang out in this area unless he had to."

She turned to face him in time to see his eyes darken, and she pressed herself back against the car door, a tremor going through her body. Had she thought he was harmless before, she was mistaken. There was more to Brant than he let on.

Almost immediately, the darkness lifted, and he replaced it with an easygoing smile. "There's more to me than you think," he said, echoing her thoughts. "Come and see."

He parked in front of one of the houses and stepped around to help her out of the car. At the top of the marble steps, he rang the bell, and Zandrea hugged herself against the sudden night chill. This was a mistake. She just knew it.

The door opened, and a woman who looked like the mirror image of Brant stood there, except she must be a good twenty years older. "Brant! My baby!" The woman threw her arms around his shoulders and dragged him into the house.

Zandrea followed slowly, looking over her shoulder and longing for a way to escape. She fingered the side of her purse knowing her cell phone was just inside.

The woman caught sight of Zandrea and sniffed the air. Zandrea stared at her. What was with these people and their sense of smell?

"Who is this, Brant?" The woman's tone held definite disapproval.

Brant wrapped an arm around Zandrea's waist like they hadn't just met. "This is Zandrea. I brought her for coffee."

"She's hu—"

"Mother!"

Zandrea wondered what the woman was about to say before Brant cut her off. "How do you do?" Zandrea nodded, keeping her cool. She was going to beat Brant's ass for bringing her to his mother's house on the first freakin' date. What was he thinking?

A look that must have spoke volumes passed between mother and son, but neither bothered to explain anything to Zandrea. Glory, which is what Brant's mother had insisted she be called, led them to the back of the house and to some stairs leading down. Zandrea clutched Brant's arm as they descended as it was dark as anything. She couldn't believe she was falling in line with this craziness. They might both be insane, and here she was following behind Brant.

They came out in a hall that was longer than it should have been. By her estimate, it had to extend out into the street above. Doors lined both sides and a soft light hung overhead. At the end of the hall, someone opened a door, and music spilled out. Brant led her toward it. The man they passed had eyes so black they seemed to draw Zandrea in. He stared at her and licked his lips. The desire she saw there was palpable, and she let out a little shriek of alarm when Brant growled at him.

What the hell?

Her cell buzzed in her pocket. From the rhythm, she knew it was a text. She pulled it out, but before she could key a reply to Stacy's message, Brant took it from her hand. "You're with me tonight. We will enjoy all night together, and then I will return you. Agreed?"

No! her mind screamed. She nodded. "Yes."

Chapter Five

Brant smelled her fear. Yet mingled with it was excitement. With every step they took into the unknown, she seemed to like it. He had asked her about why she went to the ER, but he could guess. In some ways, Zandrea liked danger. But maybe she hadn't realized it yet. Brant had always thought he lived a quiet life, nothing out of the ordinary, well for a wolf shifter that is. His routine was just that, same old thing each day. Occasionally, things got dangerous as they had the night before, but like always, Lucas was there or one of the others if he needed assistance, and he offered the same to his kinsmen. For the most part, he handled things on his own. Not until he met Zandrea did he realize he was looking for something, too. And if they could only have until Lucas called with a demand that Brant bring her to his house for the good of them all, then Brant would enjoy his time with her.

He had made the decision the second he stepped into his car with Zandrca at his side. He would tell her the whole truth, about what he was. That truth started with the pub his mother ran beneath her house, the place she had refused to give up after she had remarried after finding out about Lucas' birth. Nothing he could do about that, and it had turned out fine anyway given she had divorced only two years later. At least there was only their kind in the community.

Brant swung the door wide to the pub, and while the noise of the music didn't lessen, all conversation halted, and every pair of eyes swung in their direction. The patrons picked up on Zandrea's human scent. She would smell sweet too, a woman, sexually ready for a man. Every male would feel a hunger to taste her. His kind had healthy appetites, and he was no different.

With deliberate care, Brant tugged Zandrea to his side and lowered his mouth to her exposed shoulder. He let them all watch while he sank his canines into her tender skin in the smallest of bites. He licked the small trickle of blood, enjoying her taste.

Zandrea squirmed in his hold, but Brant hung on. When he raised his head, he met his fellow wolves' eyes sending the message he knew they had already gotten. Anyone daring to touch her would deal with him. For tonight. After Lucas erased her memory, he would have no claim over her, at least not for human men. His mark would remain so that the wolf shifters would know she wasn't available to either seduction or attack.

Brant waited for regret to wash over him for his rash behavior. No other woman, shifter or human, had made him want to mark her as his own, and he had done so to Zandrea without thinking, without considering it. Yet, if he had it to do again, he would. *Mine.*

He shuddered at the intensity of his feelings. This was crazy. She would be snatched away soon. No, he needed to focus on having fun for the moment. It would start with a beer or two.

Brant led Zandrea to the bar and took a stool. She set her hands on her hips and glared at him. "You said you were taking me to a coffeehouse. This looks like a place where they sell bootleg liquor."

Brant burst out laughing. "Bootleg? I haven't heard that word in many years. Don't worry. They sell coffee here too, and it's good."

She frowned. "Whatever. I'll take a beer, I guess." She shifted on her stool and glanced around. "This place is bigger than you would think from the layout of the first floor. Does it extend to the street?"

Brant nodded. "Our little secret. Besides, we own all of this land, so we can do just about anything we want here."

"We?"

"My kind."

She gave him a questioning look, but Brant didn't address what he meant. There was plenty time for that. Allowing her a few sips of her beer, he then hoisted her to her feet and tugged her to the small dance space in the middle of the floor. The music slowed, and Brant took Zandrea into his arms. He rested a palm on each of her ass cheeks and tugged her closer.

With her arms around his neck, and no space between their bodies, they rocked side to side in slow motion. Brant's desires ignited. His shaft grew rock hard, and all he wanted to do was seat it inside Zandrea until the desperate need eased.

He found the place where he had nipped her and he gently licked it for a while. He fought the desire to tear off her clothes and explore farther.

"You bit me," she accused him.

"I had to mark you or I would have been fighting over you all night rather than doing this." He pushed into her hips and was gratified to hear her moan. "Tell me this isn't better."

She gasped. "I'm just horny. There's nothing special about you."

"Really?" He kissed her neck, turned her head and then kissed her lips. They parted without hesitation, and he pushed his tongue into the warmth of her mouth. When he deepened the kiss, lifted her higher against his erection and didn't stop for a good ten minutes, she didn't fight him once. "Nothing special? I'm a strange man. I zipped you away from the safety of your friends. I took your cell phone and brought you to a dangerous place like this. You haven't put up a real complaint yet."

Her gaze dropped to the floor. He felt her tremor and hated himself for making her feel that way.

"I'm sorry," he whispered in her ear.

"No, you're right. I..." She shook her head. Now, Brant regretted reminding her how she had gone trustingly with him. While he didn't think of himself as a bad person, seducing a woman who might not want to sleep with him on a first date was not a good thing. He couldn't regret his actions or her trusting him. Selfish, sure, but so be it.

"Come," he told her. "I'll take you back to the club."

She seemed about to protest, but said nothing. The loneliness Brant had dealt with over the last few years—even when he had several lovers at once—descended on him. She couldn't be his lover.

Outside in the fresh air, she took in several breaths. Brant leaned against his car, arms folded, and watched the rise and fall of her breasts. Her nipples were clearly defined through the thin material, and he craved a stroke or a lick.

"You make me reckless," she said simply.

He put his head back and stared at the stars. "Truth be told, you make me feel the same."

"How so?"

Looking into her eyes, he was lost. "I want to tell you everything. I want to tell you why I had that gash in my shoulder and why if you looked now you'd find no trace of it."

Her eyes went wide and lowered to his left shoulder. With trembling hands, she unbuttoned his shirt and pushed the material aside. Brant bit down on his lip and clenched his fists at his sides to keep from taking her into his arms. Her mouth fell open, and she ran her fingertips along his skin.

"It's like brand new skin. Never been cut, never scarred. Was it a trick of my imagination? No one could..."

"I could and so can every person like me."

"Like you?"

"Wolf shifters."

They stood there looking into each other's eyes. Brant couldn't read her mind, but he was excellent at reading emotion from scent and instinct. Even without that ability, he could guess what was running through her mind—should she run or stay?

He turned one hand out, palm facing her. "Stay."

She laced her fingers with his and leaned into him, resting her head on his shoulder. "I think that you wouldn't tell me this if something wasn't going to happen later to undo it. You said your secret was most important to protect. Will you kill me later?"

"You're so calm."

He felt her smile into his shirt. "I might be in shock."

"In that case let me into your panties."

"You're an asshole."

He tangled his fingers into her hair and tugged just enough to get her to put her head back, and he covered her mouth with his. With hungry kisses, he tasted her, trailing down her cheek to her jaw, up to her eyelids, her forehead, her temple.

Having slipped a hand beneath her blouse, he unhooked her bra and peeled it off. She let him remove it, and he tossed it on the hood of his car. Sliding one hand around to cup her breast, he ran the other along her hip to the hem of her skirt and then up to take hold of her panties.

"Brant!" she gasped. "You're not going to do it here!"

"Didn't you enjoy watching Lucas fuck that woman in the alley? He said you gave him a look of approval. I assume you wanted to try public sex."

"I...well...I'm not sure." She pulled back out of his arms. "Definitely not in front of your mother's house. Are you nuts?"

He grinned and re-crossed his arms over his chest. "Trust me, my mother's done that and more in her time. Right now she's got three lovers."

The interest he'd seen in Zandrea's eyes faded. "So you're not faithful. How many do you have?"

"None at the moment."

"And if I were to become your lover?" She had turned away, but with those words, she turned back, pinning him in place with a stare. He didn't want to hurt her, but she should know what she was getting into if she was to let him into her life. He'd forgotten. This was a one night only deal.

"There are those of us who choose a lifetime mate. In some ways we're like a regular wolf. However, we do not run in packs unless we choose to or if it's convenient for a time. Few choose a lifetime mate, and most choose several lovers. Because humans can be picky about that kind of thing, we normally stick with our own kind. A female shifter often has as many lovers as a male one. That's who we are."

She sighed, closing her eyes. "I understand." She shook her head. "Listen to me saying I understand about you being a shifter. It's crazy. Either way, you're not the faithful type which is what it boils down to. Well, I guess you had better take me back to the club. No, just take me home."

Brant would be lying if he said he wasn't disappointed. He was not usually picky about women who shared his bed. If she was attractive to him, that was fine. He had reserved meaningful conversation for his friends and Lucas. Yet, lately he was always lonely whether with the guys, with a woman or alone. Zandrea was the first to give him a spark of interest, although he couldn't figure out why. It wasn't like they had discussed Einstein's theories or anything else half way serious.

With resolve, he grabbed her bra from the hood of the car, handed it to her and opened the car door for her. He guided her inside with a hand at her hip, his shaft twitching at the contact. Sex. It was just about the sex, and if that was the case, any woman would do.

Chapter Six

Zandrea rested with her head turned away from Brant and her eyes closed. She had slipped off her heels and curled her legs up against her chest. The move had forced her skirt higher, revealing too much of her legs and probably her ass, but she was battling throwing herself on Brant's lap and begging him to let her ride.

She couldn't give into wanting him. That had been her mistake time and again and the cause of heartbreak after heartbreak. Stacy could fuck a man and not lose her heart, but not Zandrea. No, she had to choose a loser who had no intention of caring for her beyond getting her in bed a few times and then giving her some lame excuse why it wouldn't work out between them.

With her hand blocking most of her face, she peeked out between her fingers at Brant. He was drop dead hot. All the men she'd gone out with had been average, in looks and in the wallet. Here she was for the first time with a man she'd bet anything had washboard abs and not an ounce of excess flesh on his entire body. From his car, clothes and even his friends, she knew he had money. That stuff on the whole wasn't a big deal to her, but to have the experience would have been nice.

At least he had been upfront from the beginning so she could make the right decision. And she had made the right decision, hadn't she?

When the car swerved enough to jostle her from her thoughts, she glanced up. "Hey, this isn't the way back to the club. You're doing it again. Hijacking me."

"Kidnap?" He grinned.

She rolled her eyes. "You know what I mean. Where are we going now?"

His lips tightened for a second, and his knuckles turned white while he gripped the steering wheel. "You were right. I cannot let you continue to know about us after tonight."

She let out a small scream. "No, please, Brant. Don't kill me." Searching through her purse for the small bottle of iodine she kept there, she figured she would throw it in his face and jump out of the car.

He reached across and stilled her hands with his. "I'm not. I promise. You'll just forget you ever met me, everything I ever said or showed you."

"How?"

"Don't worry." He squeezed her fingers. "I won't let Lucas hurt you. He wouldn't anyway. That's not what we do. We like to live peacefully among humans, and killing one would not allow that to continue."

Zandrea sat there for a while in silence, wondering if she should believe anything he had said that night. There was no proof beyond the injury, and that didn't mean anything either. She could have mistaken the patient from the night before, and maybe Brant was just having fun at her expense.

"I want to see you change into a wolf."

His eyes widened. "What?"

"Show me. Prove to me that you haven't been lying all this time, just making fun of me."

He frowned. "I can't very well do it while I'm driving. Besides, we're not allowed to let a human see us change."

"I'm sure you've broken all kinds of rules by telling me all you did tonight. All those people back at that bar saw me. They knew what I was like you said by my scent, so they know what you were up to."

"It's not uncommon for a shifter to enjoy playing with a human, especially the females. You're so soft, and your smell is intoxicating." He glanced at her, his gaze dropping to her breasts. She'd forgotten that she hadn't put her bra back on, and her nipples were hard, pushing against her blouse. Yet, she made no move to cover up. He licked his lips. "You saw the reaction of the men back there. You were so wet, they smelled it and wanted you."

She gulped. "You're kidding. They *smelled* it?"

He nodded. "Your sweet cream. It is sweet, isn't it?"

She squeezed her legs together. "Shut up."

His laugh at her expense irritated her. She didn't want him to know how his words turned her on all the more. *Resist, damn it! He's not all that!* She could yell at herself all she wanted, but the truth of the matter was, if he pushed even a little, she would give into him. And tomorrow, she would wake up full of regrets. Then again, he'd said Lucas would erase her memory. That was terrifying. To have slept with the hottest man on the planet and not remember it. But just for that time, she would enjoy every second. Should she risk it?

"This is all so ridiculous. I mean. I'm not too scared of you. I'm a little terrified of Lucas, but you. No."

"It's because you're turned on. It's overridden your fear of me."

She laughed. "Whatever. And if we slept together..."

"It would be wonderful. I would ensure that we both enjoyed ourselves to the fullest. Later, when Lucas does his thing, you won't remember what we did and would be free to go on like nothing ever happened."

Brant pulled up in front of a house so big, Zandrea thought it was safe to term it a mansion. The driveway alone was impressive, curving along a tree-lined road and opening out into a patch of grass with an elaborate fountain in front. The two story stone exterior of the house looked well-maintained, and the grounds beside and behind the house must go on for acres.

Zandrea stepped out of the car with her mouth hanging open. "Damn! What does Lucas do for a living?"

"Investments," Brant said simply. "I do as well."

She glanced at him. "Do you live like this?"

He grimaced. "My place is less pretentious. But I suppose I *could* live this way if I chose."

"Show off." She laughed.

He winked. "You asked."

He moved around the car and reached for her hand. Zandrea hesitated and then took a step backward. "I'm not sure about this. I don't want to go in there. Oh goodness, did you cast a spell? I shouldn't be here. I want to go home." To her disgust, tears welled in her eyes. What an idiot she had been all night."

As she retreated, Brant moved closer, his expression calm but determined. "I'm sorry, baby, but you have no choice."

"No!"

Zandrea spun away, but Brant caught hold of her wrist and hauled her back to his chest. She struggled in his arms, tried to knee him, but he blocked it, catching her legs between his. He tightened his hold and forced her chin up to look into her eyes. If she expected his eyes to be filled with anger or madness, she was mistaken. "I'm so sorry, Zandrea. This isn't your fault. You shouldn't have been put in this situation, forced against your will."

He kissed her lips, and she tried her best not to like it, but that was ridiculous. She craved more of his touch. Brant rested his forehead on hers, and they stood there for a long time. So many words crowded her mind.

Her decision not to go farther with him raged back and forth in her mind, and she told herself to break free, to lose him in the trees. After all, she had been on the track and field team in school. Well, before she had picked up the few extra pounds.

"The last thing I want is to have you forget me," he whispered.

She let her head lower to his shoulder. He wrapped his arms tighter around her so that their bodies melded together. A shudder went through her. His scent was enticing as well. She didn't need a super sensitive nose to enjoy the sandalwood and natural male essence.

"Why?" she answered.

"I don't know." He shrugged. "Maybe because this is the first time it's happened to me, I mean having a human needing to forget me, to undergo Lucas' treatment. It's happened with the others before, not often, as we're careful, but a few times in the last few decades."

"Decades?"

He didn't address her question, but titled her chin up. "Are you ready to go inside? We may have some time. The house is dark, and Lucas' car isn't here. We can have a drink and talk."

Swallowing her fear, although she had no reason to trust this man, she nodded. "Yes, okay. Let's go inside."

Brant flipped on the lights as he led her to a living area with tasteful decor in earth tones and a brick fireplace dominating one side of the room. On one wall was a ridiculously huge flat screen TV, and Brant used a remote to power it up and switch the channel to an easy listening music station. After that, he moved to the fireplace and soon had a roaring fire going. Although the night had been a little cool, the inside of the house was chilly. The heat soon had the room toasty.

At the bar, Brant prepared two glasses with ice and glanced in her direction. "What would you like?"

"Ginger ale?"

His eyebrow went up.

"My stomach's unsettled," she explained. Sinking down to the couch, she let her purse slide off her shoulder, and she dropped her shoes on the floor. The velvet beneath her ass was comfortable, and she wriggled around on it a little, moaning softly.

Brant growled. "Stop that. You're driving me insane."

Zandrea looked up to see the front of his pants tented and his eyes dark like they had been earlier. She shivered, in part from fear but also with desire. What would happen if she slipped out of her panties and parted her legs right here?

He seemed to guess at her thoughts and nodded his head in encouragement. Zandrea looked everywhere but at him, breathing deep, forcing her body to calm down. When he set her glass down in front of her, she zipped it up and took a sip. The cold liquid went a long way to soothing her raging hormones.

"You're afraid of me," he announced, settling on the couch beside her.

"I am not!"

"Not in the way you should be," he admitted. "But you're afraid of what I make you feel. You're not like other women I've met. All of the women I've met are ready and willing to make love with me."

She clenched her hands in her lap when he reached for one of her legs and lifted it to rest on his lap Zandrea was surprised that Brant's gaze never left her face, though she was surely flashing him with her legs apart like that.

"So I'm hurting your ego, is that it?"

He shook his head. "No, I'm just wondering what makes you hesitate."

"Every woman doesn't have to jump into bed with you."

"We give animal magnetism a whole new meaning." He raised a hand and grinned. "Hold on before you attack. I didn't mean that as arrogantly as it sounds. I mean we give off something, a hormone or some such, I guess. Lucas is into that crap. I just know it works. Anyway, we can make the opposite sex much more excited than human men can. Sometimes with a touch." He ran his fingertips along her thigh, sliding just past the hem of her skirt but not reaching her heated center. "And sometimes with words, like when I was telling you about how the scent of your cream flowing was driving the shifters insane."

Her breath hitched in her throat. "Anybody would get off on hearing that!"

His eyes seemed to glitter in the dim lighting. "But can anyone come from those words alone?"

Her mouth dropped open. "Prove it!"

Chapter Seven

Prove it, she'd said. Brant knew without a doubt he could bring her to orgasm with little more than a look and a few choice words, but it was taking an insane amount of his built up self-control to keep from plunging his fingers into her heat. What he had told her was true. Her scent had been driving the shifters out of their minds. And he was no different. She was without question flowing right now. The scent drew images to mind of how thick it would be, how it would taste, even the sound of her cries as she came seemed to fill his ears. He could scarcely put two words together, let alone try to seduce her.

It had been a mistake to come here this early. He should have taken her around town as he had intended to do in the first place and then called Lucas to coordinate a time when they could meet here. The atmosphere with the fire and the lights turned low were conducive to seduction, to all out wild, hot sex on the bearskin rug Lucas had to buy three years ago to complete his pretentious home decor.

With herculean effort, Brant removed his hands from Zandrea's body and moved across the room to stoke the fire. "No, I'm not going to do that. If I don't get to come, neither do you." At her gasp, he chuckled. "I wouldn't be able to resist taking you if you did anyway. Your moans would make it impossible not to spread your legs and take what I want. The expression, 'I'm only human' doesn't apply here."

"Meaning you couldn't be responsible at that point."

"Yes."

He heard her move about behind him, and he imagined she was straightening her clothing, maybe even planning to make another run for it. He sighed. She couldn't escape him. Even if she got a head start, he could outrun her any day or night. For some reason if that failed, his sense of smell would lead him to her. Not now, not ever would he forget her as she would forget him later. The way that thought tore at him boggled his mind, but he didn't examine it too closely. They didn't know each other well.

Her voice came from just behind him, amazing him that he hadn't picked up on her movement so fevered was his mind. "I have a knack for picking up losers who cheat on me. I almost always end up falling in love, and they always cheat, breaking my heart into a million pieces. Stacy and Nita are there to help me through it with pints of french vanilla ice cream, walnuts, whipped cream and a half cherry on top, but still, it's too much."

"Specific aren't you?"

She laughed. "Yeah, well. I know what I like."

A rustle of material and somehow he knew her bare breasts were on his back. "If I turn around..."

"You'll be able to have me."

Brant's mouth went dry. He spun to find her naked from head to toe except for her red bikini panties. He panted at the rich dark chocolate of her skin, the nipples protruding invitingly and her navel pierced just asking for his tongue to dip into it. "Damn it, woman!"

He dropped to his knees and extended his tongue while gripping her hips. Her skin was smooth as he ran his tongue over it. He kissed her belly, and she moaned, arching into him. Brant ran his fingers beneath the material of her panties and dragged them downward. The patch of black curls brought a roar to his throat, but he fought not to release it for fear of frightening her.

"Mine!" he growled instead. "All mine."

"Brant!"

Roughly, he pushed her legs apart and buried his mouth between them. Her cream coated his tongue with one swipe, and he delved deeper to find her nub. The shout she let out at first contact was the last he heard, for blood rushed in his ears, and all he could focus on was sucking her until she had no more to give. The little swollen bud deserved all of his attention, to force his lover to give him her cream.

He slid his mouth lower and pushed his tongue inside, gathering as much of her juice as possible. He laved and laved then leaned back and pressed a finger up her tunnel. Her muscles tightened. He drove another in and refocused on the nubbin.

Somewhere on a subconscious level, he heard a door slam, but Brant couldn't pull himself away from Zandrea's goodness. He wanted to consume her, to eat until he couldn't move.

"Yum, is it that good?"

Zandrea yelped and would have pulled away to cover herself, but Brant held her in place. He took two more swipes before leaning around her thigh to spot his brother. He stood there arms crossed and interest in his eyes. They had shared women in the past, but Brant would be damned if he ever let Lucas touch Zandrea.

He bared his teeth, pointed and sharp, a rumble growing in his chest. "Touch her, and I will kill you. Get the fuck out and let me have what's mine."

Lucas' eyes narrowed. "For now."

Brant didn't wait to see if his brother left the room, and he didn't give a shit if Lucas did or didn't. He could watch if that's what he desired, but Brant was getting inside Zandrea *now*. He stood and lifted her in his arms to lower her to the floor. Lucas would have words later about them soiling the bearskin carpet, but Brant didn't care.

Zandrea sat up and braced her hands on his chest when he had ripped open his shirt. "Are you sure this is okay? He...um..."

Brant slipped out of his shirt and flung it. He leaned back and unbuttoned his slacks. She bit her lip while watching his movements. Brant grinned. "Can you turn back now?"

She swallowed and licked her lips. "No, I don't think I can."

"Good." He stood up and slipped out of his pants, took hold of his erection and stroked it while she watched. Knowing she liked what she saw sent his lust into a whole other stratosphere. With forced gentleness, he lowered her until she lay flat, and then he positioned himself between her legs, nudging them wider. Even after he had feasted for so long and with such enthusiasm, she was wet all over again. He paused to watch and stretched a finger out to first dip into her and then to trace over her pearl. Her eyes drifted closed, and she lifted her hips, whining for more.

"You want me inside you?" he asked.

"Yes!"

Her skin puckered with goose bumps. He squeezed her thighs and pinched her nipples. Following his come coated fingers across her breasts, he licked the cream from her skin, savoring it and the tight peaks in his mouth. He pulled back, tugging on the nipple until she cried out his name.

"Damn it, Brant. Put your dick in me now. Please!"

He complied, inching in a little at a time. She was so tight, like she hadn't had a man in a while. Brant gritted his teeth and fought not to slam into her. It would kill him if he hurt her. All he wanted was to please her, to make her come, to hear her call his name and wrap her legs around his waist.

Soon he had all of his thick shaft seated deep inside Zandrea, and he paused to catch his breath, willing himself not to release too soon. When the sensation to come eased a little, he began a slow rhythm in and out of her. She bucked, tightened her hold on his waist and dug her nails into his back.

Brant curled his nails into his palms. Having grown out with his excitement, they would tear at her skin if he wasn't careful. Instead, he clenched them and pressed his hands into the floor while he found Zandrea's mouth and pounded into her.

* * * *

Zandrea couldn't believe sex could be this good. Brant was so big, it hurt going in, but the pleasure of being filled with a man was intense as well. She wouldn't have let him stop if he tried. Her body was on fire after he had licked her like she was his last meal, like she tasted that good. Even his brother had commented when he came in on how Brant was eating her. Men had gone down on her before, but never like that.

Now he pounded in and out of her like he had lost all control. He lifted one of her legs up over his shoulder, and Zandrea thought she would faint. Her bud pulsed, her core muscles tensed, and she forgot the ache, the soreness for the sheer pleasure of being taken in the rough way Brant had.

He pushed her knee toward her chest, and the slight change of position had him thrusting against her ass. She screamed and pleaded for him not to stop. Her fingernails digging into his muscular, hairy thighs, she pulled at him, wishing they could be one and the need she felt would be satisfied.

Without warning, Brant flipped their positions, so that he was on the bottom and she was on the top. He had her facing away from him, but he held onto her hips. He pushed her forward slightly and brought her down hard on his dick. Her head spun. An orgasm rushed through her. She sagged forward having lost all strength, but Brant held on. He sat up, wrapped his arms around her and pushed her head back on his shoulder.

He thrust in and out while he stroked her between her legs. Another orgasm took her. She could do nothing more than moan.

"Again," he demanded.

"I can't."

"Again." His rhythm didn't break for an instant. His massaging of her most sensitive part had her climaxing for the third time and then a fourth. "Come for me." His voice was rough and deep. If Zandrea hadn't been so turned on, she would have been afraid.

She gasped. "Brant, I can't. It's too much."

He slid his hand from between her legs to rest on her belly. She glanced down and noticed how long his nails were. They were sharp, and she wondered if they could have sliced her open. He guessed her thoughts.

"I was careful." He choked off more words, his eyes closing. After some time, he whispered. "Don't be afraid."

She wondered what he meant by that, and then she knew. He growled louder than she'd heard before and then at the point of his release, he bit down into her shoulder. She tried to pull away, but he held on. It wasn't that it hurt so much, because surprisingly it didn't. The sensuality coupled with his orgasm was insane, but it was violent and wild as well. Brant was nothing like any man she had ever met before.

After a while, he raised his head, his breath coming in heavy pants. His eyes were half closed, but Zandrea trembled at their color, almost black and glowing with the reflection of the fire light.

"I need to have you again," he whispered.

She gasped and shook her head. "I'm so sore. Everything hurts. I don't think I can take it."

He smiled. "Not tonight." She thought she saw tears in his eyes, but when she looked again, his eyes were dry.

Chapter Eight

"You dumbass!" Lucas shouted. "How could you fucking do that? You've made her your mate, and now she doesn't even remember you. Why didn't you say something sooner?"

Brant leaned against the wall on the balcony outside of Lucas' house and turned his face into the breeze which was picking up to the point of a wind. "I didn't plan on it. I couldn't help it. I found my teeth sunk into her sweet skin. Once wouldn't have been a big deal."

"I know that, but you bit her twice. You admitted to the one in your mother's bar to mark her, but the second bite sealed it while having sex. You've never been this careless before, Brant."

"My soul has never ached for a woman as much as it aches for Zandrea."

"Cut the dramatics."

"Fuck you!" Brant growled. "Everyone is not heartless like you. I don't know what happened. It shouldn't have gone the way it did. It was unexpected. Even at the hospital, I was all set to go outside to wait for you, and then I picked up her scent. I followed it. Later, we both figured it was the fact that I had a fever, but now I know something in her was drawing me."

"A destined mate is rare among out kind. You know that." Lucas still looked doubtful. He had been questioning whether it was just lust Brant was feeling, but deep inside Brant knew it was different. Yeah, *now* it was different. Zandrea was his mate, and he'd find it impossible to live his life without her from here on out. Yet, she would not know him from Adam if she saw him face-to-face. That knowledge, though it wasn't here fault, cut him deeply.

Brant shrugged. "Whatever the case, I need to see her. Last night, I don't know what I was thinking. I walked out when you started your thing." Brant eyed his brother in suspicion. "You didn't touch her, did you? Make her forget that you did it. I remember how excited you looked watching us make love."

Lucas' nostrils flared. "Make love? Give me a break. No, I didn't touch her. I don't go after humans that often. Too tame for my taste. I can't believe you got enough just sleeping with her last night. You'll want to get the edge off tonight. I hear one of the Eastern female shifters has come to town looking for fresh meat. I can't imagine she'd turn down my little brother."

Brant clenched his fists. "Don't patronize me. You know a true mated wolf cannot be intimate with anyone but his mate. Damn it! I've fucked up. How the hell am I going to have my needs met if my mate doesn't know me?"

Lucas's expressed showed not the least bit of sympathy. "Give it some time. See the other shifter like I suggested, and let me seek out a couple of the elders to see if there's a way to break the bond that I don't know about. It's possible since we rarely follow old customs in the first place."

"Yeah, it's the elders who said we'd get into crap like this if we left the old ways. First thing we did was toss aside running in packs, now one of us is trying to break away from a mate. I can imagine the outrage that will cause with the old-timers." Brant sighed. "Fine. One week. I don't think I can hold out much longer than that. But, Lucas, hurry! I *will* not take a lover that's not Zandrea. Period."

* * * *

Six days was all that Brant could keep himself away from the woman whose soul called to his whether she knew it or not. He hadn't slept more than a couple hours at a time, and when he did, his mind was filled with flashes of her beautiful face, her sexy body beneath him, her crying out his name as he brought her to climax after climax. Unfortunately, the hot dreams didn't translate to him getting his satisfaction. Even using his hand meant nothing. His bottled up sexual desire was nearing boiling point, and seeing Zandrea on a date with another man was not helping matters.

Seated at a nearby table so that he was within earshot of Zandrea and the asshole who should have his throat ripped out, Brant watched them with his hands clenched in his lap. He ignored the waiter who came by twice to ask if he was ready to order. Brant could have sat across the room and picked up their words, but he didn't want to have to filter out everyone else in the room. The process would only annoy him more.

Damn, she moved fast being with him just six days after they had been wrapped around each other. Then again, she didn't remember that. Frustration made him growl low in his throat, and he turned his stare back to his waiter for the third time. With eyes wide and smile frozen in place on the man's face, Brant could guess his own eyes had gone dark and threatening. Good, maybe that would make him fuck off.

The waiter spun on his heel and bolted. Brant turned his attention back to the couple at the next table. He lifted his water glass to his mouth but only managed to shatter it in his hand.

Control gone, he stood and stomped over to the table to confront Zandrea. "Why the hell are you with this loser? He only wants to get into your bed." Brant sniffed. "I can smell it. What I don't pick up is a desire from you."

"What the hell? Who are you?" Zandrea demanded. "And what business is it of yours if my date wants me? Wait, you said..." She stopped, her eyes widening and lowering to the table.

Brant noted the embarrassment on her date's face. He hauled the guy to his feet. "That's right, she doesn't want you." Relief at the knowledge flooded through Brant's body. "Get lost!"

"Hey!" Zandrea jumped to her feet and shoved Brant. "You need to back off my date. You don't know him, and you damn sure don't know me."

"You are mine!" Brant insisted, knowing he sounded like a maniac. He wrestled with his emotions, but gained no control over himself.

"You've lost your mind!" Zandrea squeezed past him and grabbed the man's hand who had not said anything yet. She dragged him toward the exit, and Brant stood there for a second before starting after them.

A waiter and the manager blocked his path. "Sir, who's going to pay for this meal?"

Brant glanced at the table of unfinished food. He himself hadn't ordered a thing. "It's not mine. Let that loser pay."

The manager remained in place. "It seems to me, *sir*, that you harassed them until they had to leave. Now in the police report, I will be sure to mention—"

"Fine!" Brant yanked his wallet from his back pocket and peeled off a few bills to toss onto the table. "That should cover it. Now get out of my way before I give you a lot more to report to the police."

Cowed, the manager and waiter stepped aside, and Brant took off for the exit. By the time he reached the street, there was no sight of Zandrea or her date. Brant slammed his fist into a lamp post and growled low in his throat.

Several patrons arriving and leaving the restaurant eyed him warily.

After slipping into his car in the parking lot, he sat in silence trying to calm down enough to think of his next move. He hadn't handled things in the restaurant correctly. While at home, he had practiced what he would say and planned to walk up and meet her all over again. Instead he came off like a raving lunatic. It was doubtful she'd forget that and ever let him within two feet of her.

He punched the steering wheel. "This is not happening!" His cell rang, and he slipped it from his pocket to see who was calling. It was Lucas. He hit the answer button. "What?"

Without preamble, Lucas announced, "There's no way to break the bond unless you or she dies. I can arrange for someone to do that."

Brant's chest tightened. "Do what?"

"Kill her, of course."

Brant disconnected the call, but Lucas called right back.

"Don't be stupid, Brant. I spoke with not two but five elders. All of them have said mating with humans is a mistake. Few have done it, but it has resulted in weak wolves and other issues. If I believed in it, I would say nothing but heartache would come from taking a human mate. If you were thinking with anything other than your dick, you'd realize that."

"It's not just that," Brant insisted.

"Oh, it isn't?"

"You wouldn't know. You've never had a mate. You've never loved anyone other than yourself."

His brother didn't deny it. "What's your point?"

Brant sighed and closed his eyes. In the rearview mirror, he picked up blue and red flashing lights. So the manager had phoned the police. He didn't need trouble. Brant started his car and eased out of the parking lot, headed in the direction of Zandrea's apartment.

"My point is," he said when he had put distance between himself and the police, "that yes, it's physical. I don't deny that I want to fuck her brains out. Contrary to what you think, I was more than satisfied with her. And I never ever wanted to take a mate. I loved having several women at once. But the moment I bit her, no before, I felt like she was more, like I could never walk away from her even if I tried. That sounds corny to a cold-hearted bastard like you, but it's true. Now that we are mates, I don't think—no I know I can't—be without her. So, one way or another, I'm going to have Zandrea.

You can help me or stand aside. But if you fucking lay one finger on her or have someone else do it, I will kill you without hesitation."

This time it was Lucas who cut the line, and Brant tossed his phone on the passenger side seat. Fifteen minutes later, he pulled up to Zandrea's apartment and parked his car. Rolling his window down, he sniffed the air. Yeah, that jerk was either here or had been recently. Brant stepped out of his vehicle and stood glancing up and down the street. He stretched out his tense muscles and crossed the road.

Chapter Nine

"I had a good time, Zandrea," Ronnie told her. "You know. At first. Before that guy..."

Zandrea paused in sticking her key in the door of her place. All the way back home, her mind had been filled with that freak who acted like he owned her when she'd never met him. He was hot as hell, but the man had a screw loose.

"Um, yeah, sorry about that."

Ronnie stared at her. "You didn't know him, did you?"

"No." She fiddled with her key in her hand. She'd been about to let Ronnie come in, knowing Stacy would be out until late. But crazy guy had been right about one thing. She wasn't the least bit attracted to Ronnie, and she had no desire to prolong seeing him. Truth be told, she had been off her game all week. Something had changed inside of her, but she couldn't pinpoint it. "I didn't know him, but that incident messed up my mind frame. Why don't we call it a night, and I'll call you?"

Ronnie stood there unmoving, and Zandrea wasn't about to open her door so he would think she wanted him to come in. She waited him out.

He shuffled from foot to foot, giving in at last. "You're not going to call me, are you? And if I call you, you won't answer or will have your roommate give me some lame ass excuse."

She didn't deny it. "I'm sorry."

Ronnie spun away and stomped down the stairs to the first level and out the door. Zandrea thought she heard someone laugh, but when she peered over the railing, she didn't see anyone on the first floor. She shrugged and opened her door to let herself into her apartment.

Stacy was curled up on the couch with a bowl of popcorn. Zandrea parked on the back of the couch and reached for a handful. "I thought you said you'd be out late. It's a rare occurrence when we all three actually have dates at one time."

"Yeah," her friend muttered. "But it's not a rare occurrence for those dates to suck." She rolled her eyes. "That guy was so freaking boring, I can't even imagine why I went out with him."

Zandrea flipped around to sit down correctly and kicked her shoes off. "I hear that. You won't believe what happened to me tonight. But hold up, I'm just remembering something."

Stacy shoved the popcorn bowl into Zandrea's lap and took a swig of her soda. "What?"

"Remember that night at the club. You know last Saturday?"

Stacy yawned. "Not really. We got smashed or something, and it's all a blur."

Zandrea nodded. "Except for the part where we met those three guys at the same time while we were coming out. And I think I saw this other man nodding to them just before they approached us, a man any of us would have jumped at. Who do you think he was?"

"Zan, like that has any bearing on the fact that we're losers."

"I'm not a loser thank you very much!"

"Then your date was wonderful, and he was just too much of a gentleman to keep you out late. Is that it?"

Zandrea flared her nostrils. "Smart ass! Ronnie wasn't bad, but I just wasn't into him. But this other crazy dude, my body sang like a freaking soprano for."

Stacy's eyes lit up. "Do tell."

* * * *

Zandrea stepped out of the shower and wrapped a towel around her body. She swiped a hand over the mirror and stared at her reflection. Running fingers through her hair, she considered her love life, or the fact that it was non-existent. So desperate was she for a man, even a nutcase had turned her on.

Not that she had fantasies about a dominant man trying to control her. She liked being in the driver seat of her life, but the way he had said she was his had her body going wild. While she searched her mind for a flicker of recognition, there was nothing. She'd never seen him before in her life, but her body acted like it knew him.

Shaking her head, she moved into the bedroom and dropped the towel before rubbing lotion on her body. She ran her palms over her breasts, annoyed that her nipples were erect. Between the sheets and the light turned off, she thought about last Saturday night. Nita and Stacy had shocked her when they admitted that there were hours missing from their night and none of them could remember where the time went or what they had been doing. Zandrea hadn't confessed to the other two, but she had been sore between her legs, and there was a mark on her shoulder that still ached a little.

She ran her hand over it and closed her eyes waiting for an image to slip into her consciousness that would explain what had happened, but none came. A couple nights later she had gone back to the club to question the bartender, but the man claimed she and her friends had drank like fish in the corner for hours. He had remembered, he said, because he had thought they were too pretty to be alone. She'd snorted and thanked him.

"But did something happen?" she whispered to the dark room. "Did someone slip us a mickey and Nita and Stacy are like me, too scared to admit that they were sore like they'd had sex?"

Shocked at the thought, Zandrea sat up in bed. She shook from head to toe. Please, no, that couldn't be true, could it? They'd been stupid and took chances way too much with their wild lifestyles, but rape?

She slipped into her robe and rushed to her bedroom door. With her hand on the knob, she stopped. She couldn't do it. If she asked Stacy about it and Stacy hadn't experienced the soreness, then she would know Zandrea had. Chewing on her lip, she thought about what to do. An idea formed in her mind. An examination would show if she had been violated, and because it was her doctor, no one would have to know anything until she was sure.

The decision made, she turned and headed back to bed but stopped when she heard a sound outside. On shaky legs, she walked to the window and pulled the curtain back to peer out. The balcony off the living room was just to the left of her bedroom window. On it was a huge dog, bigger than she'd ever seen. He howled in anguish at the moon.

"What the hell?" she whispered. "Did Stacy get a dog? Idiot shouldn't leave him on the balcony biggest he is."

She slipped back into her robe and knotted it before hurrying out to the hall. Used to strolling in the dark to get a midnight snack or drink, she didn't turn on any lights. Instead, she headed straight to the sliding doors leading to the balcony and peered between the blinds. The animal was still there. She dropped to her knees to look into his eyes. Never having a fear of animals, she wasn't afraid now, but she wanted to be sure he wouldn't attack. He looked like someone had broken his poor little heart.

Zandrea opened the door. "Come inside, baby. What's wrong? Stacy leave you out there all alone?" She wrapped her arms around his neck and nuzzled his furry neck. The dog whined and pulled back to lick her face. When he tried work his way inside her robe, she gave his nose a light smack. "Stop that."

His tail thumped, and he sat down watching her with his tongue hanging out of his mouth. Zandrea glanced down at herself noting how her robe hung open a little showing the swell of one breast. She smirked.

"Dirty animal." She fixed her clothes and stood. "Okay, you can stay inside. I'll talk to Stacy about not leaving you out on the balcony. She should know better than to get a pet as big as you. Besides that, our lease says thirty pounds and under. Your ass is way over that."

Zandrea turned and headed back toward her room. A bark stopped her.

"Shut up, idiot. You'll wake the whole building." She tried leaving again and another bark. "All right, come on. You can sleep in my room, but only tonight. Your master can handle you after that."

The dog followed Zandrea into her room, and when she had shut the door, she turned to find he had jumped on her bed and lay there.

"I think you've bumped your head, dog. Get down." He ignored her. Zandrea stomped across the room, shoved the massive animal to one side and pulled her covers back. "Your ass better not have fleas or something."

She dropped her robe and climbed into the bed. She thought she heard a moan that sounded suspiciously like delight, but she was too sleepy to investigate. In the morning was soon enough to tell Stacy to deal with her pet.

That night, Zandrea dreamed of the man from the restaurant with his body molded to hers and his arms wrapped around her waist. She had never felt so safe, so cared for, and she slept soundly until morning.

Chapter Ten

"Are you for real, Stacy? He's not yours?" Zandrea sat on the edge of her chair feeding chunks of chicken to the dog. "Then how did he get on the balcony?"

Stacy shrugged. "Beats me. What's more it's not a dog. It's a wolf."

Zandrea shrieked. "A wolf?"

Her friend nodded. "Yup. He's beautiful though, bigger than I've ever seen, and he acts like he's in love with you." Stacy laughed. "Damn, why couldn't he be a man, huh? Nita'd be so jealous that we have a man living with us."

Zandrea laughed. "Whatever. He just likes me because I let him sleep in my bed and fed him. Oh wait, yeah most men would like that." They both burst out laughing. Her canine admirer growled in annoyance. Zandrea stuck out her tongue at him. "So I guess it's to the pound then."

The moment she said it, Zandrea knew she couldn't part with the dog. There was something about him. She cleaned her hands and knelt down in front of him to take hold of his face. His big dark eyes that looked almost black bore into hers as if he was begging her not to send him away.

"You want to stay with me, don't you, baby?" she asked him.

Stacy laughed. "Did he just nod?"

Zandrea buried her face in his neck. "We'd get in serious trouble trying to keep you, and I've got an appointment this afternoon so I can't be here to take you out for another walk."

"Appointment?"

Zandrea could have bitten her tongue off. She hadn't meant to say anything about her doctor's appointment. Dr. Stevens had agreed to squeeze her in as a walk-in because she was concerned about injury during her last sexual encounter. She hadn't told him her suspicions, which probably was a mistake. She could straighten it out at his office if he confirmed that she'd had sex in the last year and a half. Hopefully he could tell one way or another.

"Yeah, I won't be long." She didn't explain, and Stacy didn't press her. "Can you take him out, Stacy? No out of town deliveries today, right? Please? I promise I'll figure something out later. Maybe take him to Nita's or something during the day."

Her friend sighed. "Fine. I don't want to let him go either. He's a good boy." Stacy scratched the wolf behind the ears and called out her good-byes before heading out to work.

Zandrea stood up. "Well, come on. You can keep me company while I shower and change. I'll think about a name for you while I'm at work, and if you behave and not rip the apartment to shreds, I will bring you some hospital cafeteria food." She laughed. "Won't that be good?"

Her new pet didn't look impressed, but seemed too eager to follow her into the bedroom.

* * * *

Brant stepped out of the shower and toweled dry. He couldn't get the smile off his face. Last night had been wonderful. He'd taken a huge risk shifting back to his human form to wrap himself around Zandrea's soft body, but he couldn't resist. She'd let him stay, and she had moaned her pleasure at having him hold her all night long. The only time he had pulled away was to go and get his clothes from his car to hide inside her room. That way, he would have something to wear when he left.

Slipping his shoes on his feet, he paused when his cell phone buzzed. He clicked on. "Yeah?"

"You sound chipper," Lucas said accusingly.

"I am. I slept with Zandrea last night."

"What!"

Brant laughed. "She took me in as a stray, and while she was asleep, I shifted back to hold her in my arms."

"That is not a solution, Brant."

"It's the only one I have at the moment. If I can spend even an hour in her presence, I'm happier. You'd know that if—"

"Stow it! So you'll live the rest of your life in wolf form?"

Brant hadn't thought that far ahead, but he considered it now. If he had to choose between never seeing Zandrea again or allowing someone to end her life, living as her pet was not such a bad thing, especially if he got to hold her and to watch her dry her naked body fresh from the shower. His shaft had gone rock solid seeing her with water droplets glistening on her smooth skin. Her sweet scent had made him pant and long to taste her.

Seeing his unwavering stare, she had only laughed and shook her head, calling him a dirty dog. But she had made no move to hide herself, so he got to look his fill of her.

"If living as a wolf is what it takes to always be with Zandrea, then I suppose I will. However, today, I'm going to go out, because I'm worried about her. She said something to her roommate about an appointment. When her friend asked her about it, Zandrea was vague. I need to make sure everything is okay, so I'm going to follow her. I'll check in later."

"Brant," Lucas called out before he hung up.

"Yeah?"

Lucas sighed. "Be careful. I don't pretend to understand, but you're wrong about me. I care about some people other than myself."

Brant grinned. "I love you, too." He clicked off.

* * * *

Zandrea sat on the edge of the hospital bed and waited for her doctor to come back in the room. She chewed a nail while reading and re-reading the various posters around the room. They were boring the first time she scanned them, and they were boring now, but she couldn't stop herself from considering the ad for a new drug on one wall, heeding the signs of high blood pressure on another, and noting that it was rude not to call twenty-four hours in advance if she was going to break her appointment on a third wall.

Finally, a soft knock sounded on the door, and Dr. Stevens strolled in. "Zandrea, good to see you again." The doctor sat down on a stool and flipped a chart open. "I do see the signs of vigorous sex, but not so rough that you caused any damage. Just be sure to let your partner know when it's too much."

Zandrea's stomach knotted. She swallowed a few times hoping she wasn't about to throw up.

"From the last time I saw you, you indicated you hadn't been sexually active for a while. I'm hoping you took precautions..."

"Precautions," she muttered. Of course, safe sex, protection. She was on the pill, but a condom? She wasn't aware she had been with anyone. Fear tightened her chest. She doubled over. In another second, her doctor would see her crying if the commotion outside in the hall and a scream didn't capture his attention.

He stood and opened the door. "What's going on?"

"A dog!" someone yelled.

Zandrea gasped. "Impossible." She scrambled off of the table, held her gown together and rushed to the door. At the other end of the hall, her wolf sat calmly staring at her. "Shit!"

Zandrea scrambled into her clothes and rushed out into the hallway at full speed. Assistants and patients were pressed against the wall unmoving, their eyes wide and their mouths hanging open. Zandrea was struck again at how big the wolf was. She imagined if she didn't know he was gentle, in this setting it would freak her out as well.

She grabbed him by the scruff of his neck. "I'm so sorry. He's mine. I didn't know he followed me. I don't know how he got out of the house. Please forgive me."

Dr. Stevens stood pale on one side of the massive desk that looked ridiculous out in the hall across from the room where he had examined Zandrea. "Don't worry about it. Settle with me later. Please take him out of here."

Zandrea dragged the wolf outside and shoved him into her car. She jumped in on the driver's side and had to suffer more embarrassment when her car didn't start on the first six tries. She slammed a fist on the steering wheel, trying not to cry. The wolf whined and nuzzled her arm.

"Oh goodness, Wolf," she cried out, the tears pouring. "I just found out I was raped. I don't know what I'm going to do."

With her face pressed into her hands, Zandrea sobbed. She didn't hear anything around her so she had a moment of shock when fingers touched a small space on her shoulder. Gentle pressure there, and she lost consciousness.

Chapter Eleven

Zandrea shut her eyes tight against the sunlight shining in the window and moaned before shifting to her side. Without thinking, she slipped a hand beneath her pillow and cupped it closer to her face. Feeling like someone was watching her, she opened her eyes to come face-to-face with Wolf.

She threw back the covers and sat up. "What the hell? When did I get..." She glanced down to find she was naked, and memories of what she had learned at the doctor's office came rushing back to her. "Oh no, Wolf. This can't be happening. It *couldn't* have." A hand pressed to her lips, she rushed to the bathroom and fell to her knees to empty the contents of her stomach in the toilet.

When she had no more strength, she collapsed on the floor and curled up in the fetal position sobbing and rocking.

"Don't. Please don't, Zandrea."

She gasped and rolled over. A man stood in the doorway, the one from the restaurant who had claimed she was his, and he was as naked as she was. "You," she squeaked. "Was it you? What are you doing in here?" She draped an arm across her breasts and looked around for a way to escape.

He leaned out and held a hand toward her. "Don't be afraid. Baby, you weren't raped, I promise you. If you'll get up off the cold floor and come and sit down, I'll explain everything."

"Don't call me baby!" she snapped. Like that was the least of her worries. Had he attacked her again after she left the doctor's office and brought her here? That meant he knew where she lived and had broken in. "What did you do to Wolf? Come here, boy! Attack!"

She had no idea if her pet understood that he had let an enemy come in to hurt her, but he was so huge, he was sure to intimidate this man despite him being monstrous in size as well.

"Come and sit down. Put something on," the man said more firmly. "You're shivering."

She wanted to tell him what to kiss, but she was at a disadvantage crouched on the floor and him blocking the exit. On unsteady legs she stood up, watching so he wouldn't make any sudden movements toward her. He backed up but not too far, a look of concern in his eyes. The man seemed to care about her, although she couldn't imagine why.

"Turn your head!" she demanded. An eyebrow went up, and he was about to say something but changed his mind. He turned his back. Zandrea darted out of the bathroom and scooped up the clothes she'd worn earlier in the day. She slid into her pants at record speed and screwed up the buttons on her top, but didn't stop to fix them. She wanted to be fully dressed in case she had to run.

When she pulled the laces on her sneakers in place, she looked up. "You put something on, too."

He faced her, making no move to cover the huge package he displayed. Zandrea averted her eyes, and he grinned as if he was proud. "I'm sorry, I can't. I left the clothes I wore out of here in someone's yard about a mile away. I had to hurry to meet you."

"What?"

He sighed. "My name is Brant. We met last week at the club—"

"You're the one!" She stumbled backward and would have run out of the bedroom if he didn't rush to take her hand, holding her in place. He pushed the door closed, and the soft click might as well have been a vault slamming shut for all the fear it sent through her body that she was trapped with a madman.

"Please, calm down. Let me explain."

He kept his voice low and steady. Zandrea forced herself to swallow and take deep breaths. Panic would not help her.

Brant continued. "We met and hit it off. We were intimate." He rushed ahead. "It was mutual consent. But I made a mistake. I admitted my family's secret, and because of that, my brother insisted on removing the fact that we had ever met from your memory. That's why you don't remember that we made love, that I made you my mate."

Zandrea eyed him like he'd lost his damn mind. "You think that makes sense, don't you? Or that I believe you."

"It's the truth." He ran a hand down the side of her face, but Zandrea ducked away. "Baby, you are my mate. Now and forever. I claimed you fully that night, and I realize that was wrong, but it cannot be helped now."

"What are you talking about!" Zandrea shoved his chest, and it was like pushing against a wall for all the impact it made on him.

"I am a wolf shape shifter. The wolf you have had as a pet was me." He ran a hand through his hair and offered a guilty grin." Without telling her what he intended, his body began to change. The eyes that intrigued her turned dark, and his bones cracked and popped. Hair sprouted everywhere.

Zandrea threw herself back against the door, a hand over her mouth. In seconds the man who had been standing before her was now the wolf she had let sleep in her bed, had let into the bathroom when she showered. He had watched with avid attention while she put lotion on her naked body.

This couldn't be happening. It wasn't real!

Zandrea threw open the bedroom door and slammed it behind her, trapping the wolf inside. She sprinted across the apartment, grabbing her purse and keys on the way. When she hit the stairs, she jumped several at a time and ignored the twinges in her ankles. Out on the street, she opened up her run and bolted for her car. The doorway of the apartment building was still empty when her tires screeched as she turned the corner.

Half hour later, Zandrea let herself in Nita's dorm room and threw herself on the bed to cry. At least she wanted to cry, but the shock had not only sapped her energy, it seemed to have dried her tear ducts. Zandrea lay on the bed face up and stared at the ceiling.

"Shape shifters don't exist," she mumbled. "That stuff is for the movies."

For a while she lay there calming her breathing, directing her thoughts to more peaceful circumstances. There would be no more problems. Nita's last class for the day would end in forty-five minutes, and they would laugh about the huge misunderstanding. No big deal.

A knock sounded on the door. Zandrea went still. Her heart thumped in her chest, making it hard to hear. Still that knock seemed to drown out everything. Nita's fellow students and the staff knew Zandrea. As long as Nita had been going to school, refusing to leave really, they just ought to. She had often come here to escape her life and pretend she had no issues. So who would be knocking at this time?

"Who is it?" Zandrea called. No one answered. The knock came again. With caution, she moved toward the door and then opened it slowly. The second most gorgeous man she'd ever seen—second to Brant, she had to admit—stood at the door.

Where Brant might have been crazy, he had gentle eyes. Compassion and warmth was reflected there. This man's stare was cold, and his mouth was pressed into a harsh line. He raised a hand and took hold of Zandrea's arm.

"Get your fucking hands off me," she demanded.

"Let's go."

She glared at him and yanked on her arm to no avail. His hold tightened until it was painful.

"I have no wish to hurt you."

"Could have fooled me."

He growled. "You can come with me quietly, or I can knock you out. It's your choice."

"W-Who are you?"

"I am Brant's half-brother."

She gasped.

His hold loosened. "Which will it be?"

What choice did she have? Pointing with her chin over her shoulder, she indicated her purse and keys. "I have to get my stuff, and I won't make a fuss."

He stared are her as if to gauge if she was telling the truth, and then he released her. Zandrea wracked her brain to come up with a way of escape, just like she had done with Brant, but nothing came to mind. This man wouldn't hesitate to crack her head, she thought. He'd get her to whatever place he had in mind one way or another. What had she gotten herself into?

In his car, Zandrea sat still not saying a word. She watched the scenery closely so she could tell the police where to find this jackass that is if he didn't kill her. She trembled at the thought. Not one time in her life had she gotten into a fight. She'd always been the one to joke her way out of everything, and if that didn't work, she had Stacy to kick ass. Stacy didn't take crap off of anyone. Later, they had met Nita who could probably buy her way out of stuff if the need ever arose and if she hadn't blown through her trust fund allowance by then.

"Where are you taking me?" she asked him. "And what's your name?"

He didn't bother answering her questions. "I would have insisted Brant bring you to me again, but the fool left his clothes somewhere, and he couldn't very well chase you down the street naked or track you in daylight as a wolf."

She stared at him. "H-He really is a wolf shape shifter?"

He didn't answer.

"Tell me something, damn it," she yelled. "I want to know what's going on."

"What's going on is I'm going to clean up the mess my brother has made and make you forget you ever met him—again."

Chapter Twelve

Brant kicked the door to his brother's house open at the same time Seth, one of the other shifters was opening it. They met face-to-face growling at each other.

"Back off, Brant," Seth told him.

"Like hell I will. Lucas has my mate. I'm coming in to get her."

Seth shook his head. Two other shifters stepped up, both beefy and able to take on Brant if they needed to. "You know the rules," Seth reminded him. "Our existence must stay a secret from humans no matter what. Just be happy we're not killing her."

"Fuck you!" The pain at that thought cut through Brant until he thought he would faint. He clenched his fists and tightened his jaw to keep focus. He needed to see her, had to hear her voice and breath in her sweet scent. She was his, damn it. They knew that. "I'll fight whoever I have to, to get her."

"You'll take us all on?" Seth indicated the men.

After a stare off that lasted several minutes, Brant took a step back. "Don't hurt her. Please, just tell Lucas not to hurt her. Clear her memory of me if he has to, but, Seth, don't let him make her cry."

Seth dropped a hand on Brant's shoulder. "Don't worry. Your brother's a first class son of a bitch, and he doesn't like humans much, but he won't deliberately hurt one. Your mate will be safe. You just concentrate on getting used to the fact that you'll live the rest of your life without her. We've agreed that even staying with her as a pet is too risky. You can't have any contact with her whatsoever."

Brant considered bucking against the decision made without consulting him but decided against it. What would be the point? None of these single men could understand what it was to find a destined mate, to feel her even when she wasn't there, calling for him to join her. Zandrea might be human, but their connection was spiritual. No doubt about it. She was his through and through, and Brant suspected, although she would never be able to pinpoint it, Zandrea would suffer without him if they stayed apart. He didn't care who didn't like it, he would not permit her to suffer.

"Fine," he said at last. "I'm going. But if I find out—"

"Yeah," Seth interrupted. "I got it. Heads will roll or something equally clichéd." The door slammed in Brant's face.

Brant turned his back on the house and glanced up at the darkening sky. First he would return home, and then he would begin to plan his next move. *It won't be too long, baby. Don't worry. I'll be with you soon.*

* * * *

Zandrea went over the want ads for the third time and sighed. She didn't qualify for squat, and she began to wonder if she should go back to school like Nita. Too bad she couldn't borrow one of her friend's advanced degrees to get a nice paying job. Nobody wanted just a high school diploma anymore.

Stacy strolled into the room. "Why are you even looking for something new? You have benefits, and you always liked working in the cafeteria."

Zandrea rolled her eyes. "Don't get crazy. *Like* is a strong word. I tolerated it."

"Well visiting the ER always seemed to satisfy you," Stacy told her. "What changed?"

Nita paused in polishing her toenails on the loveseat across from Zandrea. "Yeah, you used to tell us stories about the people you met there and all their issues. The hypochondriacs were the funniest."

"It doesn't mean anything anymore." Zandrea whined and threw herself down on the coffee table, sending magazines and Stacy's centerpiece flying. "My life is crap!"

Stacy smirked. "Girl, I know you better straighten up that table after I killed myself cleaning up. Your ass didn't do anything except complain. What's gotten into you? You act like you lost your best friend, which is impossible because I'm right here."

"Funny, Stacy," Nita snapped. "I'm her best friend."

Stacy held up a hand and went to picking up the magazines herself. "What's up, Zan?"

Zandrea shook her head. "I don't know what's wrong with me. I feel like something...or someone...is missing. I feel like I'm all alone, which is crazy because like you said, we've all been together forever. I've always been generally happy."

"Maybe you need to talk to a therapist," Nita suggested.

"Or my pastor," Stacy offered.

Nita jumped up and swiveled her hips with her toes splayed to keep from touching while her polish dried. "What you need is to get your swerve on, girlfriend!"

Zandrea and Stacy burst out laughing.

"Girl, you stupid," Stacy cried, wiping her eyes. "Nita, you need to stop talking like that before it becomes real and all those stuck up lawyers and accountants that run your life get worried and send you off to Upper Crust Ville."

Zandrea snorted. "Okay, okay. Now I feel better. You girls are crazy. I'm going to take this paper and look at it while I take a nice relaxing bubble bath."

Stacy snatched the paper away. "That defeats the purpose. Go relax. It will be here when you get back."

Taking her friend's advice, Zandrea left the paper and headed for her room. She undressed quickly and glanced warily around the room like she expected someone to be watching. There was no one there. After running the water and pouring in her favorite lavender scented bubble bath, she slipped beneath warm surface and settled back She jumped a few times until her back and the water warmed the porcelain, and then she closed her eyes.

As had happened so many times when she relaxed or lay in bed with her eyes closed, a shadowy image came into her mind. She knew it was a man but not what he looked like. At first she'd assumed it was a memory, but then it seemed too alive, and unless she was going insane, he spoke soft words to her, words that were too low to be clear, but soothing all the same. He wanted to ease away her loneliness and help her not to be so depressed all the time. More and more, during these odd sessions was the only time the ache receded. She hadn't shared with her friends the depths of her despair so as not to worry them, but if something wasn't done soon, Zandrea was fearful of what would happen to her. What was it that was missing? Was it this man?

"Who are you?" she asked him in her mind. *"Why do I feel so lost except when you're here like this? And yet even then it's a temporary relief. What's wrong with me?"*

He responded, but she couldn't make out his words. Hot tears filled her eyes and spilled down her cheeks.

"Come for me soon. Please," she said in desperation.

* * * *

Zandrea stood at the perfume counter demonstrating the newest fragrance and fighting against a splitting headache. What had made her decide to take this job she didn't know. She was not big on wearing fragrance—or makeup, which had been the counter she had covered the day before. She hated how they used her as a floatie, switching from position to position, wherever there was a need. But she was the low man on the totem pole, she guessed, and that's how they did things at this department store.

A powerful sneeze, followed by a low growl caught her attention. She glanced up into the watery eyes of the sexiest man she'd ever seen. The poor thing whimpered with a hand pinching his nose. She wondered how he could breathe.

Rushing around the counter, she held up a tissue. "Are you okay? Allergies, huh? We get people walking by here all day complaining of the smell. They forget to detour through another area in order to get out to the mall."

She was aware that she was rambling, but just being near him lifted her spirits, and it seemed so right. She grinned in his face like an idiot.

"I'm great," he muttered. "Now."

Zandrea blinked. He stared at her as if he was feeling the same relief from the fog she'd been locked in for the last three months. "Um..." she began. "You should probably move away from the perfume counter. If you pass by the shoe section, the smell won't reach you, and you can get to the mall out through the men's section."

He didn't move although it was clear he was still suffering. Zandrea took his arm to show him the way. She found herself clinging and fought to get a hold of herself. In front of the store, on the mall side, she stopped.

"Have lunch with me," he blurted out.

"Yes."

Forgetting everything else, Zandrea strolled at his side down to the food court. They drifted from place to place, looking for something to eat, neither saying a word. When they settled on a slice of pizza and had added a coke, they sat down side by side. Zandrea couldn't believe what she was doing, and with a stranger.

"I'm Zandrea. What's your name?" she asked him.

"Brant." He looked hopeful. "Do you know it?"

She frowned. "What, the name Brant? No, I don't think I've ever known anyone by that name." She tilted her head to the side and gave him a coy smile. "But I'd like to get to know you."

His breath seemed to catch in his throat. He nodded and stuffed his pizza into his mouth. Zandrea watched him chew. He was all hard muscle, big chest and powerful arms. She imagined it would be incredible to be flat against that chest with him stroking and kissing her. When his eyes met hers, she blushed, feeling like he knew what she had been thinking.

"I'm not opposed to it," he whispered.

She stared. "Opposed to what?"

He shrugged. "You looked like you wanted to kiss me just now."

"Oh." Zandrea ducked her head and continued to eat her pizza, anything to keep from jumping onto his lap and begging him to make love to her. This was so strange. All this time, she'd barely been in her right mind, lost and scared. Now here this strange man came along, and she was over the sadness. Unlike before, she didn't even feel the pain around the edges of her consciousness like when that man in her mind appeared to help her get through another day.

"Zandrea."

She glanced up. "Yes?"

"I know this will sound strange, but hear me out, okay?" Brant's eyes were pleading. She nodded. "I want to date you. I want to keep it a secret from everyone, even your girlfriends."

She stared. "My girlfriends?" How could he know? Of course, he would assume she had girlfriends. Most women did. But wasn't it dangerous to just go out with a man like this, especially when he didn't want anyone to know. "Are you married?"

He took her hand. "I am for you and only you. Say you'll date me."

She nodded. "Yes. Without hesitation, yes."

Chapter Thirteen

Brant felt like he was going to burst. He and Zandrea were going away to a cabin owned by his mother's friend. The extra precautions for secrecy were important. Because he had stayed away from Zandrea and only visited her in her mind for three months, Lucas had called off the wolves that had been following him around.

His abilities were not like Lucas' so he found it hard to connect with Zandrea on a mental level when he was not with her. And knowing she was still not comforted enough had torn him apart. If Lucas hadn't backed off when he did, Brant didn't know what he would have done.

And now, he was going to be able to freely hold her in his arms, to make love to her for the first time in forever. His shaft hardened at the thought.

"What are you thinking, mister?" Zandrea demanded, pointing at the tent in his pants.

He grinned. "Nothing. Come on, you." He gathered up their bags after removing them from the trunk of his car and wrapped an arm around her waist. His shaft twitched in anticipation. He didn't want to do a damn thing when they got inside other than to rip her clothes off and lick her from head to toe.

She rolled her eyes at him and laughed. "I know you have dirty thoughts in your head, Brant. What if I don't want to sleep with you? We've only been going out a couple of weeks. That's soon, and I made a vow not to jump in the bed too soon with any man. I've been used in the past doing that."

Brant stopped, his eyes wide. He hadn't even considered that she would turn him down. A woebegone expression must have been on his face, because she burst out laughing and dragged him into the cabin.

"Don't worry, baby. I've been hot for you ever since I laid eyes on you in the mall." She winked. "Isn't it weird? It feels like we've known each other longer. It feels so right." She blushed and looked down at the floor. "That sounds lame."

He dropped the bags and took her into his arms. Nuzzling her neck, he breathed in her heady scent and pulled her head to his shoulder. "Not lame at all, and it's true. Everything about us together feels right." Could he get away with not telling her what he was? Maybe somehow it could work. The thought of her running from him again was too much to bear.

Taking a deep breath, she stepped back out of his arms and looked him in the eyes. "Well, in that case, let's not pretend we're not out here for one thing and one thing only. She lifted her hands to her T-shirt, and with a look that dared him to follow suit, lifted it over her head. The hot pink bra cupping her perfect breasts nearly brought him to his knees.

Brant reached out to stroke her soft brown skin, reveling in the way it felt beneath his fingertips and the way she trembled at his touch. Zandrea often had defiance in her eyes like she dared anyone to judge her, but she was sensual and loving too. This woman was strong and independent, yet at the same time, he felt her need for him, and it warmed him.

Rather than undress, he stood there frozen in place, watching while she peeled off the layers of clothing. Her jeans followed the T-shirt to the floor, revealing matching panties. She kicked off her shoes and flicked away her socks. Brant stilled her in front of him, studying the rounded curves of her body. He turned her around and ran his hand down over her ass before moving close to rub against her. A rumble started in his chest. "Your ass drives me nuts."

She peered back at him, a coy look with lowered lashes and her bottom lip caught between her teeth. He growled again. "You like that, huh?" she asked him. "All that ass."

"Every bit of it. Take off your bra and panties. Let me look at all that is mine."

His lover obeyed, but now she looked nervous and hesitant. "It's more than..."

"No, don't do that." He laid a finger over her lips. "You're incredibly beautiful. I love looking at you naked."

The confusion was plain on her face. "This is the first time, goof."

"I've seen you a million times in my head." That was true. He'd been fantasizing about her ever since he'd first laid eyes on her, thinking that she was little more than a lay like every other woman, but unable to get her out of his head or his heart. He paused at that thought. He loved her. For the first time in his life, he loved a woman, one sweet woman. "Zandrea."

"Yes?"

He swallowed. "I love you."

She gasped. Her eyes widened, and she put her hands up over her mouth. Maybe he had spoke too soon and scared her. He wanted to take it back and not allow her to fear or be hurt, but he couldn't. It was true. He loved her with all his heart.

"Are you sure?" she said at last. "You're not just saying that to sleep with me. I mean we were going to do it anyway."

Stepping close and drawing her into his arms, he forced her to look into his eyes. "I love you, baby. So deeply. I know it's fast—"

"No, it's not too fast." She shook her head. "I can't explain it either, but I love you as well. I want to be with you in every way."

Brant followed as she led him toward the single bedroom, and quickly he slid out of his clothes. The appreciative scan she gave his body made him harden all the more. With a boldness that was more likely because her body remembered their night together than anything else, she took hold of his staff and stroked it from the base to the top. Her thumb glided over the head, smearing his pre-release around.

"Ah, Zandrea," he breathed.

She dropped to her knees. He thought about telling her she didn't have to suck him, but the words wouldn't come out. When her lips enclosed around him, taking him deep, he refused to deny himself the pleasure her warm mouth offered.

Tangling his hands in her hair, he pulled her head gently forward. "Take me deep, Zandrea. That feels amazing, baby. You're so good."

"You taste amazing," she told him when she drew back a moment. As he had instructed, she took him deep into her throat, moaning and sucking until he was sure he would burst forth any second.

When he couldn't take it any longer, he pulled away and helped her to her feet. "I need to come inside you. I want to feel you wrapped tight around me when I release."

They lay together on the bed. Brant guided her to her back and lifted one of her legs while pushing it outward. Her sweet center drew his attention, so wet and ready for him and him alone. Driving a single finger up her tunnel, he watched her face. Her eyes drifted closed, and she arched her back, pushing out her stiff nipples. He leaned down and captured one in his mouth, sucking while pumping his finger into her.

"Brant!"

He drew back just enough to flick his tongue over her tight little peak, but he paused in his stroke in and out of her. "Do you want me to stop, baby?"

"Never!"

With a grin, he continued to dip his finger into her and added another, then another. When he couldn't bear waiting any longer, he shifted his weight to lie between her legs and hoisted her knees up higher. Her sweetness opened to him, and he watched with his desires threatening to make him lose control because her cream was running heavy for him before they had even gotten started.

With deliberate care, he pressed his shaft's head against her opening. Her folds parted, and she stretched to fit him. It felt so incredible, he panted to hold on until he was seated inside her. Inch by inch he slid deeper. Zandrea whined and squirmed. Her fingers clenching the sheets, she raised her hips for more. "Come on, Brant, don't make me wait. Please, put your dick all the way in me. Now!"

"Easy, baby. I have to take it slow or I'll come too soon. Wait for me, Zandrea. I promise I'll do everything I can to please you."

At last he was buried to the hilt, and he collapsed on top of her, breathing hard and willing his body to wait. The sensations eased, and then he lifted himself on an elbow in order to stare into Zandrea's face while he pumped in and out of her. He watched the ripple of emotions in her expression, how her mouth fell open, and she alternated between licking her lips and biting them. How one minute she grabbed hold of his ass, forcing him to pump harder and the next she seemed to lose all energy to move.

Brant's climax raged forth. He couldn't hold back much longer, but he fought to hang on. Zandrea's screams and her trembling told him she was near to her orgasm. He wanted to wait for her. He nibbled her neck and bent to capture a nipple between his lips. Sucking it brought on more of her screams, and then she wrapped her legs around his waist, squeezed and then shouted her release.

Not hesitating for a moment, Brant picked up his pace until he was pounding into his lover. He reached around to grab her ass and drag her tighter against him. His growl grew deeper, and his teeth extended into sharps points. Before he realized he would do it, he bit down into her shoulder, but Zandrea was too lost to the pleasure to feel the pain. In another second, Brant released, and he had to clamp his mouth shut to keep from allowing the beast in him to howl all the way through it.

After swiping his tongue across the small wound on Zandrea's shoulder and making sure he changed fully back to his human form, he rolled to her side and pulled Zandrea close to him. "I'm sorry. I got carried away."

She snuggled into him. "Don't worry. I have to admit, I don't come easily so coming twice with you in me was amazing."

He glanced down at her like she was crazy. During that first night they had spent in bed, Zandrea had come at least half a dozen times. She must be mistaken.

She laughed. "You look like you don't believe me. Trust when I tell you, there have been countless times I had to do it myself afterward."

Brant narrowed his eyes. "You will never have to do it yourself with me, even if I have to use my fingers. It's my job to please you sexually."

She moaned. "Promise?"

"Promise."

"And what do we have here?"

Brant jerked at the sound of his brother's voice. He looked around to find him standing in the doorway, arms crossed and brows lowered. Several other shifters were behind him, but Lucas blocked their view, stepped into the room and shut the door.

Zandrea yanked the covers up over her body, and still hid behind Brant. "Who the hell is that?"

"My brother," he muttered. "So you found out, Lucas. What are you going to do?"

Lucas shrugged. "Me? Nothing. I wash my hands of you. But you will stand before your peers and give an accounting of why she is more than all of us, our safety."

"Shit!" Brant spat.

"So I advise you to get dressed and get your fucking story straight, because whatever happens now, that's the end of it. For good."

Chapter Fourteen

Zandrea scooted to the edge of the bed and grabbed her clothing that Lucas had gathered from the front room and tossed at them before going back out and shutting the door. She hated dressing right after sex without taking a shower, but the urgency in Brant's demeanor didn't brook any arguments. She had no idea what was going on, but those men, his brother and the others she had spotted behind him, looked like they meant business. What the hell had she gotten herself into?

Brant grabbed her hand when she would have moved past him to go to the door, and he gently pushed her down on the bed again. When he had drawn a chair up close and straddled it, he let out a heavy sigh. The fear in his eyes had her shaking.

"What is it? What's going on, Brant?"

He closed his eyes a second and then seemed to force them open, training his dark gaze on her. "I wanted to keep my secrets and pretend everything would be okay between us. But no relationship could be built on lies. Not a good one anyway."

"W-What do you mean?" Her stomach knotted. She didn't want to know that there were secrets, and his words sounded too much like he was going to leave her. Did he set up this elaborate scheme of his brother showing up in order to break up with her after she'd slept with him? No, that would be over the top. At least, she hoped it was.

He took her hands in his and squeezed them before taking them to his lips one at a time and planting gentle kisses on each. "Remember above all else that I love you. I didn't think I could ever feel this way about a woman, but I do with you, Zandrea. You are my mate, but I don't love you just because of that. Or maybe I do since that means we're right with each other. I don't know."

"You're confusing me, Brant. Just say it." She pulled her hands from his and clutched them in her lap. "Are you breaking up with me?"

"Never!" He stood, moved the chair aside and sat down beside her, but he didn't attempt to take her hands again. "Zandrea, this will be hard to believe, but I am a wolf shape shifter. That means I can change my body form into that of a wolf. I was born that way, and I can do it at will. There are others like me, and it is against our rules to let humans know of our existence."

Zandrea just sat there unmoving, staring at the floor. "Humans," she whispered.

He explained other facts, that all of the men out front, including his brother, were like him. That they had met and made love before, that he had spent time with her in his wolf form living as her pet, and worse of all, that Lucas had erased her memory of everything not once but twice.

Zandrea surged to her feet and paced away from him. "How can I... Why should I..." She spun around to face him and then turned away again. She couldn't look at him. Her love for him warred with the pure insanity of what he was telling her, of how if it was true, he had manipulated her. "So you made me love you, bit me...used me?" She touched her shoulder where it was still tender.

"No, never." He stood as if he would come to her, but she backed away. His shoulders slumped in defeat. "I can feel it, your longing to run away from me. If it would help, I would take you away from here, far away and let you live your life, but you would never survive."

"What the hell does that mean?" she demanded, whirling around to face him. "What fucked up thing did you do to me, Brant?"

For a moment desperation filled his eyes, and he reached for her. But then he dropped his arms to his sides, his eyes darkened, and all the warmth she had seen in them before was gone. He looked almost exactly like the ice king his brother had seemed to be when he walked in earlier.

"I'm sorry. There's nothing else I can say. I screwed this all up big, but you will have to stand before my people, and we both will have to accept their decision whatever it may be. So, let's not delay our fate any longer."

Zandrea put her hands on her hips. "I don't have to do a damn thing and..."

The door opened. She fell silent at Lucas standing there, a look of impatience on his face. "Ready to go? Good. Let's move. You'll both be riding with me. Jed will take your vehicle and gather the rest of your things."

When Lucas would have taken her arm to guide her out, Brant growled, and he backed off. Zandrea shivered. They really were animals. She thought back to the day she first met him. No, that wasn't the first day. Lucas had erased the first time from her memory. But that day at the perfume counter,

Brant couldn't stop sneezing, and he had covered his nose with an expression on his face like he was about to die. Now, she knew. His heightened sense of smell. That perfume must have made him feel like he was dying.

Zandrea didn't know if she hated him for his lies, for tricking her and for not being human, or if she still loved him. The emotions were there, beneath the surface. They weren't going away. Yet, this was too unreal, too much like a dream from which she'd wake up soon.

And what was Brant feeling now? She glanced at him after they were inside Lucas' Jeep headed back out to the main road. Brant's expression was closed. She couldn't detect any feeling at all from him, least of all love. But he had said, just before he explained everything, that he loved her. Was that still true now that the full impact of what he was about to face came through to him? Did he resent her?

* * * *

When they arrived at a small townhouse in a not so great neighborhood, Zandrea thought maybe they were making a stop over before heading on to wherever they would meet with Brant's people. Somehow she had imagined a grand hall that could hold five hundred people or something, somewhere out in the suburbs or the country where no one would see the goings on.

Instead, she slipped from the Jeep to be hit in the face with the smell of good cooking somewhere and blasting rock music coming from the house next door. Several houses up, a young girl was riding her tricycle while her mother sat on marble steps watching and chatting with a girlfriend. This was all too regular city folk-like to Zandrea, and again she questioned whether this was a dream.

Lucas walked up to the door and rang the bell. A woman with blonde hair and eyes that looked like Brant's opened the door. Her mouth had smile lines at the sides, but her expression was serious. She took a step back to let them by. "Good to see you again, Zandrea."

Brant frowned. "Mother, she doesn't remember you or coming here."

Zandrea gasped. "I've been here before? This is a trick, right?"

"No, come on." He placed light fingertips at her elbow and led her to the back of the house, down some stairs, along a hall that seemed too long for the style of house and then into an open area. The scent of alcohol filled her nostrils, and a bar stood in the far corner. She imagined the lights were normally somewhat low, but right now, they were turned up high, making her feel like she was on display.

Two chairs sat in front of the bar, and a small crowd of people were standing around talking. When Zandrea and Brant had entered, they fell silent and stared. Zandrea scanned the crowd and spotted only one woman other than Brant's mother, who brought up the rear of their little group.

Lucas indicated for Zandrea and Brant to take a seat in the chairs, and he moved to the side. "Let's get right to it. I have business to take care of."

Brant grunted and stood his ground. "Who the hell put you in charge?"

His brother narrowed his eyes on Brant. Zandrea thought they were about to fight right there, and all she wanted to do was bolt. After a while, Lucas spoke. "If you were not busy with your human, you would have known that we've voted to reinstitute the old ways and that is to have an Alpha lead. The unanimous decision was that it be me. You have a problem with that? Would you like to challenge me?"

Alpha? Zandrea looked from one to the other. They were like animals, and the men watching gave off just as wild an aura as the brothers did. Zandrea inched toward the door, but Brant reached out and drew her to his side.

"Fine," he grumbled. "I won't challenge that decision. I have no wish to lead. However, I'll be damned if anyone thinks they can decide whether Zandrea and I remain together." He swept the room with his gaze. "She is my mate. Period. Nothing can change that."

An uproar broke out in the crowd. Zandrea caught "human" and "weak" in the murmured comments. She still had no proof that what Brant had told her was true. As if on cue, one of the men stepped forward and dropped a hand on her shoulder. Zandrea screeched in surprise.

Brant let out a growl that was pure animal, and Zandrea's eyes widened so much they hurt when his canine teeth grew longer than the others and all of them sharpened to points. His eyes shifted to black, and hair sprouted on his body. Brant tore the man's hand from Zandrea's shoulder and slammed him against the wall. In seconds, the man changed as well, growling and snarling like he wanted to rip Brant apart with his teeth alone.

"Enough!" Lucas bellowed.

The fight was over before it started. Brant released the other shifter and turned to glare at Zandrea as if this was all her fault. She took a step back, but his eyebrows lowered, and he snapped. "Come here."

She wanted to smart off, telling him to kiss her ass, but she didn't dare with the mood he was in. Instead, she shuffled over to him, praying he wasn't about to rip her apart like he seemed to want to do to his own kind.

Surprising her, Brant wrapped an arm around her waist and drew her close. He whispered in her ear, "Remember what I told you."

He loved her. Warmth spread throughout Zandrea's body. She closed her eyes and rested her forehead on his shoulder a moment. Despite what she had just seen, and what she felt like doing, which was running far and fast, she realized that she loved Brant still. None of this situation was clear, but one thing was, she couldn't leave him. The pain, the longing, she had felt was because Brant wasn't with her. From what he had said, she was his mate even when she didn't know him. Her emotions knew, her heart knew. And that's what she would follow.

Zandrea cleared her throat. "I don't know what your rules are and what you are thinking about doing. All I know is that I love Brant with all my heart, and I cannot, I *will not* live my life anymore without him. So do what you will. We're staying together, and even if I have to fight a pack of wolves to stay with him, I'll do it."

For what felt like hours, no one said a word. Zandrea was waiting for them to all burst out laughing at her thinking for one minute that she could take them all on let alone one of them. And then it occurred to her that they could also just take her out back and kill her, and no one would be the wiser. Then Brant could get a new woman and forget all about her. She clung to his arm, hoping the latter had not entered anyone's mind.

"What say you?" Lucas asked them all. The murmurs rose, and Zandrea willed them to hurry before she fell on her face in a dead faint.

They seemed to come to a consensus, and Brant's mother stepped forward. "You will be allowed to stay with Brant, but you are sworn to secrecy about our existence. You cannot share it with anyone, including Nita and Stacy." At Zandrea's gasp, she nodded. "Yes, be assured we know everything about you. And if you tell anyone about us, you will be killed. Period."

Zandrea sagged into Brant, and he held her up, tightening his hold on her. He kissed the side of her head and released a shuddering breath.

His mother grinned. "For me personally, you better not hurt my baby, or I will hunt you down. Got it?"

Zandrea squeaked out, "Got it."

"Beer for everybody!" the woman yelled, followed by cheers all around the room.

For a long while Zandrea didn't raise her head from Brant's shoulder, and he didn't loosen his hold. If he did, she would have fallen, but she suspected he held on with just as much desperation as she did. Brant's words were strong, that he would defy anyone who would try to separate them, but he would have enough common sense to know he couldn't win against that many shifters, let alone Zandrea.

At last, Zandrea raised her head to look into his eyes. Where they had been angry, cold and at some point troubled, now they glowed with joy and warmth. Zandrea grinned. "What?"

"I'm wondering how quickly I can get you moved into my place," he told her.

"What?" She rolled her eyes. "I didn't say anything about living with you. I'm an independent woman, thank you very much."

He chuckled and squeezed her. "We'll see about that."

She flared her nostrils and smirked. "Whatever. Can we go now? Our little vacation was interrupted. Maybe we can zip back out to the cabin?" She wiggled her eyebrows suggestively.

Brant touched her lips in a feather kiss and then drew back. "Sounds wonderful, but the meeting's not over."

Zandrea glanced around. "They're all drinking like they're celebrating. It seemed to be over. Quick, but over."

He shook his head. "No, these bums will grab any excuse to drink. But you really must swear to keep our secret, and"—he gritted his teeth—"since they are instituting the old ways, we'll have to be officially united in a ceremony presided over by Lucas."

"Sounds like you have a problem with Lucas being the Alpha, whatever that means."

Brant didn't comment on it. "Don't worry. Everything will be fine." He tossed an annoyed look in the direction of his brother and then focused again on her. "First things first. We become official mates before the Alpha and elders, and then we figure out how best to spend many hours locked in each other's arms. Naked!"

Zandrea laughed and smacked his arm. "I'm ready when you are, baby."

He kissed her. "Love me?"

She nodded. "With all my heart."

"And I will love you always and protect you with my life. That's a promise."

City Wolf 2

Chapter One

Lucas leaned back in his chair and took on an expression of boredom. He let his gaze sweep the room, categorizing every woman as he went, who would be good to fuck, who he already had—and of course, who to avoid at all costs.

Deliberately ignoring Gloria meant nothing to her. She slunk to his side and rested long manicured nails on his thigh with a pout planted on her red lips. Even before her hand slid higher to stroke his shaft, he had begun to harden. No matter how she had betrayed him, he still loved her. She was the only woman he ever would love, maybe even the only *person* he'd ever care about outside of his half brother Brant.

"What the fuck do you want, Gloria? Run out of lovers for the night?" he spat. He'd displayed too much vehemence when he should have been indifferent.

Her smirk told him she had noticed. "Aw, still pining for me, baby?" She stroked him harder, and damn if he wasn't ready to come. He shoved her hand away and stood. Gloria wrapped her arms around his waist and rested her forehead on the back of his shoulder. At one time he thought it sexy as hell her being that small.

"Get lost, Gloria," he muttered with more control this time. "I'm meeting someone here. My newest bed partner, so don't get in my way."

"What?" She lifted her head and searched much like he did. "Which one is it? No, matter. You can tell her you're taken for the night. Remember how we used to fuck all night long?"

"Not really." He freed himself and walked out onto the dance floor, looking for a likely target, anyone he could use to put some distance between himself and Gloria. If she hung on him much longer, he'd give into her and wake up with a shattered heart the next morning. He may have liked to walk around like he was made of ice as the others had described him, but the truth was a whole other story.

A young woman with her back to him, swaying to the rhythm of the music, caught his attention. From his vantage point, she had an ass he'd like to ride and smooth brown skin that looked sweet like sugar. He scanned the area near her and found no man lingering close enough to claim her—not that it would have mattered—and he sidled up behind her.

Matching her movements, he swayed with her and leaned down to kiss her neck. She gasped and would have moved away, but he caught her around the waist. "No, don't move. Just turn your head and let me get a taste of that mouth."

"What?" She elbowed him and spun around with her hands on her hips and eyebrows lowered in a scowl. "How dare you presume I want to kiss you?"

Lucas blinked and took a step back. The studious one. What was her name? This was one of Zandrea's friends. The name slipped into his mind. Nita. He stood there staring at her while she railed at him, probably going through the expansive vocabulary she had picked up in all the years she'd been in university. He wondered what fears kept her from actually living rather than hiding out as a student for so long.

Whatever the reason, he needed her right now, whether she knew it or not. He had seduced many women in his time, and this sexy little thing wouldn't be any different.

While she continued to complain, Lucas reached across the space between them and scooped her up close to his chest. He was aware that he was exuding the pheromones that would make her melt in his arms, and that was just fine with him. Without hesitation, he lowered his head and covered her protesting mouth with his own. The second he slid his tongue between her luscious lips, she melted.

Deepening the kiss, he tightened his hold and ran a hand up her back to cup her head. His shaft, which had begun to calm walking away from Gloria, hardened all over again with his body pressed to Nita's. She was not his type, if he truly had one. He liked petite blondes, aggressive little wolf shifter females that could give as much as they got. But the sweet thing in his arms was leggy and tall. Her handful sized breasts, pressed into his chest was nothing like what he usually went after, yet still, he was about ready to burst kissing her.

"Come to one of the back rooms with me," he demanded when he pulled back.

Her large brown eyes were unfocused, and her lips were swollen from his kiss. She nodded unsteadily. "Yes."

"Hell no!" someone snapped.

Lucas looked up over Nita's head to the angry woman behind her. This was the other friend, the toughest of the three who would probably attempt to kick his ass should he try to take Nita for his own pleasure.

"This has nothing to do with you," he told her. "Nita is a grown woman who can decide who she takes as a lover."

"Whatever." Stacy snatched his prize from his arms. "She's not going anywhere with you. I saw you before." She nodded to a point somewhere behind him. "Over there letting that woman rub all up on you. So when you got bored with her, you came over here to get Nita. I'm not having it."

Lucas felt his eyes darken in anger and was glad of the low lights to hide the change. He breathed in and out a few times to calm himself, but it wasn't working. Instead, dislike of this woman ran through him. He glanced down at Nita. With his anger up, his seduction had eased. Nita blinked as if her mind was clearing from a fog. *Damn.* He still wanted her, and this woman wasn't going to keep her from him.

* * * *

Nita blinked and stood up straight. She watched a little dazed at Stacy arguing with the sexy man who had kissed her earlier. Wait, kissed her? She couldn't imagine that she had let a stranger rub all over her body and stick his tongue in her mouth. She was a little on the desperate side lately, and more than a little jealous at the fact that Zandrea had found a man and was hiding out somewhere in a bed with him, but to let this guy use her this way?

She focused on Stacy's words, and became more alarmed with each word.

"I saw you letting that woman over there rub you. So you think you're going to get my friend in the back to do the same thing? Not!"

Nita turned to him, realization dawning. "What did you do to me? Some kind of hypnosis? Who are you? And how did you know my name? I'm sure I didn't tell you."

His lips tightened, for some reason reminding her of how he had tasted. Whatever he had done to her wasn't present now, and yet, she ached to crawl back into his arms and offer her body and soul to him. Then again, the man was gorgeous, the epitome of dark and dangerous male. Almost black eyes, dark thick curls atop his head, hard muscles, and he dressed with casual grace in a collared black shirt and slacks. The shirt sat open at the neck, giving her a peek at matching black curls on his chest. A vision of running her fingers over that delicious expanse rose in her mind, and she turned away.

She needed a drink. Without another word or waiting for him to answer, she headed to the bar. Stacy could handle him. A man like him wouldn't look twice at someone like her. Maybe he was trying to make his girlfriend jealous. Whatever. Easy come, easy go.

Nita slid onto a stool at the bar and ordered her favorite drink, a Redheaded Slut. When the bartender placed her shot glass in front of her, she thanked him and scooped it up to down in one gulp. She squeezed her eyes shut and waited for the burning sensation in her throat to pass before she slammed the glass down on the counter.

"Yeah, I needed a stiff drink after the first kiss with Lucas, too."

Nita looked around to see a beautiful blonde standing beside her. The woman gave the man occupying the stool a look, and for some reason he cowed and fled. She sat down like the whole occurrence was typical for her.

"Excuse me?" Nita said.

The woman smiled, although truth be told, the coldness in her eyes could freeze a person. "Gloria Rampart. You?"

Nita hesitated. "Nita James. Nice to meet you."

Gloria waved a hand. "What I was saying was the first time I kissed Lucas, I was lost. Until I realized he would never give me his heart." She stuck a cigarette between her red lips but didn't light it. Nita watched to see if she would, given that smoking here was prohibited. "You see, Lucas is the ultimate Alpha male. He barks commands, expects you to follow and he doesn't give a shit about anyone, least of all women. He likes to have several women a week, sometimes several a night. So, if you had aspirations of getting with him—don't."

Finding no words right away to respond with, which was a rarity for her, Nita said nothing. Yet, even a blind woman could see Gloria was jealous and that maybe things weren't like she wanted them to be between her and Lucas. She paused in thought. *Lucas? Sexy name.*

Glancing back over her shoulder, she spotted him just turning away from Stacy and smiled. No one could out argue her friend. That was for sure. Nita refocused on the woman at her side and took on what Zandrea had termed her school marm attitude to beat down the pretentious. "Don't worry, sweetheart. Soon enough you'll come to realize that a man like him isn't conducive to a strong and healthy self-esteem. I would not direct my attentions on Lucas for all the money in the world."

Chapter Two

Lucas stood in the trees outside Nita's dormitory. What the hell was she doing still in school? And why were they allowing it? It could be that her family had money. When he was trying to clean up behind Brant, and his debacle of taking a human mate, Lucas had done a thorough background check on each of the three friends. Zandrea had worked at the hospital, Stacy for a car rental place and Nita was a perpetual student living off a trust fund.

He should have let it go after the scene her friend made on the dance floor. After all, he did not do human women—ever. In no stretch of the imagination could she ever meet his sexual needs, and yet here he was lingering like a fucking pimply-faced teenage boy, hoping for a glimpse of her.

Laughter somewhere nearby caught his attention, and he shrank back farther in the trees. Two men, probably barely into their twenties strolled up and came to a stop in front of Nita's building.

"Where are you headed, man?" the shorter of the two asked.

The other man hooked a thumb over his shoulder. "Gonna get me a piece of this woman named Nita. She stays here. Older woman, by five years, but she's ripe. Boy is she ripe."

"I hear you, dog." The first man grinned. "Give me a call tomorrow, tell me all the details."

"You know me."

They touched fists and went in different directions. Lucas felt the beginnings of a growl rise inside him without conscious thought. If that fool thought he would get his hands on Nita, he had another thought coming. Lucas would have no qualms about ripping him to shreds. The vehemence of his feelings gave him pause, but he ignored it. He would be just as violent toward another male sniffing around any other woman he wanted.

He considered shifting but thought better of it and instead ran across the street and entered the building. The door should have been locked, but someone had wedged a wad of tape in the gap where it closed, probably waiting for a lover to come. Lucas took advantage of it and slipped inside.

Just as he passed the threshold, a low tapping caught his attention. The man was already on the third floor, knocking at Nita's door. Lucas tensed. How the hell had he gotten there that quickly? Lucas had been only a step behind. No human could. He sniffed the air, picking up the scent of cheap cologne that wafted behind the man, but nothing else. Maybe it was his imagination.

Lucas climbed the stairs without making a sound, his ears strained to pick up anything unusual. One flight down from Nita's room, he paused. The rattle of the lock being undone reached his ears, and the door opened.

"Deandre, what are you doing here? I'm just about to go to bed." Nita yawned. Lucas poised himself ready to spring up the last flight of stairs if the fool dared try anything.

"Hey, baby, is that any way to greet a friend? I thought were getting closer the last few times we were talking." The guy chuckled. "And there was definitely some vibes passing back and forth earlier tonight after Chemistry."

"Were there?"

Lucas smirked at the vagueness in her voice.

"Uh..." All the bravado drained out of Deandre's mack. "Well, anyway, I knew you were going out with your girls to the club, and I didn't want to sweat you, you know. A woman has got to have time with her girlfriends. I understand that. It's the kind of guy I am."

Lucas peeked up over the stairwell to catch a glimpse of Nita resting her hip against the doorframe, her head tilted to the side and a slight smile on her lips. She could not be falling for this. He frowned and clenched his jaw.

"Is that right?" Nita chuckled. "You realize I'm older than you, right? Like what six or seven years?"

"Five," Deandre corrected. "And I love older women."

"Okay, well, I'll give you a chance." She ran a finger along the sleeve of his jacket. "Just because I think you're kinda cute."

Lucas released a low growl and had to duck down before they spotted him. Deandre made an exclamation, and Nita gasped. Lucas descended the steps to the first floor and waited in the shadows of the space beneath the stairs.

"Slow down, Mr. Eager," Nita said after a few minutes, when they had obviously assured themselves no dog was about to attack. Lucas imagined

Deandre had thought she was about to let him into her room. "We can go out to eat or something, maybe catch a movie. That's the deal. Take it or leave it."

Deandre grumbled. "You're direct, aren't you?"

"That's the kind of girl *I* am," she affirmed.

"Okay, then. I take it." Deandre's step sounded on the stairs. His mack had returned. "Be prepared to fall hard for me, baby. That's a promise."

Lucas waited in his hiding spot while the man came down and passed him. When he was directly in front of Lucas, he inhaled and still there was no scent from this man other than the cheap cologne. From his experience, all humans had a scent, and his sense of smell was one hundred times that of a human's. He should have been able to pick something up.

Deandre turned his head to look directly at Lucas, and although his expression didn't give the impression that he could see Lucas, that Deandre knew he was there and didn't consider him a threat irked him to no end.

Deandre chuckled low in his throat and shoved the door open. While Lucas waited a beat before he followed the man, he watched as if in slow motion as the tape that had kept the door open fell to the ground. The lock clicked in place.

Lucas pressed the door handle and eased the door open a bit. After a moment, he peered around the edge of the door and scanned the street. No one was in sight. When he had stepped out on the sidewalk, he stiffened at the click of heels on the cement. A woman rounded the corner of the building. She pressed a hand to her chest at seeing him and then strolled up.

"Hey, sexy. You scared me."

Lucas barely acknowledged her, but passed by and crossed the street to his vehicle. He tapped the unlock button on his key chain and snatched the door open before hopping inside. As he pulled off, his tires screeching, he realized two facts. One, the woman also had no scent, and two, there had been that lingering cologne in the air around her. He put both observations down to being tired and sexually frustrated. He would have to find someone to take the edge off and fast.

* * * *

With the sun shining in his eyes and a sense of being watched, Lucas opened his eyes. A sexy blonde whose name he couldn't recall lay at his side, leaning on his elbow while she stared in his face. He took stock of his libido. While he could take her a few more rounds, he felt somewhat satisfied. She was a shifter, so they had fun the night before. And the activity had served to free him from the temporary obsession he had had with Nita. She was human. He had no need of them. Case closed. Let her friend Stacy protect her from whatever creature the guy from last night had been. She seemed like she was time enough for him anyway.

Lucas threw back the covers revealing his morning erection and swung his legs over the side of the bed. A growl sounded behind him before his lover wrapped her fingers around his shaft.

"Oh, looks like someone's all raring to go," she cooed.

"I just have to pee," he grumbled. "Let go. What we did was a one time deal. I don't do seconds."

"Not what I heard." She followed him when he stood and pressed her big breasts into his back. A flash of his fingers kneading them while he sucked her nipples went through his mind. His shaft pulsed, but he pushed the thoughts away.

"Okay, I do seconds, sometimes even thirds. However"—he shoved her hands off of him—"I have no desire to fuck you again."

She gasped. "You cold bastard! I should have known not to sleep with you. I should have ignored your call. Fuck you, Lucas."

He bowed in her direction, his face impassive. She snatched up all her clothes and stomped toward the bathroom knowing he had been headed in that direction. The door slammed in his face, and the shower came on a second later. He tried the knob but it was locked. With a grunt he turned back to search the motel room for his clothes. He'd have to wait until he got home to relieve himself. These were the hazards of the single life. For a second, he considered following in his half brother's footsteps and getting himself a mate, but then he dismissed the idea. None of the shifter women he knew was the faithful type, and crazy as that seemed for a man like him, he knew if he did take a mate, he'd never want to share her with another wolf. Ever.

So life as usual. It wasn't so bad.

Chapter Three

Nita sat daydreaming about the night before while chewing on a thumbnail. Her professor's voice droned on, and while usually she was riveted to the lecture, having a great love of ancient history, today she couldn't concentrate. A pair of dark eyes filled her mind, eyes that were almost black and lips so firm and good, she could feast on them for months without taking a breath.

She had been flip with that woman. What was her name? Gloria. She'd been flip with her about not letting herself get into Lucas, but the truth was, she wanted more. Even if it was for one night of wild hot sex. That would be more than what she had come to expect in her life. Her lovers had been few and far between, and none of them were above average looking.

With effort, she shifted her thoughts to Deandre. He was cute, but young. She was not at an age yet where she wanted to date younger men, to see if she still had it kind of thing. Then again, two men after her in one night was a rarity indeed. A girl would be out of her mind not to play it up a little, just for the fun of it.

She grinned thinking of the train of her thoughts. Zandrea and Stacy would be rolling around on the floor laughing if they heard how she had picked up more of the relaxed way of speaking and thinking like they did. How could she not? Her life had been damn dull and filled with endless books before she met her two best girlfriends. She liked to think she was more down to earth now, and there wasn't a thing wrong with it.

"Ms. James?"

Nita coughed and sat up straight. Her professor repeated his question, and she was clueless as to what he was talking about. Her cell rang. She held up a finger and gave an apologetic smile before darting out of the room. From the corner of her eye on her way out, she spotted Deandre. He winked. She didn't acknowledge him beyond a nod but pressed her connect button to answer the phone.

"Hello?" she whispered, shutting the lecture room door behind her.

"Hey, girl. What are you doing?" Zandrea called through the phone.

Nita grinned. "Z, you're alive. I can't believe it."

"Haha. Funny. Want to have lunch with me today?"

Nita checked her watch. "It's like eleven thirty. You don't plan ahead, do you?"

"No, you do enough of that for us all. Besides, I just managed to crawl out of my man's bed for five minutes. I missed my girls, but that damn Stacy isn't answering her cell. Probably forgot to charge it and she's off in Timbuktu somewhere delivering a car."

Nita nodded. "Probably. Okay, where and what time? I had another half hour in this class, but I can just leave if I have to go any distance. This is my second time through it anyway."

"Damn, girl," Zandrea complained. "Let the schooling go. Get a real job like everybody else. Or just lay around spending your money like regular rich folk."

Nita burst out laughing. "I'm not that rich. I have to live on a budget like everybody else. Plus I love learning. I was thinking about traveling next year, visit all the places I've only learned about in a classroom setting. The problem is, I don't have anyone to go with me, and I'm a little nervous about going alone." Inspiration hit her. "Maybe if I can secure a boyfriend he could go with me. That reminds me that I have to talk to you about something, and it's a good thing Stacy won't be there. She won't think rationally if she knew."

"Oh, do tell," Zandrea gushed.

"In person. Where?"

Zandrea gave her the details, and they agreed on the time before she hung up the phone. She had just enough time to run over to her room, shower and change before jumping on the highway to get to the restaurant where Zandrea wanted to meet. She had said they had some amazing steak dishes, which she wanted since it seemed to be all that Brant ever craved to eat.

Nita couldn't wait to hear about how things were going with Zandrea's man and if she felt like he was the one. She doubted it because it seemed like all he wanted to do was have sex. That was good and all, but how did they learn more about each other and if they had common interests if their lips were locked together twenty-four seven?

As Nita stepped into her shower securing a cap around her shoulder length chestnut curls, she recognized the green-eyed beast for what it was.

She wanted a steady man in the bed just like anyone else, and if they had a lot in common that would be great too. She wouldn't begrudge Zandrea for fulfilling one of those desires in her own life.

* * * *

"Nita!" Zandrea screamed as she ran up to her. Her friend's arms wrapped around her in a hug that threatened crack a few ribs and squeeze out the last bit of air in Nita's lungs. "I've missed you so much, sweetie."

Nita groaned. "I can tell. Easy. What did you do, go on steroids or what? You're so strong and buff. I thought you'd have gained a little not leaving the bed all this time."

Zandrea chuckled and ran her fingers through her hair. It was several inches longer than when Nita had last seen it. Her friend's hair never grew that fast before. It was a tad freaky.

"Oh sorry. No, I'm used to Brant's roughness. The man is insatiable, and I admit I love it. Plus, he has an exercise routine you wouldn't believe to keep in shape." She waved a hand in the air and rolled her eyes as she pulled Nita to a table. "But never mind that. Spill. I want to know what you have to say that you didn't think it would be a good idea for Stacy to know. She's like a mother hen to you, so what's the baby bird been up to behind mama's back?"

Nita squirmed in her chair, looking down at her hands. Of the three of them, Stacy was the bold one, Zandrea was the wildest, but still bold, and Nita was the studious one, the woman with the least amount of experience with men. She knew that was why Stacy watched over her. Especially after she had nearly tied the knot with a broke guy who had just been after her money a few years ago. She would do well to be cautious, but she wasn't looking for a husband or to hand over any money. She just wanted companionship. That wasn't such a bad thing.

"Well it's about men," she began. "Two of them."

"Two!" Zandrea whooped, drawing the attention of several other patrons, and Nita sank lower in her seat. Her friend laughed. "Sorry, girl. I just got excited. Okay, so who are they? You get busy with either of them yet? Are you sure you want to take on two at once?"

Nita held up her hands laughing. "Slow down. No and no. I haven't gotten busy yet, and no, I'm not sure about either one. One is named

Deandre, and he's cute. Younger, but I don't know. Something mysterious about him that just draws me. Weird I know. And then there's Lucas. He kissed me last night at the club—"

"Lucas!" Zandrea's eyes grew wide. "*My* Lucas? I mean Brant's brother, Lucas? Which club?"

Nita chewed her lip. "The one we always go to of course."

"Oh goodness, no baby. No way. Not him." Zandrea shook her head back and forth so vigorously, her hair swung across her face. "Go with the other guy. Trust me. Lucas is the last man you want to take into your bed."

The same jealousy Nita had felt earlier came creeping back. Had Zandrea been intimate with Lucas and not liked it for some reason? But then again, when would she have? None of them had a man for a long while until Zandrea had gotten with Brant. And from what she'd heard about the man's appetite, there was no way Zandrea could handle two sex hungry men.

"What's the big deal, Z? You...uh... you haven't slept with him, have you?" Nita hated how she sounded like she was pleading for it not to be true."

"Fuck, no!" Zandrea exclaimed. "Not on your life. That cold bastard? In fact, I find it hard to believe he kissed you. He'd have to chip away the ice to meet your lips."

Nita smirked. "A lot of love for your brother-in-law."

Zandrea rolled her eyes. "Girl, don't even." She leaned back to study her menu a few minutes before laying it down and reaching across the table for Nita's hands. "I'm sorry to be like Stacy would be on this one, sweetie, but she'd be right on the money. Lucas is bad news. You're sweet and sensitive, and I know for a fact that his kind...I mean, the men in his family are charmers. They'll get you naked in five seconds, before you even know what happened to you."

Nita considered that. It was true. One minute she had been telling Lucas off for thinking he could just rub up on her and kiss her neck, and the next she had thrown her head back and was letting him slide his tongue down her throat. A shiver ran over her body at the memory. She couldn't help it. She wanted so much more. And she was pretty sure that woman who had warned her off of him just wanted more as well. Nita wasn't looking for love with Lucas. Just sex. From the looks of things, she would have to keep her relationship with him a secret from her girlfriends. If it got serious, then would get their advice.

She squeezed Zandrea's hands. "Okay, I will take your advice and concentrate on the other guy. He seems safer anyway."

Zandrea beamed. "All right. Now, let me order because I'm famished, and you can tell me all about him."

Chapter Four

Irritation rode Lucas' back like a growth, and he shifted his shoulders for the hundredth time trying to get a release. For the last week, he had been avoiding Gloria with the last crumbs of willpower he had, but today he knew he would go to her. Why? Why the hell couldn't he get her out of his damn system? Why her of all women?

He had been leaning against the outside wall of the club he frequented trying not to look like he was waiting for her to show up. She'd taken to bouncing around from place to place, and he had no idea where she was staying. Tonight a long sleek black limo rolled up to the door, and when the driver opened the back door, he wasn't surprised that Gloria stepped out. Her date, from the scent of him, was human. Lucas frowned. If a human female couldn't normally handle a male shifter, a human man damn well couldn't. And definitely not Gloria.

Squinting his eyes, Lucas noted the puffiness around the man's eyes and the way he shuffled slightly when he walked. He smirked. Gloria had worn the man to a frazzle, and he was only holding onto her for how she looked dangling from his arm.

As they passed, Gloria caught his eye. The invitation was clear. She hadn't gotten enough the night before and wanted him. Like the whipped puppy he was beginning to feel like around her, he started forward and then stopped at the fragrance that hit his nostrils. He turned his head toward the street to spot another car and another set of long sexy legs that were just unfolding from its interior.

Thoughts of Gloria floated away when he spotted Nita. She couldn't possibly satisfy him and yet, his mouth watered to have her, to hold her and look into those big warm eyes. *Idiot*, he chastised himself. She might not be of Gloria's caliber, but she wouldn't be any different. The proof was in the way she melded herself to the man whose arm she was on, those small soft breasts pressing against him, and the man practically drooling over the offering.

Suddenly feeling worse than he did knowing he would give into Gloria, Lucas pushed off the wall and rudely slid ahead of the advancing couple to enter the club. He ignored the curse the guy threw at his back and the sharp gasp from Nita's sweet lips. He needed a drink or several right now.

His drink in his hand and his eyes on Nita's hips, Lucas leaned an elbow on a table and tried not to be too obvious in his desires. It wasn't working.

"Whoa, dude, you want that? She's human you know?" Nash, one of the men in his pack strolled up with a wide grin on his face. "You've been staring her down all night. That idiot she's with isn't much, scrawny. Why don't you go over and take her?"

Lucas suppressed a growl. "What I do or don't do with her is none of your business." He played with his glass a few minutes before speaking again. "Have you noticed he doesn't smell human?"

Nash frowned. "Huh? I haven't noticed anything. I try to tone it down as much as possible in here. Sweat and other scents on people's bodies can get to be a bit much in this atmosphere. So if he doesn't smell human, what does he smell like?"

Lucas shrugged. "Not sure. I thought I'd leave it alone, but...well, I'm curious."

"Just curious, huh?"

Lucas gave him a look that said leave it alone. He would have no qualms about dragging the floor with his friend's sorry ass to make a point about not fucking with him, especially when he was in the mood he was in tonight. If his damn brother would drag his ass out from between his mate's legs for five minutes, he could talk to him about this guy, but Brant wouldn't surface for a while. Lucas knew he damn sure wouldn't if he had a mate.

Shaking his head to clear it of those dangerous thoughts, Lucas frowned and redirected his gaze to sweep the club, checking out who was in attendance tonight. Right away, he spotted Gloria in a corner booth on the lap of her lover. The man looked like he was passed out, and Gloria appeared to be ready to explode in anger at not having her needs met. She liked public sex. He considered going over there and must have moved as if to go because Nash caught his arm.

"Do you really want to do that, man?"

Lucas eyed the other man's hand on his sleeve. "Do you want to interfere with your pack leader?"

Nash didn't back down, one of the reasons Lucas kept him close. He didn't kiss anyone's ass, least of all Lucas', and he told it like it was. "We both know how it was the time you found her in bed with another wolf. You hunted until you were nearly dead and didn't shift out of your wolf form for two weeks. Brant and I went through a lot of shit to get your head screwed back on straight. You don't want to go that route again."

Lucas shook his arm off. "And I don't need to remind you that I am your Alpha. You don't tell me, I tell you. Now step aside."

Nash didn't move for a full thirty seconds, and then he seemed to think better of crossing Lucas. He bowed his head slightly and swept his arm out as an usher would. "Don't say I didn't warn you."

Ignoring the remark, Lucas threaded through the crowd, headed for Gloria. Sensing his approach, she glanced up, and the knowing look that came over her lovely face did not slow Lucas' steps despite the resentment of her hold over him increasing inside of him. When he was within feet of her table, Lucas found his attention shifting again. Someone rushed through the crowd, jostling another person into his chest. Without a thought, his hands came up to steady the woman before she fell, and he found himself nose to nose with Nita. Or not quite nose to nose. For the second time he was struck by her tall lithe figure. Why did she appeal to him so much? And how could she be the only woman able to break the spell Gloria seemed to have over him?

"Oh, excuse me." She paused noting it was him, and her lips parted in a soft gasp.

Lucas stared down at those warm chocolate lips, remembering how they tasted. His fingers tightened on her hips. They stared at one another for a long time before they were interrupted by an angry voice.

"I suggest you get your get your hands off my woman, chief."

Nita was obviously irritated by the possessiveness in her date's words. "I am not your woman, Deandre. But"—she glared at Lucas—"you do have a habit of putting your hands and your body where they don't belong."

He grinned, his heart light for the first time that evening. "Oh, I don't know. My hands feel like they belong right where they are. Don't you agree?" He continued before she could answer. "In fact, my lips are thinking my hands have the right idea."

Deandre's brows crashed low over his eyebrows, his lips tightened, and he laid a heavy hand on Nita's arm. All the feelings of possessiveness that Lucas had felt that first night he'd kissed her came pouring down over him now. A growl started in his throat, and while he knew he must protect the secret of what he was above all else, he couldn't think of anything beyond tearing Deandre's arm off with his teeth.

Two men stumbled up, both seeming to be drunk and unsteady on their feet, but Lucas knew differently since they were both shifters, and one of them was Nash. With a loud hiccup in Deandre's face and an arm thrown around his shoulders, Nash and his buddy noisily invited the mystery man to a round of drinks at the bar. Lucas, knowing what a steel barrier it appeared to be to resist against the shifter's muscle, watched as Deandre was dragged away.

He turned his attention back to Nita. "Dance with me, beautiful."

She scoffed. "Sounds like a command. I don't obey orders. I'm a grown woman."

"Wouldn't know it by how much time you've spent in school without focus."

She gasped. "If that's your way of charming a woman, you have a lot to learn yourself."

He stepped closer to her and lifted her chin to bring her lips up to his. "Let's get this straight right from the start, sweetness. I want one thing and one thing only from you." He lightly touched her lips with his own and was gratified to find them trembling. Not with fear alone but with desire. He could sense that a mile off, from any woman. "I want to fuck you. If you prefer, I want to make love to you. Either way, I want into your bed. I have no doubt that I can please you. If it's really good, we can continue in that capacity for a few sessions. What do you say?"

Lucas knew he had released pheromones. In the shifters it was extremely powerful and potentially dangerous. He could lure a woman he did not mean to and cause all kinds of trouble. Younger shifters had that kind of trouble more often than the older ones, but sometimes he could forget if he was too focused on the object of his desire. Like he was now. With effort, he attempted to calm his raging desire in an effort to allow Nita to make her own decision regarding whether she accepted him as her lover. If he didn't, she would be drawn to him like a bee to honey and wake up tomorrow wondering when she had consented. In a human, that could be devastating. Shifters were used to wild nights and mornings after. It came with the territory which had been what led to his conflict with Gloria.

Nita blinked several times, and Lucas knew her mind was clearing of his sensual hold over her. He resisted the temptation of tasting her lips again or running a thumb over her taut nipples so close to his chest. Waiting was excruciating.

"Well?"

"I..." she began. "Uh, Stacy wouldn't like it."

He frowned. "How old are you?"

"Twenty-seven. Okay, forget Stacy. Yes. My answer is yes. We can be lovers. But first I have to talk to Deandre."

"Forget him." Lucas whipped her around to face the door. He wouldn't wait another second to her to himself. That loser she had come with could go sniff out some new woman. Nita was his for now, as long as he desired her.

Chapter Five

Nita bit her thumb nail, something that was becoming a habit lately, while she stared at herself in the mirror. She could not believe she was in Lucas' house. She would have thought a man like him who probably had a different woman every week—hell every day—would never bring one to his house. And what a house it was, too. The place was a mansion and so tastefully decorated.

She ran her hands over the thick terry towels on the rack beside the sink with its gauzy bows tied around each. The deep, rich burgundy looked too good to dry her hands on, so after she'd washed them and patted water over her face, she had shook them dry.

The fact that the man had money was not what was bothering her. It was her lack of experience or rather her limited experience. Lucas was certain he could please her, but what about her pleasing him? Would he get up and tell her to get out if she couldn't excite him the way he wanted? Her stomach knotted at the thought. What the hell had she been thinking coming here?

Spotting her bag on the back of the door where she had hung it, she dug inside and pulled out her cell phone. Maybe she should call Stacy and have her come pick her up. Then she could put this whole episode behind her and spend the next few hours studying for the test she had on next Wednesday. After all, that was what she knew, what she was used to doing when she was sexually frustrated.

Just as she flipped the phone open, a knock sounded at the door. "Nita, you've been in there a long time. Are you coming out any time soon?"

She cringed and backed away from the door. Lucas was hot, but he was rude and cold too. A man like him couldn't possibly satisfy her. Sex was more than just bumping and grinding. It was gentleness and caresses. It was sweet words whispered in a woman's ears. She couldn't even imagine that man saying something nice, let alone gentle.

"I...uh...I think maybe...."

The words died on her lips when she heard the lock click like he had stuck a key in it. When the door opened, she stared at him wide-eyed and dry-mouthed.

"You're scared," he announced unnecessarily. "I'm not going to hurt you. Come here." He held out his hand, but his words were a command.

Alarm made Nita chew on her bottom lip. She was going to cry! *No, no, no!* She could not cry in front of him. A tear rolled down her cheek and plopped onto her blouse. Another followed.

Lucas crossed the space between them, slipped her phone out of her nerveless fingers and deposited it into his pocket. With no show of strain, he picked her up in his arms and carried her out to the living room. When he sank down on the couch, he rested her on his lap.

Nita struggled to quiet her sniffles and sighs to no avail. When she peeked up from her hands clenched in her lap, she found Lucas preparing what looked and smelled like hot chocolate in a mug on the table. A small saucer of cookies sat near it.

With precision, he snapped a cookie in half and guided it into her mouth. While she chewed, he lifted the mug, blew the steam away and held it before her lips. She took a small sip, and the rich warm chocolate went a long way to soothe her hurt feelings.

After she had eaten most of the cookies and drank down half the chocolate, Lucas wiped her mouth with a napkin as if she was a child and leaned back. "Better?"

Dumbly, she nodded.

"Good." He pushed away the dishes and turned to her to pull her closer into his arms. His mouth rested against the top of her head, and she felt his breath stir her hair. "Now, you're here because you want me as much as I want you. I think we can be good together. I'm confident you can please me."

He paused, and she swallowed, not so certain.

"I'm an excellent judge of a woman's skill," he boasted. She rolled her eyes but didn't respond. Fear was still gripping her so much so that she couldn't speak. The treat had calmed her, but she was no more confident now than she was earlier. Lucas seemed to read her mind. "If you like, I can make this easier on you."

She pulled back and looked at him. "What do you mean?"

He grinned. "Found your voice, huh?" He hesitated. "Call it a knack. I can...seduce...you until you forget your fears. You forget everything except having my hands on your body, my lips on yours, my dick—"

"I get it," she squeaked. "But trust me, there's no way my stomach will unknot at this point. I think you're out of my league, Lucas. And it's too bad that I have to admit it because you've already got a huge head. You don't need to get any fuller of yourself."

She expected him to go off on her or make some pompous speech, but instead he put a hand on either side of her face and forced her to look into his eyes. Nita didn't know what was happening, but just as Lucas promised, the fear began to dissipate. In its place was desire so strong, she knew she could not resist it.

Her fingers drifted to her blouse, and she began unbuttoning it with trembling fingers. The one thought that occupied her mind was getting naked for him, wrapping her legs around his waist and being so full of his hard-on that she would scream with delight.

"What are you doing to me, Lucas?" She groaned, arching herself to him. She ran a hand down over his chest to the solid erection in his pants. Someone whined, and it was shocking to find that it came from her throat. "What's happening to me? I need it now. Please," she begged.

Lucas stood her on her feet and without hesitation, stripped her of all of her clothes. Just as quickly, he stripped himself, and Nita feasted on the hard plains of his body, the thick erection extending up from a nest of dark curls and his wide chest, ripped abs and hard thighs. She panted.

And just that quick, the wildness inside of her left. He caught her beneath her chin and made her look at him again. "Now, beautiful, we are both raw before each other. I find you the most delectable woman I have ever seen. Every inch of you makes me want a taste. See the evidence here."

She dared not look now that her nervousness had returned.

"I want you cognizant of what we're about to do. You still want me don't you?" There was no doubt in his words.

"Yes," she breathed.

Without a word he dropped one hand on her shoulder and then drew his fingers up into his palm, all except one. His pointer finger skimmed down over her tender skin to stop at the tip of her nipple. All the while he watched her face for her reaction. Nita's legs grew weak. Arrows of desire shot down between her legs, and it was all she could do not to grab onto his hand and force him stroke her entire breast. The man knew what he was doing. He was an expert. If she had doubted whether she was in his sexual league before, now she was certain. She was far below him.

"I-I..." she stuttered.

"Huh-uh.' He wagged the same finger in front of her face. "No talking. Only feel."

What could she do except obey? He stepped back a little and ran the other hand down over her belly. When the tips of his fingers brushed the hair at her apex, she gave one last hiccup, and her eyes widened in surprise and embarrassment. He merely smiled and dove in with no shame.

An expert at his task, he parted her folds without looking and pushed into her wetness. Nita chomped down on her tongue to keep from crying out. She might have wanted to maintain control, but her body was on a whole other wavelength from her brain. Her legs parted, and she swayed forward, driving Lucas' fingers deeper.

Moaning, she reached up to grasp his shoulders for support, and he began a slow, agonizing stroke in and out of her. She fell into the rhythm, her hips arching forward and back, loving the feel of him fucking her with his fingers.

Before she knew what was happening, a climax shattered all remnants of constraint. She cried out and lifted one leg up to his hip where he held it until she had ridden out the pleasure cascading over her body. When the orgasm died down, she drew back, and Lucas removed his fingers.

"Excellent. Now, are you ready to please me?"

Nita swallowed, staring at his chest, suddenly too afraid to look him in the eyes again. "Yes, I'll do my best."

He snapped her chin up, his eyes narrowed and she thought, maybe darker than they were before. "You will please me, Nita. I have no doubts about that. Even if it takes us all night long."

Chapter Six

All night long? Was he crazy? Nita thought maybe he was. He had led her into his bedroom, a haven of masculinity and yet the king size bed with its silky black sheets and softness that seemed to wrap around her, was made to comfort male or female.

While Nita lay in the middle, feeling like a lost lamb waiting for the wolf to attack, she watched as Lucas circled the room, lighting candles. The thought crossed her mind that he was about to cast a spell, not unlike the one he appeared to have cast over her in the living room when all fear had left her to be replaced by naked lust. That was absurd of course because spells and magic didn't exist. Lucas was nothing more than a man, a man with skills to woo a woman like her, dumb enough to fall into his trap. Yes, he would be pleased tonight. Something told her he would not stop pursuing her until he was good and satisfied.

The bed rocked and sank down where he placed his knee. Somehow the candlelight gave his handsome face an eerie glow, and Nita swallowed thinking he looked dangerous, like he wanted to eat her rather than make love to her. She opened her mouth to say something, she didn't know what, but no words formed either in her mind or on her tongue.

Lucas slid a small tray over closer to the bed, on which sat several small bottles and a bowl with water in it. "Relax," he told her. "You'll enjoy this." He unscrewed each bottle and sniffed the contents before replacing the cap. When he came to the last one, he sniffed, nodded and added a few drops to the water.

With a small sponge, he soaked up some of the liquid and squeezed out the excess. She trembled when he touched her hot skin to gently push her back to a full recline.

In a low, mesmerizing voice, he explained what he was going to do. "I have a keen sense of smell. Certain scents set me off. Some in a positive way, some not so positive. This scent, a special blend I made myself in my greenhouse, is a favorite. I think you'll like it." He ran the sponge over her breasts, and Nita caught her breath. He might as well have been teasing her nipples with his bare hands because the sensuality of his movements heightened her desire. She moaned, and Lucas smiled and nodded his approval.

Nita breathed deep. "It smells like vanilla and something else I can't put my finger on."

He grinned. "And you won't. A secret ingredient."

"Are you a witch doctor?" she wondered and then lost all train of thought when his gentle washing lowered to her belly and on down toward her apex.

"Mmm, your cream will be even sweeter when I lick this off you," he muttered. His concentration was wholly on spreading her legs and carefully saturating her wet folds.

Nita grasped the covers and closed her eyes. She thought she might have drawn blood when she bit down into her lip, but she didn't care. Lucas lowered his head between her legs, and the sponge tossed aside, he fed noisily at her center. Nita screamed in ecstasy when he lifted her ass to drive her closer to his hungry mouth. She came without warning the second he drove his tongue deep inside her.

"Lucas, oh, what are you doing?" Impossibly, she came a second and third time in rapid succession. This was not just some scented liquid he had used on her. She'd never come so fast and so hard. Tears filled her eyes, and she thrashed about, struggling to hold on to her sanity in the midst of the intense pleasure. "It was supposed to be your turn to come," she panted out.

He didn't lift his head more than an inch from her. His voice was rough and deep, sending a bolt of fear through her. "Do you think for a moment that I'm not enjoying this? I could eat you all night!"

She climaxed again and again, pleading with him to stop. Not because she wasn't enjoying it or that she was sore, but a woman could only take so much before she exploded. Right? Nita practically howled his name countless times, and then he rose up and sat on his haunches.

This time she knew his eyes had changed. They were coal black, and there was menace in his expression. Roughly, he dragged her toward him and positioned her so that his dick pressed against her opening. She thought about protesting, but it was too late. He plunged into her, deep and fast. His head went back, and he shouted "yes" over and over as he ground into her.

Her lover being so well-endowed, Nita expected his entry to hurt since it had been a while, but along with the stretch and her tight muscles gripping his shaft like it was a gift from the gods, she felt only bliss.

Lucas paired her ankles in one hand with her legs straight while he pushed in and out of her, his balls slapping against her ass. In a fluid movement where he didn't lose connection with her, he rolled her to her stomach, hiked her ass in the air again and pumped her from behind. She groaned into his pillow, muffling her cries as much as she could when all she wanted to do was scream her head off. She hoped—she prayed he was enjoying himself because she didn't ever want him to stop now. It was too good.

Another orgasm hit, and Lucas' growl matched her moan before he fell down on top of her. At the same instant she felt his warm release inside her, he sank his teeth down into her shoulder. She cried out in shock at the sting, which should have been more of a pain but wasn't.

"Shit!" he grumbled, this time in a voice she didn't recognize at all. She tried to turn to face him, but he moved his head to the other side of hers, panting and holding her in place. "Just a minute."

* * * *

Damn! What the hell had he been thinking? Not once, not one single time in all his long life on this earth had he slipped and bitten a lover. And yet when he was close to his climax, his teeth had sharpened, and he had found himself sinking them into Nita's shoulder. Whoever had created the wolf shifters had done him a huge favor in requiring two bites and not one for him to take his mate. He would just need to be careful and not bite Nita a second time.

Lucas rolled off of her and lay on his back now that he had calmed down some and forced his teeth to return to normal, his claws, which had grown out as well, to retract. There was nothing for it. His best bet was to treat her like she hadn't pleased him in the least. That would get her to call a cab and leave in a huff. He didn't know what he had been thinking in bringing her to his home in the first place. He never took his lovers anywhere but to their houses or to a motel. That had been the rule for years, and there had been no reason to change it now.

The sooner he got rid of Nita, the better. Of course, the problem was he was already growing hard again, and the smell of sex in the air, thinking of their come mixed together inside her was making his mouth water to eat her again. He hadn't tried out several of his favorite positions as yet.

Once more, Lucas thought. No twice more and that was it. He would push her to leave, and he would never see her again. No harm, no foul.

Chapter Seven

"So how did the date go last with what's his name. Deandre?" Stacy grinned and winked at Nita. "You got in kind of late. I would have stayed up to wait for you and talk a little, but that last trip took it out of me, especially with Kevin acting like an idiot lately."

Nita bit her lip. Late? She'd gotten in at a quarter to five that morning. When Lucas had said he could eat her all night, the man was not kidding. He could do that and more, and his weird potions or whatever they were only enhanced the experience. When she thought about the reaction his body had in response to them, way beyond the erotic boost she had experienced, she shivered with the delicious memory. And she was sore all over. Of course, she couldn't tell Stacy any of that.

"Okay, I guess. Not sure about him." She'd be lucky if the man called her again. She had abandoned him in the middle of the date to go sleep with Lucas. Who could forgive that? "It was great of you to let me stay here, Stacy, but I think I need some quiet time at the dorm for a while. I have a test on Wednesday, and men are not on the plan before then."

Stacy shook her head. "I can't believe you. You're not going to give me details, are you?"

"Not really."

"Witch!" She rolled her eyes. "I'll get it out of you sooner or later. You don't have that doe-eyed look, so I think you're safe for now. If I see it, we're definitely talking."

Nita waved her hand on the way out the door. She had skipped the first class of the day, but she couldn't miss the later afternoon one. "Sure. I'll talk to you later."

As she jogged down the stairs to the first floor of Stacy's apartment building, headed out to her car, she thought about how she had woke up after a short half hour nap with Lucas to sneak out of his house. A few blocks down the road, and she had called a cab to pick her up. Contrary to what Stacy and Zandrea thought, she had learned her lesson with giving her heart to men. Lucas would have gone back to his old cold self when he woke up for sure and then kicked her out or dropped her off at her dorm without a backward glance. She had beaten him to the punch, and it felt good like for once she was the one in control. The feeling might be an illusion, but she was going to hold onto it for as long as it lasted.

Sliding into her car and then turning over the engine, she rubbed her shoulder where Lucas had bit her right when he came inside her. He was a weird one, and yet, if he asked, she just might give herself to him again. And that scared her more than anything. She might not be doe-eyed right now, but she could be—with him.

Right as Nita turned into the parking lot at her university, her cell phone rang. She kept her eyes on the road while she fished inside her purse to retrieve it. Punching her horn at a driver backing out in front of her without looking, she flipped the phone open and pushed the connection button. "Hello?"

Only after she heard his voice did she realize she should have checked the caller ID. "Hey baby, what happened last night?"

Nita's throat closed. What was she going to say? "Hi, Deandre. Um, I am so sorry about running out on you. I had a family emergency and was so distracted that I forgot to let you know I was leaving. A friend took me home."

A long pause. "A friend. Hm. Because it looked to me like you were stepping out on me with some other guy."

Nita's eyebrows shot low. She didn't like being caught in a lie, and she rarely did it. Irritation rose inside her at both being caught and at what she had done to Deandre. It was low, not the kind of thing she did. "He is a family friend. His brother is engaged to my best friend." That was somewhat true.

A buzz sounded in her ear. She lowered the phone to glance at the caller ID this time. She didn't recognize the number, but suspected it was Lucas. The phone seemed to yell at her to choose whether to swap over for the other call. She swallowed hard. "Could you hold on a sec, Deandre? I have another call, and it could be important."

"Same as last night, huh?"

"Yeah," she snapped and switched over. "Hello?"

"You ran out on me," Lucas announced without preamble.

"Lucas." Damn, how did she get herself into this bind? She cleared her throat and tried to take on the female player attitude that she so was not.

"Come on, it was just sex. It was good, granted, but that's all. We didn't need to wake up holding each other. And I had an early class to get to. Rather than disturb you, I called a cab. No big deal."

Holding her breath, she waited for his response.

"You're right. I like a woman who understands it's just physical. No emotions need get involved at all. So, I'll call you maybe next week. If you're available great, if not, well you did please me last night."

Nita rolled her eyes. All about him. "Well I'm not sure. You pleased me as well, but I'm not into casual sex." And she had just blown her whole player persona. "I think we can put it down to an experience." Before he could say anything else, she blew him a kiss and shut her phone and then threw it into the passenger seat beside her.

As she pulled into a parking space, her phone rang again. Deandre! She had forgotten she had left him on the other line, and come to think of it, how did Lucas get her cell number? She didn't remember giving it to him. *Men!* Zandrea was right. She could not handle two men at once.

She answered the phone.

"Wow, you hung up on me. My feelings are hurt. I'm beginning to think you don't like me," Deandre whined, although he didn't sound hurt in the least.

"I'm sorry. I think I forgot to charge it. It might go out again." She thought fast while she stepped out of the car. "Listen, why don't I treat you to dinner tonight? We can go wherever you'd like. Just name the restaurant."

Deandre chuckled. "Okay, I'm going to hold you to it. You can't run out on me, and you've got to give me a kiss to make up for everything."

Nita yanked the door open to her classroom. "I won't run out," she told him firmly. "Got a class. Leave me a voicemail or text message with the name of the restaurant so I can call ahead if I need to. Talk to you later." She snapped the phone closed and then turned it off.

* * * *

Deandre slammed his fist into the wall of his room and then winced in pain. Nita was playing harder to get than he had anticipated, and it was all because of that other guy she had walked out with. He wasn't a fool. Anyone with half a brain could smell the lust rolling off of those two when they left. He had not been so distracted by the guy's friends that he didn't see what was going on. But if he had pushed he would have revealed what he was. And that was not an option right now.

Above all else, he needed to secure Nita. He had chosen her, and when he set his mind on something, nothing could change it. He would have her one way or another, even if it meant taking out the competition. He grinned. He knew just how to do that too. Of course with that cold son of a bitch, it wouldn't take much. Nita would no doubt already suspect he had no heart. Deandre would seal that belief in so that she wouldn't look twice at that fool. Then the door would be wide open for Deandre, the wronged lover. He laughed at the possibilities. This would be fun, and he needed some fun after laying low for so long at the university. Things were about to heat up big time.

Deandre punched in a speed dial code on his phone and waited for his friend to pick up. When the groggy voice came on the line, he said, "Hey, got that info I wanted?"

"Damn, D, you just asked for it like two hours ago." A yawn distorted his next words.

"That was last night, Kevin. I need to know where he hangs out. I need to know where he is right now. If you'd get your ass out of the bed for five minutes, you could get me what I need."

Kevin yawned again, and Deandre picked up the sound of aluminum cans being kicked aside as his friend shuffled to wherever he had the information waiting. "I had a long day yesterday, and I'm trying to catch up on my sleep. Besides, I've got girl troubles of my own."

Deandre sighed. "Tell it to someone who gives a shit."

Kevin grumbled. "Would it kill you to be nicer to me? I know I owe you a lot, but still. Damn! A person can only take so much before they lash out."

"Is that a threat?"

No response for a full minute. "No, it's not. Just...lay off. Okay, he and his boys hang at this club—"

"I know about the club! There's got to be somewhere else, maybe during the day. I want to touch him before tonight."

"You're disgusting," Kevin spat. "How did I get mixed up with you?"

Deandre laughed. "Shall I go over it? Recite just how much I did for you that night?"

"No, that won't be necessary. You saved my ass. I owe you. I get it. You have the nerve to call us friends sometimes, but we both know I'm now your lifetime lackey."

"See, we understand each other, don't we? What do you have, Kevin? I'm losing my patience. If you fuck it up with Nita and I, I swear I'll—"

"A country club," Kevin blurted. "For the rich and snooty. On the north side. Let me give you the address. There's a good chance he'll be there right now, drinking with his buddies and celebrating how lucky he got last night."

Deandre slammed down the phone. When this was over, he was going to kick Kevin's sorry ass and maybe get himself a piece of the woman he was obsessed with. He laughed. Maybe. That depended on how devoted Nita would be to him after he got what he wanted from her.

Chapter Eight

Nita knew something bad was coming the minute a cold breeze blew past her in the restaurant with her friends Zandrea and Stacy. The day was warm, and not a wind was stirring. Besides that, they were nowhere near the door when she felt it. She shivered and drew her jacket up around her, which she had discarded upon sliding into the booth.

"Whew, did you two feel that?" she asked her friends. "Felt like someone walked over my grave."

Stacy snorted. "Since you're not dead, that's hardly likely. And what are you eighty-five talking like that?" Stacy bumped Zandrea's arm. "Maybe we need to keep a sharper eye on Nita. I think she's losing it."

Nita rolled her eyes, and Zandrea shook her head. Their friend hadn't spoken much since they had arrived. She seemed preoccupied with something on her mind. "I'm sure she's fine," Zandrea muttered.

"Come on, Z. Give me a break," Stacy complained. "We finally get to duck out for lunch all together, and you can't get your mind off your boyfriend. Have some pity on your manless friends."

Nita didn't want to correct Stacy. She did have a date with Deandre tonight, and Lucas hadn't said he wouldn't be looking her way anymore. Not that she was going to let herself get mixed up with him too much.

Zandrea sighed. "It's not Brant I'm thinking about. Not exactly. There's been some unrest among his...uh...people. Not sure, just something doesn't feel right to them, like something bad's coming."

Stacy frowned. "What are they psychic?"

Zandrea glared. "Never mind."

"I know what you mean, I think," Nita put in. "That feeling I just got was like that, but it was like it was about me, not Brant's people. Maybe I am losing it. I don't know. I had a date after forever, and you'd think I'd never been out with a man. I feel so off in my head. I can't explain it."

Zandrea made a noise of understanding. "Like being with him and talking to him has disordered your emotions to the point that you don't know if you're coming or going. And you find yourself clumsy for no reason or absent-minded when you're not even bogged down with a lot to do."

"Yes!" Nita stared in surprise that Zandrea had hit it on the head. She had been just like that since that first kiss from Lucas. She was pretty positive it was not a result of meeting Deandre, which was a shame. Her emotions had been roiling out of control, and had gone even further out of whack after she had slept with Lucas. That was the reason she had taken the initiative to wake up and leave his house before he could do anything. It was the reason she had led the conversation they had had on the phone. Yet, even with those measures, her insides churned with both nerves and longing to be with him again. If he didn't call again, or if she didn't see him, then what?

Zandrea's expression froze in place along with her fork halfway to her mouth. She was looking past Nita's shoulder. "What the hell is he—?" she whispered.

That same foreboding rippled over Nita's body, giving her goose bumps. She turned slowly in her chair and was shocked to see Lucas bearing down on them. *No, not now. Please, not now.*

His brows were low over his eyes, and his jaw was set. Her gaze dropped to his hands clenched at his sides, and she would have fallen if she wasn't sitting. This was more than irritation. This was all out anger. Could she really have set him off that much with how she had dismissed him?

Stacy surged to her feet, but not before Lucas took hold of Nita's arms and dragged her to her feet. He shook her a little so that her head rocked back and forth.

"Tell me I am wrong in thinking you're seeing another man!" he shouted. She stared at him.

"Take your fucking hands off my friend," Stacy roared.

Lucas ignored her. "Answer me, Nita."

"Y-You're hurting me," she managed to utter. "Let me go, Lucas. Who I see is none of your business. Our night together was—" She broke off her next words before she could alert the others about them being intimate.

Lucas' eyes had gone wide as if her hinting at them having sex was a surprise to him. She glared up at him wondering what had come over him. His dazed look disappeared, and he shook her again, harder.

"You can spend tonight in my bed as well, but if you deny me and go out with someone else, you will be sorry." He released her and raised a hand above her head. Nita screamed and put her arms up.

Stacy charged him, knocking him off balance until he landed on his ass on the floor. He glanced up blinking, and before Zandrea could grab her, she kicked him between the legs. Lucas howled and rolled to the side holding his nuts.

Zandrea yanked money from her wallet, tossed it on the table, and herded both Nita and Stacy out the door. They were in Zandrea's SUV, speeding down the highway in seconds with Stacy in the back seat cussing up a storm and Nita shaking from head to toe in the passenger seat.

Nita couldn't get her mind to settle, to assess what had just happened, but one thing she knew without a doubt—there was something very off about that scene just now.

"Z, we left my car back there," Nita croaked with a dry throat.

"You're in no condition to drive," she snapped. Her attention turned back to the road and she fished her phone out of her pocket, pressed a button and held it to her ear. After a few minutes, she growled, "Your no good piece of shit brother just attacked my friend, and if you don't get his ass in check, I'm going back there and put him out of her misery!"

She explained briefly what happened and then fell silent, and so did Stacy, leaning forward to try to catch what Brant was saying in response.

Finally, Zandrea blew out a breath. "Okay. Yes, all right, Brant. I'll meet you there. But we're settling this, baby. I mean it." Zandrea disconnected and put her phone away. She reached across the seat and patted Nita's hand. "Don't worry, sweetie. Brant's just as pissed as I am. He wants me to meet him and go over what happened. Then we're going to go find Lucas. Brant has a way of tracking him down."

"What GPS or something?" Stacy asked.

"Something like that," Zandrea answered. "Okay, Nita, I'm going to drop you at Stacy's. You just get some rest. We won't discuss right now the fact that you went and slept with him after I warned you about him. But trust me, I never suspected he would act like this. I would have told you flat out if I thought he was abusive. Brant has some explaining to do as well behind this shit."

Nita took a shuddering sigh. It was all she could do not to burst out crying. She found herself wanting to defend Lucas, but that was ridiculous. She was not the type of woman, she thought, to get caught up in a domestic violence relationship. Cutting all ties with Lucas was the best course of action. She should have listened to the warnings in the first place.

Absently rubbing the spot on her arms where Lucas had gripped hurting her, she said, "I'd like to go back to my place, please. My dorm room. I just want to be alone and sleep."

Stacy made a soothing sound and hugged her, reaching between the seats. "Of course you do, sweetie. I'll talk to you a little later on. And I promise, I'm not going to judge you. You are grown, and you can make decisions for yourself. I just want you to know I'm here."

Tears filled Nita's eyes, and she scrubbed them. Uttering a quick thanks when Zandrea pulled up to her building, she jumped out of the car and ran up to the door. Her hand shook so much she couldn't get the key in the lock, but another student came to assist her. Nita took the stairs two at a time and barely made it into her room before she was sobbing uncontrollably.

Nita had been crying for a half hour when the tears lessened. She lay flat on her bed staring at the ceiling and replaying the whole scene at the restaurant in her head. Something was off about Lucas that was for sure. He had been surprised when she mentioned them sleeping together. Yet, he was out of his mind thinking she was with someone else. But he had already known that the night he dragged her away from Deandre, and she hadn't been on another date with the man.

The whole episode didn't make any sense. Still, whatever his issues were, she could not see him anymore. He could deal with his family and see a therapist if that's what he needed. Maybe his psychotic break was what his people had sensed coming.

She rolled to her side and sighed with her hands tucked beneath her chin. The bite he had placed on her shoulder ached. She rubbed it remembering his touch, how he filled her and made her come countless times. What a horrible waste.

Soon, her eyes drooped, and she fell asleep thinking it was a good thing she had Deandre.

Chapter Nine

Deandre's shaft hardened in his pants at the first sight of Nita stepping out of her door. Her long caramel brown legs were exposed beneath a short dress that was cut in a style that hugged her small breasts. *Yum!* He groaned knowing she couldn't hear him as he hadn't yet stepped out of his vehicle. Soon he would be lying between those luscious legs, and he would enjoy hearing her cry out his name while he pounded deep into her.

Before he could spill in his new faded jeans, he pushed thoughts of Nita's naked body from his mind and climbed out of the car. "Hey, sweet thing. You ready to go?"

He held out his arms, but when he touched hers, she flinched and lowered her head.

"What's up? You feeling okay?" he asked her.

She nodded. "I'm fine. Can we go? I don't like standing out here." She glanced around her like someone would jump out of the bushes. The night was warm and breezy, and no one was about. He expected that all the eggheads that lived over here had their heads buried in a book. Deandre shivered. His purpose had been focused for a long time now, and attending college was a means to an end. When he got what he wanted, he would leave this stuck up facility for good. Whether he would take Nita with him he hadn't decided.

"Shall we go?" Deandre opened the passenger side door, prepared to play the role of understanding and sensitive lover. In no time at all, his sweet, innocent Nita would fall into his arms and his bed.

* * * *

Nita squirmed in the passenger seat of Deandre's car. She wanted to ask him where they were going, but couldn't find the energy to speak up. Her nap earlier hadn't helped matters at all. She was still depressed as hell, and her choice of dress wasn't making her feel anymore comfortable. The moment she had sat down the material rose, showing off too much of her thighs. And while the inverted pleats looked great standing, sitting they had flared only enough to hug her hips. She must have gained a little since the last time she had worn the Maggy London Ikat print dress. That meant more shopping, which she didn't like to do, but only because her trust fund was limited. Whoever heard of a person coming into their inheritance only when they turned thirty?

Resigned to being too exposed for the moment, she splayed her hand over the side of her leg and stared out the window. Thoughts of Lucas came to mind, but she was distracted from tormenting herself over him by Deandre's overpowering cheap cologne.

"Mind if I roll the window down a bit?" she asked him.

He ran a gentle hand down the side of her face and caressed her lips with the pad of his thumb. She fought not to pull away.

"Go right ahead, baby. Anything for you."

She lowered the window and closed her eyes. At last, Deandre returned his hand to the steering wheel, and the breeze rushed in to clear the air in the car and to clear her head. Only a hint of the scent remained. At this level, it seemed familiar, like she had smelled it before. Of course she would have. Deandre had been sniffing around her for a few weeks now. But the thought that she had smelled the cologne earlier in the restaurant at lunch time slid into her mind. *That's ridiculous. He wasn't there. Only my perfect lover, my insane ex-lover, Lucas.*

* * * *

Irritation rose inside Lucas making him feel like his head would explode at any second. Nita had made her position plain regarding him. There was no more need of torturing himself over the woman, and yet, when he had picked up her scent on his way out of town to put her, Gloria, and every other woman that tempted him out of his head, he couldn't help stopping to check on her.

Since that single bite on her shoulder, Lucas had been free of the crushing hurt in his chest that he had lived with ever since the night he caught Gloria in bed with another man. Now when he thought of Gloria, he felt nothing but disgust. In a single evening of making love to Nita, he had been freed. That had not been the case with any of his former lovers. Could it be because she was human? Was there something special about them after all?

No, he couldn't believe that, and yet here he was, obsessing over her. He wanted to get a glimpse of that sweet face, those wide brown eyes. Never had he once desired to bed a black woman. It just didn't enter his mind. And he'd seen several today alone who were beautiful, but the craving he had was for Nita.

He growled, slamming his fist against the center of his steering wheel. "Nita."

His staff grew hard almost to the point of pain. Tugging his pants to give himself room that no longer existed did little good. "This is just lust," he told himself. "Nothing more." With a sigh, he slid out of the car and stood alongside it. "One look. A single look at her cannot hurt anything."

Weaving through the oncoming traffic with horns blaring at him, Lucas crossed the street to stop in front of an Italian restaurant where he had caught Nita's scent. Rather than step into the lobby where he would be too conspicuous, he moved to the side of the building where there were more windows through which he could look in. The glare from the lights, though low, would allow him to see in but make it hard for the patrons to see out unless they pressed their faces close to the glass.

At a table in the back of the room, he spotted her, with the guy who had no scent other than that disgusting cologne he wore. Lucas picked up on the lust mirrored in the man's eyes as he seemed to stare down at Nita's cleavage. A growl started in Lucas' chest. He felt the shift in his eyes, knowing they had turned black, but he fought not to change any more. Nita wasn't exactly his. She had made that plain on the phone.

He watched her twisting her hands on the edge of the table and staring down at them. Was she still uncomfortable with men? After all that they had done together, her even taking the initiative to lick him and suck his shaft into her mouth, then later riding him to abandon, he thought the shyness would have passed somewhat.

Lucas sniffed. Along with her normal scent, he picked up something else, something he couldn't identify. She wasn't happy, maybe even sad. The tension around her mouth and eyes spoke volumes, and not only that the date wasn't going well. He had said he would leave town for a while, but remembering that he was the Alpha leader of his pack now, and that he couldn't just abandon everyone, he waited. Protecting his pack and watching Nita had nothing to do with one another, but he had no intension of admitting that to himself right now. She filled his senses, and was all he wanted to focus on.

At ten, the couple stood and moved toward the exit after Deandre had settled the bill and tip. Lucas hadn't missed how he stiffed the waitress on the amount he gave her for her services. The growl in his throat escalated to a snarl when Deandre rested a hand on Nita's waist, his fingers splayed too much in an obvious attempt to fondle her ass.

Lucas was gratified when she sidled out of his hold and walked ahead. Out on the street, he hid in the shadows not too far from them and picked up on the conversation.

"Why don't we go back to my place, Nita? We can talk, get to know each other better." Deandre smiled, a hopeful look in his eyes.

Nita shook her head. "I'm sorry. I'm just not good company today, Deandre. Something happened earlier that...well I don't want to talk about it." She laid a small hand on his chest. "Can I call you? We can do this again when I'm feeling better. I think I'm going to walk down to Stacy's work place. She's just a block over, and I know she told me she would be late leaving there tonight for some reason. I can catch a ride with her, probably stay at her place tonight."

Deandre chuckled. "Just what kind of relationship do the two of you have with you spending the night at her apartment all the time?"

Nita's eyes widened. "You're not serious, are you?"

Lucas suppressed a laugh of his own. Idiot should keep his mind on the sweet woman in front of him instead of fantasizing about two women together, which a fool could figure out was exactly what Deandre was imagining.

"Naw, baby," Deandre joked. "I was just joshing you. Okay, I'll see you tomorrow, I hope. Let's do something then. I think you're really special, Nita, and I want to build something good with you."

She backed up a step, her hands raised. "Slow down. I'm not sure I'm ready for that, and we don't know how compatible we are. I just...like I said, something bad happened, and I'm trying to deal with it. I'll call you."

With that, she turned and headed south along the street. Lucas had no intension of letting her walk at night alone, even if she was on a busy street where several stores lined the walk, and people were coming and going. He reminded himself that she was his priority and not the man staring at her ass with his mouth slack and the front of his pants tented. Lucas would deal with Deandre later.

When Deandre had jumped in his car and peeled out of his parking space in the opposite direction, Lucas fell into step behind Nita. He too wanted to watch her swaying hips he realized, but he pushed his desires aside. She was upset, and he wanted to know why. If someone had hurt her, they would pay.

Chapter Ten

Nita became aware that someone was following her, and her heart began to pound in her chest. When she reached inside her purse for the pepper spray she kept there, he spoke up.

"Easy, Nita. I'm not going to hurt you."

She gasped and turned around. Lucas stood there bold as anything after what he had done to her earlier in the day. "W-What are you doing here? Did you follow me?"

He nodded with no shame. "Yes, I wanted to make sure you were okay."

"No thanks to you!" she snapped. Her heart continued to pound, but now it was because he was close and all she wanted to do was run into his arms, to taste his mouth again, to feel the hard muscles of his body pressed against hers. This was ridiculous. The man had threatened her, had left bruises on her arms, and she did not bruise easily. "Get out of here, Lucas. I never want to see you or talk to you again."

"Why are you so mad at me?" he grumbled. "You are the one who dismissed me."

"Before you could do it to me." She rested her hands on her hips. "Admit it. You would have. You've probably done it to countless women in the past, leaving broken hearts all over the city."

"So your heart is involved?"

She squinted at him and rolled her eyes. Deciding he wasn't about to attack, she turned and continued her walk. He fell into step beside her, and she sighed. The man would not be dismissed easily. That much was obvious. She should pull out her cell and call Zandrea and Brant, but she hesitated. Doubts had assailed her all day long, and she wanted to get to the bottom of one particular one before she turned him into his people, or whoever.

"What do you want with me?" she asked him.

"Isn't it obvious?"

"Oh here we go, you back to your normal cold-heartedness. Do you think that acting that way will win me over? Or is it your way of protecting yourself?"

"What about you? You stay in school year after year, with no major, no direction."

"That's none of your business."

"Tell me why," he insisted.

At first she wasn't going to answer, but she hadn't even told Zandrea and Stacy the reasons behind her perpetual schooling. Her inheritance had stipulated that her school bills be paid for as long as she was in school. Back when she was eighteen just entering college, she had realized that the wording would allow her to delay life for as long as the money lasted. And if what her trustees said was true, it could conceivably last for several lifetimes.

She sucked in a deep breath and blew it out. Her fingers curled into her palms like they always did when she thought of her parents, even after all these years. "From a baby, my parents loved to party. It was their life. They couldn't get enough, and they were devoted to one another." She hesitated, not wanting to sound self-pitying but wanting to be truthful to how she thought of her mother and father. "Their love for one another produced me, but it did not extend to me."

His eyes widened. She thought they were very dark again tonight, but didn't put too much in it. When the normal coldness seemed to drain from his face, and he reached across to take her hand, she let him. Relief that he didn't offer empty assurances that her parents did love her in their own way made her go on.

"They dumped me in boarding school as quickly as they could and jetsetted around the world, from one upscale party to the next. The club you like to attend is partly owned by an old friend of theirs and another guy I don't know. Anyway, one time when I was twelve, they had picked me up from school and spent the weekend with me. It was not a good experience to say the least. Their drunken friends weren't the friendliest. Anyway, my parents blamed me for the incident and dumped me back at school early." The pain restricted her heart. She rushed on.

"That same weekend at a party they attended, a parcel bomb went off and killed almost everyone in the place, including my parents. In an instant I was left an orphan, raised mostly by my trustees who made every decision in my life, except one. School."

Lucas pulled her to a stop and turned her into his arms. At first Nita resisted, but she needed to feel his strength. She melted against him and breathed in his pure animal scent, something she couldn't exactly identify, but that seemed erotic and untamed. A lump grew in her throat, and her eyes moistened. Lucas murmured words she couldn't understand with his mouth buried in her hair, but their tone was soothing.

"I made the decision to stay in school where it was safe," she muttered. "Stupid, I know, but there's no accounting for how a psyche pushed to its limits will react."

Lucas drew back with his hands resting on her shoulders and a smile on his lips. "Learn that in school?"

She grinned and wiped away the tears. "Yes. Sometimes I get all school marmie, according to my friends."

"Feeling a little better?" he asked.

She did a mental check of herself and had to admit that she did feel better. Admitting to someone the real reason why she had hidden away from the world for so long was liberating in a way. It loosened the grip that fear had wrapped around her since her parents' deaths.

While logically she knew that just participating in the world in a real way would not destroy her in some way, the fear had still bound her. Nita didn't feel like calling up her school and telling them she was dropping out, but she was pretty sure, there would be some changes.

"Yes, I guess I am feeling better. Admitting how my parents' deaths affected me was a huge step. I had been in denial for a long time. I won't pretend I'm cured, but I can take steps in that direction." She smiled up at him. "Thank you for that, Lucas."

He lowered his head and pressed his lips against hers. She should have resisted him, but she didn't. She wanted more. Opening her mouth, she let his tongue slide between her lips. A moan escaped her when he caressed the warm walls of her mouth with his tongue and teased the tip of hers with his.

After a few greedy kisses where they clung together and moaned out their pleasure, he drew back. "Come to my house."

Her memories flood back, and she swallowed. "If I say no...."

He frowned. "I get the impression that you're expecting me to react a certain way. What happened to you earlier that you referred to when you were talking to your date?"

She gasped. He had heard them? And didn't he remember the way he had behaved when he grabbed her and threatened to beat her? She licked her lips. Lucas caught the action, and the desire that flared in his eyes was no less than what roared inside her, despite what it all seemed to be. She should be terrified of Lucas, running for her life from him, and yet she didn't want to. Stacy would cuss her out if she knew.

"If I say no to you, Lucas, and mean it. What will you do? If I say I prefer Deandre, the guy I went out with tonight, to you, what will you say to that?"

Lucas let her go so fast she almost lost her balance. He turned away stuffing his hands in his pockets. Confusion clouded her mind. Was he trying to reign in his violent temper?

"Are you trying to play me for a fool, Nita?" he growled. "I've been there, done that. I don't share my women."

She placed her hands on her hips. "Oh, that's rich because you damn sure don't have a problem with women sharing you."

"You don't know anything about me!"

She spun on the ball of one foot. "Go fuck yourself."

He caught her by the waist, whipped her around and lifted her up so that her eyes met his and her feet dangled above the ground. "I don't want to fuck myself. I want to fuck you."

Her breath caught in her throat. Not with fear, but with desire.

"I want to fuck you," he said again. "No hearts. No promises. Just sex. Great, hot, sweaty, exhausting sex. Nita," he groaned almost desperately.

"Yes." She panted. "Let's go."

Chapter Eleven

There was much between them. Lucas suspected she didn't trust him not to hurt her, although he couldn't figure out why she would feel that way. She had maintained control of the relationship, such that it was, from the beginning. He was just going along for the incredible ride. And although he should stop long enough to demand why she was behaving the way she was with him, as if he had done something wrong, he didn't want to. Not now. First he had to have her. Just this once, maybe the last time.

He had taken her to his home again, another mistake but he couldn't see taking a woman like Nita to a motel, not when she had freed his heart, had healed him to a certain degree. He carried her across the threshold of his home, and with her legs wrapped around his waist and his lips molded to hers, he directed them both toward the bedroom.

Her dress was pretty with its black and white print and its low cut to show off her cleavage, but it needed to come off. He knew a bit of frustration when he fumbled for a zipper in the back and found none. "Where the hell is it?" he growled against her lips.

She laughed and pulled his hand to her side. The zipper was there with a button-and-eye closure at the top. He fought to keep from ripping it off as he lowered her to the bed. When he had gently stripped his lover and then himself, he leaned up to stare down at her sexy body. Her soft creamy brown skin made him hard as a rock, and he thought he could come just looking at her alone.

Her dark chocolate nipples were tight buds that beckoned for his mouth, and he licked his lips before lowering his head to have a taste. She cried out at first contact and arched her back while pulling his head closer.

"Lucas," she moaned. "Suck my nipples, please. Make me come. I can't get enough of you. All night and day is not enough!"

"For me as well, my love," he whispered and could have kicked himself for calling her his love, and yet, it sounded right on his lips. He sucked harder at her nipple before moving to the other and tracing the path down her belly to the curls at her apex. His shaft jumped knowing he was so close to the place it ached to merge with.

She was soaking wet, her cream dripping down on his fingers as he sought to bury them inside her tunnel. She raised her legs and pleaded for more. He didn't want to deny her anything. While the first time, he knew he had pleased her, his mind had been filled with thoughts of pleasing himself. Now, all he wanted was to make her come, to watch her face while she exploded at his touch. She liked it slow sometimes and then hard at others. He wanted to pick up on her wavelength and fulfill all of her fantasies.

Sinking his fingers into her, he watched her eyes moisten with tears. He would have pulled back, but she grabbed his hand and drove him deeper. "Don't," she begged. "Don't stop. I need it."

Had he thought she weakened him with need? She was just as vulnerable with him, he noted, and for once in all his sexual escapades it didn't make him swell with pride, but with gratitude, that such a perfect woman would find her pleasure with him. Damn, he was doing it again. Falling in love. What a fool, and he went willingly.

"Nita." He lifted her higher on the bed and followed with his body above hers. He positioned his knees beneath her lovely thighs and then pushed his erection into her. His wolf's roar was torn from his throat at the feel of her enclosing around him, welcoming every inch of his shaft with warm delight. "Damn, you feel incredible. Hold on. No. Don't move."

A shudder rocked his body, and he battled to keep from releasing too soon. Her tender inner walls seemed to stroke him, to encourage his erection to grow still more, to let go of the pressure building inside of him. He couldn't allow that. She needed to reach her peak first. He was determined that she did. Impatience to possess her sweetness had driven him, but he should have waited.

When he would have drawn out of her because he was losing control, she lifted her legs and wrapped them around his hips. Her arms locked him in place while she delved into his mouth with her tongue. She found his tongue and sucked gently on it, giving him visions of her beautiful mouth swallowing his shaft. His claws grew out on his hands and feet. His teeth sharpened, and he had to pull back and bury his face in the pillow beneath her head to keep her from seeing him change.

Blowing deep breaths in and out, he waited frozen inside her. She stroked his back and crooned to him. Lucas thought he heard her say she loved him, but when he focused on her words, she didn't repeat it. Wishful thinking.

No. This is sex alone. Sex! He shouted the word in his mind, hoping it would help. But the tender feelings that threatened to consume him continued. In an effort to convince himself—and her—this meant nothing, he reached beneath her and grasped her ass to thrust her upward. She shouted her pleasure as he pounded deep into her, fast and without reserve. In seconds she came, with him roaring behind her.

After a few more pumps, Lucas drew out of Nita, but he was still hard. His transformation under control, he glanced at her. The eager lust in her eyes told him she was still raring to go. She was unlike any human he had ever met. Or he had been wrong in his assumption that they could not keep up with the wolf shifter's libido.

Lucas extended his arms toward Nita, and she sat forward. He scooped her up into his arms and whipped the two of them around until he could scoot to the end of the bed with her on his lap. He reached in front of her to take hold of her tiny nub and massaged it between his thumb and forefinger. She caught her breath and squirmed on his lap, making him harder.

"Lucas, what are you doing?" she whimpered.

"Getting you ready for round two." He set her on her feet and pulled her back so she had to lean against him with her hands on his thighs. He slid his hand lower to part her folds and drove himself inside his favorite place to be. Even after they had fucked like bunnies, she was snug around him, slick and warm, welcoming him in. Her muscles clamped down to milk him anew, and he began a slow pump in and out.

With her ass bumping on his lap and driving him to the edge of another explosive orgasm, Lucas ran a hand up across her belly to allow her nipples to tease his palms while they bounced. His reasoning, his very sanity was slipping with the sheer pleasure of being with her. No woman, absolutely no woman had been this good before, that made him want to...bite her.

His teeth sharpened. The low rumble in his throat increased. Before he knew what he was doing, he had curved his mouth over the old wound where he had bitten her the first time. He was so out of it that he would have sank his canines into her soft flesh for the second time, making her his mate if she didn't turn her head and catch sight of his face.

Her piercing scream both shattered his ear drums and snapped him out of his trance. Nita leaped from his lap and pressed herself against the wall facing him. One hand covered her mouth, and her eyes were huge in her face. Before Lucas could gain control of his transformation, Nita screamed again, shaking her head.

"W-What are you?"

When he stood, she held up her hands in defense.

"No! Don't come near me. You're...you're a..." Tears flooded her eyes, and the way she clutched her stomach, he thought she would wretch, but instead, her legs crumbled beneath her.

Lucas darted across the space to catch her before she hit the floor, but his touch seemed to wake her up. She struggled in his arms, smacked at his face and tore at the skin on his shoulders with her nails.

"Let me go, damn it! Let me go!"

"My sweet Nita," Lucas whispered, pain threatening to cut off his air supply. "I'm so sorry." With no other words necessary, he gathered her tight to his chest and dipped his fingers into a pressure point that would render her unconscious. Nita slumped in his hold, and he stood to lay her on the bed.

Standing over her, he watched the gentle rise and fall of her chest as she breathed. He memorized the long lashes that brushed her cheeks, the soft brown skin, the delicate curves. He took in the sight of her dark nipples and the thick black curls at her apex. Gently, he ran a hand down the side of her face and bit hard into the side of his cheek. With a heavy sigh, he reached for the phone on the nightstand and punched in a speed dial code. After two rings, the phone was answered, just as he expected.

"Nash." Lucas knew his voice had gone back to its normal coldness, something he had dropped the moment he was here in his home with Nita.

"What's up, boss?" Nash asked good-naturedly.

"I need you for cleanup. Get over here to my house on the double."

His friend chuckled. "A cleanup? Which fool fucked up this time? I thought we all learned our lesson for a few decades after Brant's stupidity."

Lucas growled, resisting the temptation to shred the phone in his hands, wishing it was Nash's skull. "Just get your ass over here now!" With a burst of temper, he threw the phone across the room and watched it smash into pieces against the wall. He sighed and turned back to the beautiful woman on the bed, the woman he loved with everything inside him.

Chapter Twelve

Nita came to consciousness in degrees. Voices seemed to swirl about her head, and a bitter flavor was on her tongue. She suspected it was the cause of her feeling like she was off balance and about to black out again. Instead she fought to stay alert, to remember what had happened to her and to know what was going on now.

Lucas' voice broke through the fog in her brain. "I don't need your fucking comments about what happened. I called you here only as a precaution as my second in command. I am surprised you didn't sense trouble."

Second in command of what? An army? She wondered what they were up to and what it had to do with her.

"I thought Brant was the second in command," the other man commented.

Lucas grumbled. "Brant and I have not seen eye-to-eye lately. Now, watch her while I go to my storeroom. For some reason this mixture I have is not as potent with her." There was a pause, and then Lucas spoke again. "Don't touch her. If you do—"

"I got it. I got it." The man chuckled. "I will keep my hands to myself, but she is lovely. I'm sure you had a great time with her tonight. Although I am surprised you would slip up and reveal what we are."

Fear gripped Nita's chest. *"...what we are,"* he had said. Memories flooded her mind, fuzzy as if it hadn't just happened tonight. She and Lucas had been making love, and it had been out of this world. In fact, she had begun to think...no, she had been *sure* that this man was the one she could give her heart to. But when she had looked back at him, the handsome face she expected was not the one she saw. Lucas had transformed into some kind of demon, a beast. No, it couldn't have happened. Could it? Should she just open her eyes and tell him she was okay, that maybe she had fainted but everything was fine now?

Some internal sense told her to keep still, to pretend that she was still unconscious. A few minutes later, the clink of glasses reached her ears. She remembered similar sounds when Lucas had brought in his various bottles containing herbs and scented oils that he had mixed to stimulate their love-making. Apparently, he had brought in more, but she'd be a fool to think these he had now were as harmless as the others. The man must be some kind of witch doctor or some such, an herbalist? Her heart slammed against her chest, and she fought to calm it before he noticed the pulse that threatened to jump out of her throat.

"This should work," Lucas said nearer to her. She nearly jumped when his fingers curled beneath her chin and he guided a spoonful of liquid between her lips. Like before, it was bitter. Nita pretended to unconsciously reject it, letting it run down the sides of her face into the pillow beneath her head.

Lucas would not be deterred. He climbed on the bed and gathered her up onto his lap. His massive chest pressed to the side of her shoulder should have sent her over the edge in terror, but she felt somewhat comforted for the moment, breathing in his familiar scent.

He filled her mouth with the liquid a second time, and this time, he held a hand over her mouth to keep it in while he stroked her throat. She couldn't help it. She fought him, scratching and crying.

"Wow, she's certainly different," the other man commented.

"Shut up!" Lucas shouted. "Get out until I'm done."

"But—"

"Now!"

A door opened and closed.

Lucas began to rock Nita, and then he stopped abruptly as if he didn't want to get caught up in comforting her. He traced an odd symbol on her forehead, and when he spoke, his voice was still hard, sending shivers over her skin. "Forget everything you know about me."

Forget?

"Forget it all," he repeated. His words were like physical commands, reaching inside her mind and drawing out the time he made her hot chocolate, sat her on his lap and fed her cookies. While the scene slipped along a wavy road in her head, she reached a hand out to grasp it, but it was too late.

"No," she whispered crying. "I won't forget."

More bitter liquid. She choked, and she thought she heard an anguished sound from Lucas, but it had to be her imagination. The man had no heart. He wanted to trick her, to cast some spell or something to make her forget using that symbol he drew and the herbs.

But Nita was different. Lucas had said so. His normal concoction hadn't worked on her for some reason, and if he made a habit of wiping women's memories when they learned what he and his other monster friends were, then surely it would work more smoothly than this. That meant she could fight it.

So she laid there in his arms, unmoving. Not sure if she should say something or not, she remained silent. Lucas spoke more commands, and Nita felt the same near irresistible pull as before with that other something that she couldn't remember, but she hung on with all her might. Being motionless and fighting seemed incongruent, but she gave it all she could, praying that she hadn't already forgotten things.

She recited their first meeting in her mind, when he had walked up behind her and kissed her, when Stacy had argued with him. She recalled the first night they made love but not before they were in bed. Sorrow washed over her to know that some part of that night was missing. How she had gotten here was also missing. The most important part, that he wasn't human, was the strongest memory of all, and she clutched it tight in her head. She wouldn't let go.

After some time, Lucas placed her in the bed and let out a long sigh. "It's done," he whispered. His weight was removed from the bed, and she heard the door open. A quiet conversation ensued, but she couldn't make out what they were saying until Lucas walked back into the room.

"Here are her things, her keys. Make sure she gets back to her place safely. I have to report to the elders." He paused and sniffed. "Nash, I'm trusting you to get her there."

"Don't worry, boss. I promise to take good care of her. Nothing will go wrong. Your concoction keeps them out until morning, and they never know what happened afterward."

Lucas grunted. "Good. Get going. Report back to me when you can."

* * * *

So the other man's name was Nash. Nita filed the info away in her mind while Lucas carried her to what she assumed was Nash's car. She was laid gently in the back with a blanket spread over her shivering body. Neither man commented on that, so she assumed it was natural. But the night air had managed to clear her mind somewhat. By the time they reached the curb outside her place, Nita's unsettled stomach had calmed, and she was sure no more memories were in danger of fading away.

When Nash threw the car in park, he let out a growl that only now Nita realized she had been hearing Lucas make much of the time they had been making love. Nervous, she opened her eyes a crack in time to see a sexy woman strolling over to the car. A vague memory of speaking with the woman before came to mind but she lost it that quick. Nash lowered the passenger side window.

"What are you doing over this way, Gloria?" Nash asked.

Through the gap between the seats, Nita caught sight of her pout. "I was looking for Lucas. I know the human he's into lives over this way, and I know damn well he didn't take the whore to his house."

Nash chuckled.

The woman ran sharp nails along the paint job. "He didn't!" she growled.

"You're going to pay for that," Nash told her calmly. "Anyway, I don't have time for you, Gloria, as tasty as you look tonight. I don't do my Alpha's leftovers."

"What?" Gloria screeched.

Nash laughed again. "You were about to offer me some, weren't you?"

"Go to hell, Nash."

The man slid from the car unperturbed by Gloria and came around to open the back door. Before long he had scooped Nita up with care in his arms and was headed inside the building. Nita had thought Gloria would ask questions, but she didn't follow them. For that Nita was relieved because she thought she would go off if that woman had called her a whore again. She'd never been in a fight in her entire life, but there was a first time for everything.

Then she began to replay their words in her head. There was no doubt about it. Gloria was like Lucas and Nash. So there were female creatures. She shook, and Nash's hold tightened.

"Hold on, lovely lady. We'll get you tucked into bed in no time."

Soon Nash had settled her into her bed and slipped her clothes off only when he had covered her with her blankets. To his credit, he didn't even try to feel her up. When he clicked the lights off and tossed her keys on her nightstand, he moved to the window. Nita watched with curiosity, wondering what he would do.

He lifted the window, bent over the sill to check the area and then climbed up and leaped out. Nita stifled a scream. She was on the third floor, and a person could break a leg jumping like that. She threw back the covers and peered out into the night. There was no sign of Nash.

Her heart pounding, Nita sank down on the side of the bed, only just realizing that Nash had left her completely naked. In the morning if she didn't remember a thing, she would have wondered why she would sleep that way. Feeling like her world was coming to an end, she slipped back into her clothes and picked up the phone.

Zandrea answered on the ninth ring. "Yeah?" she barked with a voice thick with sleep.

"Z." To Nita's shame, her throat closed, and tears welled up in her eyes. She coughed and tried again. "Z, I think I'm in trouble. I don't know. I'm not sure. It's Lucas, Zandrea. He's not human."

Nita thought the line had gone dead, but after a while her friend spoke. "Tell me everything."

Nita went through the events of the night all the way up to the fact that Nash had jumped from the third story and apparently had been fine. Zandrea commanded her to stay put, and that she would be there as fast as she could. Nita nodded dumbly and hung up the phone.

"So, you know the wolf shifters' secret, huh?"

Nita jumped at the voice. She twisted around to find a dark shadow in the corner of her room by the closet. Flicking on the bedside lamp, she was shocked to see Deandre. "W-What are you doing in my room, Deandre?" she demanded but with little force as her strength had left her body.

He crossed the room to stand in front of her, a look of naked lust in his eyes. She prayed he hadn't seen her before she dressed, not in the darkness.

"I'm here for what's mine," he told her, stroking her face.

She pulled away. "What are you talking about?"

"I've always intended for you to be the one. For four months I watched you, and no disgusting wolf shifter will take my prize. Tonight, baby, you will give me what I have been waiting on for eighty-five years."

And right before her eyes, Deandre changed too.

Chapter Thirteen

"Fuck!" Brant roared. "I can't pick up a scent."

Zandrea rang her hands, worry tightening her chest. "Try harder, baby, please. She can't just have disappeared."

Brant sighed and began to remove his clothes. Zandrea, like she usually did, watched appreciatively as her man's solid naked body came into view. He handed her his clothes, and she took them. In seconds, he shifted to his wolf form and began to pad around the room sniffing in every direction. He scratched at the front door, and Zandrea crossed over to it to let him out. They were extremely careful about letting anyone see him in this form, but since it was night time, it was likely that anyone wandering about at this time would just think he was a regular dog.

Zandrea locked the door to Nita's room and descended the stairs behind her lover. He was moving fast, but she was confident he wouldn't get too far ahead of her. They were like two halves of one person. Since they had embraced the fact that they were mates, they hadn't once been out of each other's sight. Zandrea had even had to let her job go, but that low-paying dead end was no loss whatsoever. Right now, she was in the process of setting up her own Internet business. Brant was generous with his money, but she wanted her own.

On the front walk, Brant had stopped. From the sadness in his eyes, she knew he hadn't been able to pick up a fresh scent for Nita. She had disappeared, and no other strange smells had been in her place except for Nash's. So where the hell was she?

"Do you think maybe she went back to Lucas' since his voodoo didn't work on her?" she asked Brant.

He growled, no doubt annoyed that she had called it voodoo. What Lucas could do was impressive. She could admit that now that she didn't hate his guts for almost ruining her chances with Brant. But she still didn't like his ass, especially after this shit.

She and Brant climbed into his SUV, and he transformed and dressed.

His mouth was set in a hard line, and he gripped the steering wheel between clawed fingers. Zandrea suspected he would rip into his half brother the second he laid eyes on him. She would be right behind him.

Brant kicked the front door in so hard, it hung from its hinges. Lucas did not seem surprised that they were there. He stood in the hallway with bared sharp teeth and a drink in his hand. From the scent, Zandrea figured he'd been at it a while.

"You've been avoiding me, brother," Brant spat.

"Fuck you," was Lucas' reply.

"You've got a lot of explaining to do. I don't give a flying fuck if you are my Alpha. I've been looking for you ever since that bull you pulled on Nita at the restaurant, threatening her, hurting her."

Lucas' eyes were glazed. "You knew where I lived. And what are you talking about? I never hurt her or threatened her." He sighed and waved his hand, sloshing the liquid in his glass over the side. "Whatever. It doesn't matter. All that is over for good. I didn't fuck up and make her my mate before I got rid of her."

"Got rid of her!" Zandrea screamed. She launched herself at him, but Brant caught her in the air and whipped her back behind him. "You son of a bitch!" Zandrea curled her fingers, trying to get around Brant. She might not have claws, but her tips could do some damage.

Brant growled. "You cold bastard. You're slipping. Whatever you used on Nita didn't work. She remembers everything. She knows what we are, what you did to her."

Lucas slumped down on the stairs leading to the second floor. "Impossible."

"Not impossible. Brother, she's missing," Brant told him. "And you're going to sober up and help us find her."

* * * *

Lucas' stomach stirred, and he felt like he was about to throw up all the alcohol he had consumed in the last hour and a half. He had thought to make himself forget, but wiping that sweet face from his mind was impossible.

He shook his head to clear it. "No, that's not possible. I know it took. I did have trouble. My usual batch didn't work on her. She resisted, but then the second one—"

Brant squinted at him. "You said you didn't make her your mate. Did you bite her once?"

Lucas grumbled. "What does that have to do with anything?" He knew, but he couldn't face it. If anyone knew about the affects of blood mixing, it was him. He'd studied it along with herbs for years. It was his life's passion until Nita.

"You know damn well what I'm getting at, Lucas," Brant insisted. "Biting her once means you tainted her blood. She will have heightened ability even if she is human. Zandrea's five senses have improved dramatically. She used to wear reading glasses, but now her vision is twenty fifteen. Your memory potion is formulated for humans with no trace of wolf DNA in their blood. You lectured me on it enough times. So now you're surprised that Nita resisted it? Tell me the truth. You bit her, didn't you?"

Lucas ran a hand through his already disheveled hair. He had caught sight of it sticking up all over his head when he passed the hall mirror but didn't give a damn at the time. He still didn't. "Yes," he admitted. "I bit her once. I lost control. I was about to bite her again tonight, but—"

Zandrea gasped. "You were going to make her your mate?"

"No, damn it! I lost control I said. I couldn't help it. She's so...Never mind. What do you mean she's missing? If you're lying and you're hiding her from me, so help me I'll slit your throat, Brant." Another thought occurred to him. "And what do you mean about threatening her? I never did. I would never."

Zandrea's hands slipped to her hips, and Brant eyed her, apparently assessing whether she was about to attack Lucas again. He let her move out from behind him. "Don't give me that. I was there. I was having lunch with my girls, Nita and Stacy, and you barged in and started accusing Nita of seeing another man. You put your hands on her like you were going to shake her head off, and you threatened her. You telling me somebody put some voodoo on you to make you forget that?"

Lucas stood up and stalked back and forth from the dining room to the living room while racking his brain. No one had slipped him anything. No one he knew had the skill, except a couple of the elders, and they wouldn't act against the Alpha of the pack. None of the other wolves had challenged him to be the leader. The only one who had seemed close to doing that was Brant, and he had backed off since he had taken Zandrea as his mate.

The bottom line was, someone had been impersonating him, and that someone might very well have Nita. When he found him, Lucas would rip him apart. He spun to face Zandrea. "You said you were there. The man who walked in looking like me was an exact duplicate? Nothing stood out to give a warning that it might not be who you thought?"

She rolled her eyes.

He snapped his fingers. Some senses never lie. "Brant said you have heightened senses. What did he smell like?"

She frowned. "What you always smell like, I guess. Look, I'm not a freaking bloodhound."

"Concentrate, damn it. Nita may be in deep trouble, and I'm depending on you to give me a clue."

Zandrea's eyes went wide, and she shook. Brant tucked her to his side with a nasty look in Lucas' direction. "It's okay, baby. We'll find her. If you don't remember anything..."

"Wait, I do," she squealed. "The cologne. I remember thinking if you were going to go all macho on my girl, the least you could have done was wear some decent cologne and not that cheap shit you had on."

Brant stiffened. "Lucas doesn't wear cologne. None of us do. The scent can be too much."

The strength left Lucas' body. He almost sank to the floor before he took a strong hold on himself. "Deandre. That's the guy who's been trying to date Nita. I interfered with his plans, so I'm guessing it was him who came in there looking like me."

"Hm, so you think he's a shape-shifter?" Brant asked. "Shifted to look like you in an attempt to fool Nita into hating you and breaking it off?"

Lucas sighed. "If only it was that simple. All the shape shifters I've known have had scents. Deandre has none. It's almost like he's not real, not really there."

"A skin walker," Zandrea piped up. At Lucas' and his brother's odd looks, she explained. "I saw it in a movie once, and Nita, crazy girl, thought it was interesting enough to look up and recite some of the facts to Stacy and me when we had already been freaked out by the movie. Apparently, they can take on the form of whatever they touch. Lucas, did he ever touch you?"

The blood drained from his head leaving him woozy. "At the country club I frequent. He used my name to get in and pretended we were old buddies. I had him thrown out, but not before he had slapped me on the back a few times and shook my hand with this big stupid grin on his face. Now I know what he was up to. He was going to take on my form."

Brant turned to his mate. "Any other facts, sweetie?"

She shook her head. "No, but I know where we can find out."

Chapter Fourteen

Deandre yanked Nita close to him and ran his hands down over her ass. She pulled at the bonds around her wrists and strained to get away from him. He chuckled as if her resisting turned him on all the more.

"I see the hope still burning in your eyes, baby," he said between small kisses he planted along her neck. "But give that up. Your ex-lover can't track me. I don't care how good his dog's nose is." He laughed again. "You see how I can change?"

He demonstrated, and she turned her head. He snatched it back to face him. Instead of a young black man, younger than she was, this time he was white, taller and older. It was unnatural.

"Not only can I change, I have no scent. That asshole could sniff for years and never pick up my smell."

"What do you want me for, Deandre? A lay? Since you can look anyway you want, you can get any woman you want. You can just become whatever her fantasies are."

He nodded. "You're right." In that instant, he became Lucas, and Nita's heart shattered.

"No," she moaned.

"No?" he teased. "I thought you would like that. Me fucking you with your ex-lover's face. Thought it would get you off. Well never mind. I don't want you thinking of him anyway while I have you." He stroked her cheek. "And to answer your question, I want you for reproduction."

"Say what?" she screamed.

"Yup, brilliant isn't it? See I'm a skin walker, and my kind cannot reproduce with each other. We can only reproduce with those who can do it by 'natural' means. I want my legacy to go on so to speak, and I've chosen you to be the mother of my children. Now, don't you feel special?"

She spit in his face. "I'm not having your children!"

Deandre smacked her and shoved her down on the bed. He had stopped at this hotel because they had been driving for hours, and he was tired. And now from what he said, he wasn't afraid that Lucas would find them.

Nita closed her eyes when Deandre landed on top of her and pushed a knee between her legs to force her to spread them. He was rock solid against her pelvis, and she swallowed to keep from throwing up. Why had she ever found him attractive?

"I had intended to play it slower, get you to care about me so you would happily raise my child the way I want him raised, but you had to ruin it all by being a whore with that wolf. Bestiality doesn't gross you out, huh?"

"It's not bestiality," she snapped. Her words were true. The love burning in her heart for Lucas wasn't going away just because she had found out he wasn't human, that he could shift into a wolf. She had been terrified at first, sure, and she was angry about what he did. Yet, as she considered what had happened, the thought occurred to her that Lucas was suffering as well. He had apparently thought she was better off forgetting what he was rather than living with his secret. But she would bet her entire trust fund and the money coming to her in a few years that Lucas loved her just as much as she loved him. More than anything, she ached to see him again and verify it.

When Deandre's head lowered toward hers to kiss her again, she blurted out, "He can track my scent."

Deandre drew back. "What?"

She swallowed. "You said you have no scent to pick up, but Lucas can track my scent can't he? I mean he knows me pretty well."

That last part seemed to tick him off. "Yeah, too well!" He held up a small vial. "See this? Got it off a guy I know. Guaranteed to screw with the wolf's nose. Not just the wolf, any tracker who uses his sense of smell to find people. I don't normally need it, but as you can see I've thought of everything. You and I, my sweet thing, will disappear forever. You'll raise my brood. Yeah,"—he seemed to be picturing it in his mind—"more than one, I think. A few. Oh how sweet it will be making them."

The hope that Nita had been harboring, that Deandre had recognized in her eyes, died a quick death. Lucas would not be able to find her. That meant she would have to take matters into her own hands. One way or another, she would have to trick Deandre and get away. She would have to do it all on her own, with no money or resources because the very person she depended on could be Deandre in disguise, and she would be right back here facing a life of misery.

She blew out a breath she hoped sounded resigned. "Well, in that case, let me go to the bathroom and take a shower." He gave her a suspicious look, and she frowned. "You're between me and the door, damn it. There's no window in the bathroom."

After a few minutes, he nodded, leaned back to untie her hands, and rose off the bed. He bent over to unzip the bag he had brought into the room and reached in before pulling out something black and silky. He tossed it to her. "Put this on after."

Nita held it up. It was a charmeuse babydoll. The thing looked like it would barely extend past her ass. Anger rose inside her at him using her for his pleasure whether she liked it or not, but she tamped it down. In order to get out of this predicament, she would have to stay calm and use her head. She grabbed for her purse to take with her to the bathroom, but Deandre caught her wrist and searched the interior. He brought out her cell phone and her PDA and pocketed both before handing the purse back. Nita snatched it and stomped into the bathroom before slamming the door in his face. The chuckle she heard beyond the door made her grit her teeth.

"I have to get out of this," she whispered, sitting down on the toilet and staring at the wall. Deandre was a small built man but he was also strong. She could not overpower him. Longing for Lucas overwhelmed her, and she blinked her eyes in rapid succession to ward off tears.

There was no hope of anything permanent between them. He was a wolf shape shifter, and it was certain that as soon as he had the chance, he would try his charm on her again to make her forget him. Nita dropped her head into her hands. She didn't want to forget Lucas, not now and not ever.

"Hey, what are you doing in there?" Deandre called.

Nita jumped to her feet and turned the shower on, but she ignored Deandre, not answering his call. Thinking of Lucas being a shape shifter reminded her that Brant was his half brother, and now she recalled how she had heard Zandrea mention that she was Brant's mate. Nita had thought that terminology was an odd way to put it. Now she realized that Zandrea knew their secret. How could she not, sleeping with the guy? Did Brant grow claws, sharp teeth and extra hair when he got too turned on? He probably did which would have been a call for much explanation if Zandrea didn't know the truth. Something told Nita she would not be allowed to keep knowing the truth unless Lucas was willing to make her his mate.

"Fat chance," she muttered in misery. "He's too much of a ladies' man." She sighed. That was neither here nor there if she didn't get out of this predicament.

She stood and undressed then slipped into the babydoll. After a few minutes, she turned off the shower. No sense washing right now, although she really wanted to. She stuffed her clothes inside her purse and forced the zipper closed, hoping Deandre wouldn't notice how overfull it was. If for some reason she had to make her escape without pausing to get dressed, she didn't want to spend too much time out on the street dressed as scantily as she was now.

With a deep breath, she tugged the door open and pasted a slight smile on her face, hoping it appeared to be genuine. "Well, here I am. I'm not one to cry long over anything. We can make the best of it. After all, you're not bad to look at, and you can look anyway I want, right?" She raised an eyebrow in Deandre's direction.

His own grin spread across his face. "Damn, you look good! I knew you would. Turn around and let me get a glimpse of that ass."

Nita suppressed a flinch at his crass words and spun around while dropping her bag on the floor. She put a hand on her hip and spread her legs a little in an attempt to keep his attention on her and not the purse. It worked. Deandre let out a long whistle.

"Yeah!" he crooned in excitement.

When Nita spun around again, he was already shuffling out his clothes. She directed her gaze around the room in search of something heavy to bring down on his disgusting head when the time was right. The heavy motel phone on the nightstand would be perfect. It was a cliché from too many movies, but if it worked that's all that mattered.

She positioned herself on the edge of the bed and extended her arm to him. Deandre couldn't get across the room fast enough as he stumbled over his pants still around his ankles. He kicked them away and almost fell on top of her, bumping her shoulder with his chin where Lucas had left his mark. She closed her eyes, her heart aching for the man she knew without a doubt that she loved.

Bile rose in Nita's throat at the contact of Deandre's hard-on. He grumbled at finding her panties still on.

"Take them off!" While he fumbled, first trying to rip her panties off and then yanking them downward, Nita felt for the phone. Damn, why was his head on the wrong side? She couldn't see where she was reaching, and Deandre was raining little kisses along her shoulder. At any second he could figure out what she was up to.

She squeezed her eyes shut and then reached down between them, her hand just above his erection. Her voice shaking, giving the impression of arousal, she hoped, she said, "Let me suck you, lover."

Deandre whopped. "Oh, Nita, girl, I knew you were the one. But not too much. I can't waste my seed."

She pushed him to his back on the bed and kissed along his stomach. To give the man credit, he did have smooth brown skin that stretched over taut and defined muscles. Then again, that could be another illusion of the skin walker. She took her time going down his body. The pleasure of her touch got the better of Deandre. He groaned and closed his eyes.

Nita took her opportunity, snatched up the phone and brought it down with all the force she could on Deandre's skull.

Chapter Fifteen

Tears streaming down her face, Nita didn't wait a second before she tore out of the room with her purse clutched under her arm. She sobbed as she ran, not even knowing if she was headed toward the motel office or not. When she had rounded the building out of sight of the room, she stopped to yank her clothes from her bag and only then realized she should have paused long enough to retrieve her cell phone from Deandre.

Fear drove her on when she had shoved her feet half way into her shoes. She sprinted across the parking lot toward a Laundromat she spotted in the lot next door to the motel. Inside, a woman leaned a hip lazily against a table while thumbing through information on her cell phone. Nita rushed over to her.

"Please, I beg you. Let me make an emergency call. I will give you twenty dollars if you do." The woman's face brightened, and she held out the phone. Nita grasped it and pounded in the numbers to Lucas' cell in lieu of the police. They would never know how to handle a skin walker, and she wasn't sure if Lucas knew, but he was the best option.

On the first ring, Lucas barked into the phone. "Yeah?"

"Lucas," she rasped out. "P-Please help me."

"Baby, where are you?" It could be her imagination, but he sounded worried, angry and desperate all once. "I will come for you. I promise. Tell me where."

Nita focused on the woman whose phone she was using. Her curious stare didn't waver, and she made no pretense of not listening.

"He needs to know where I am," Nita told her.

"I-45," the woman supplied. "Exit 14 toward Halibird."

Nita relayed the instructions and told him about the Laundromat. Lucas instructed her to stay around lots of people. The information that he was able to pick up was that Deandre could take on any form of anyone he touched, but Nita already knew that. She assured him she would do what she could until he arrived, which would unfortunately take a while.

"Nita, I know you won't understand why I'm saying this, but don't call the police," Lucas told her. He was quiet a moment. "I'm going to contact some people I know in the area where you are. I will give them a password so you know it's them."

She was about to question that but realized what he meant. Deandre again. If she was fooled...no, she wouldn't. If he was still alive, and he came after her, she would kill his ass before she ever let him touch her again. Lucas told her the word, and with reluctance she hung up. After passing over the twenty to the woman, she drifted to the back of the Laundromat and sat down on a bench occupied by an old man who looked like he didn't know if he was there washing clothes or back home watching TV. She heaved a sigh, praying she wouldn't burst out crying again.

"Lucas, please hurry up," she whispered.

* * * *

Lucas hit the ground on all fours, not giving a shit who might notice a wolf sprinting along the road. When he could, he kept to back roads and even farther off paved streets running through treed areas and through fields. This way he could open up and give all his speed while taking short cuts that the manmade paths didn't allow for. He prayed all the way that Nita would be safe until the shifters he had contacted could reach her. And when he knew she was safe, he would rip Deandre's throat out so he could never threaten her again.

With his paws eating up the miles, his mind was free to mull over what he would do when he found Nita. Should he try to erase her memory again to make her forget all about him? He thought of Brant and Zandrea. They were making things work out between them, and they had committed to no offspring so that the wolf line would not be diluted and produce more problems. But what about him? Should he or could he take Nita as his mate?

He was the Alpha. He and the elders had conferred and decided to pass a law within their community that no shifter was allowed to take a human mate from here on out. It was too dangerous and truly since they would outlive their human mate by many decades, it would only produce heartache in the end. For him to take Nita would be a violation of the standard he had set and just plain foolhardy.

Still his heart didn't give a shit. He had tried to drink himself into a stupor when he had sent her away. This was worse, exponentially worse than it had been with Gloria. The emotions that tumbled over his consciousness felt like Nita was his whole life, his whole world.

Fuck! He ran faster, his lungs burning, his throat dry. The only thing that mattered at this point was getting to her and making sure she was all right. Other decisions could wait.

At midnight, Lucas picked up Nita's scent. Now he knew that Deandre must have done something to block their being able to track her. Whatever it was hadn't been used this far out. Exhausted beyond belief, he padded on sore feet into the woods. His people out this way liked a rural setting, away from the hustle and bustle of the city. With his nose to the ground, he picked up three others along with Nita. They were without question wolf shifters.

Through a clearing a small cabin came into view. He sniffed the air. Nita was inside. Two men sat on the porch outside the place. They stood when he came into view, although he knew they had scented him long before that.

He changed, ignoring his nakedness. "Thank you for saving her."

The taller of the men nodded. "You Lucas, I guess."

"Yes." He shook the hand of the man he sensed was the Alpha of his pack. All shifters knew the locations of the various packs although most stayed within their own and didn't know each member personally. "May I go in?" he asked out of courtesy.

The man nodded, and Lucas tried not to tear the door off its hinges when he rushed forward. There she was lying curled up in the fetal position, her hand beneath her chin, track marks from tears on her face. His chest constricted. Like hell he would ever give her up. Even if he had to walk away from being Alpha. Nita was his, at the risk of heartbreak later or being tossed out of his pack for violating their laws.

Lucas crossed the room and scooped Nita up onto his lap before he remembered that she had been terrified of him when he was half changed. His heart ached. What if she rejected him?

"Nita? Baby?" he whispered. "Wake up. I'm here."

Her eyelashes fluttered, and after a moment she focused on him. The strength left his body, and he tucked her tight against his chest.

"Lucas, you came."

"Always," he muttered in a thick voice.

"I'm sorry. I—"

"Shh, this isn't your fault by any means," he told her. "I'll take care of everything. Don't worry."

She struggled to sit up, and he let her although she remained on his lap. "By that you mean you'll try again to erase my memory."

"No."

With a tiny gasp she looked up at him, her luscious lips parted, making him want to sip her sweetness from them. He gave in and took a chance, lowering his mouth to hers. If he thought she would pull away in disgust, he was pleasantly surprised when she wrapped her arms around his neck and arched into his chest. His groin grew tight.

"I'm...uh...not sure how you feel about me, Nita, but—"

"I love you," she said in a matter of fact tone. "Can't change that whether I want to or not. So, you're a dog. What's a girl to do?"

He chuckled. She was making light of the situation, but the slight tremor beneath her words told him the situation had taken its toll. He needed to get her back home, but before that he would put Deandre in his grave.

"A girl," he instructed," is to become my mate." He stared down at her with a serious expression. "Do you want that, Nita? This is a big decision, and I'm not all that sure either of us should make that decision now and not some other time when you've had more time to think things through. But I confess that I can't wait. I want you for my mate more than anything. I love you, Nita, and I always will."

Nita heaved a sigh. "One of the shifters who picked me up was a woman. I don't know where she disappeared to, but she was telling me all about what it means to be your mate. She said from what her brother told her when he talked to you on the phone that it was likely that I was already meant to be your mate. And she explained how I would be tied to you."

"We'd be tied to each other," he corrected. "It's a whole different experience from human marriage."

"Even so, I love you with all my heart, and whatever I have to experience for us to be one, I'll go through it."

Lucas nodded and gently began removing her clothing. She squeaked.

"What are you doing, Lucas. Those guys are just outside, and they could come in here."

He grinned, stroking her cheek. "They know I am about to claim you as my mate and what that means. They won't come in."

She stared at him as it dawned on her what he meant. The shifters outside on the porch could hear what they said and smell their arousal. They would also sense that Lucas had put his mark on her but not yet sealed the deal. For a male shifter to take his mate, he needed to bite her twice while making love to her.

Nita's teeth chattered she was so nervous. She dug her nails into his bare arms, and he winced but waited in silence for her to make her decision. He knew she wanted him from the tight points of her nipples making an impression through her blouse. After some time, she nodded, and Lucas continued to undress her.

Chapter Sixteen

The thought of perfect strangers standing right outside the door able to hear every sound she uttered made Nita bite her lip and suppress the moan she wanted to loose when Lucas parted the two sides of her blouse. Her breasts rose and fell in rapid succession when he yanked her bra down to reveal her swollen nipples.

As if they called to him, he dipped his head to take first one into his mouth and then move to the other. She caught her breath as his tongue laved her aching buds. This time when his growl began, it didn't alarm her. He was what he was, and she embraced him as such.

"Ah, Lucas," she moaned and tried to hold it in.

"Don't hold back, my love," he told her and lifted her off his lap to lay her flat on the bed. He moved above her, parting her legs with his. "I long to take my time and show you how much I want to please you, but I feel like we've been apart for ages, a feeling that shouldn't be considering we're not one yet."

"We are one." She pulled him closer to her so she could nuzzle his stubbled jawline. "In heart, we are already one. Fill me, Lucas. Please. I need all of you right now."

He kneed her legs higher, and since she was soaking wet, his shaft glided in between her folds with no hindrance. Nita shouted her pleasure, and Lucas' growl burst forth. He changed, his teeth like daggers and his claws matching. Where he had only small stubble from not shaving, longer hair sprouted.

"Don't be afraid, baby. Please," he begged in a rough voice.

"I'm not. I love you. Pump me hard," she demanded. "Fuck me, Lucas."

His eyes went wide at her boldness, and he lifted her heels in the air and drove forward until he pumped in and out at a lightning speed. Nita screamed and writhed against him. Lucas howled like the wolf he was but didn't stop. Somewhere in the back of her mind, Nita registered the answering howls outside the cabin, but she was too engrossed in the intense pleasure her lover was giving her.

Lucas yanked back, flipped her over and drove in again. He held onto her hips and pounded his thick shaft deep inside of her. Nita wished she had claws to rip at the sheets beneath them. Oh fuck, she couldn't get enough. She didn't ever want him to stop. All fear of having an audience listening in drained away, and she freely cried out encouragement for Lucas to fuck her harder, faster, to make her come right now.

Lucas smacked her ass, and Nita came screaming. He pulled out of her, bent down and kissed away the sting on her skin before he began to lap at her flowing juices. A second orgasm gripped her core, and she whined while he pushed his tongue up inside her and then sucked at her tender nub.

When she was through a third orgasm, Lucas pushed her flat on the bed and followed her down. He eased his way inside her with a tighter fit since her legs were straight, and Nita thought she would lose consciousness from the pure ecstasy. The man was incredible even without the enhancing oils he had used last time. As soon as he was buried to the hilt, he ran his tongue over the spot on her shoulder, and she knew he was about to make his final claim.

Nita stiffened, but Lucas shoved a hand beneath her and stroked her belly. "Shh, relax, my love. I won't hurt you."

She tried her best to loosen up and release the nervousness, but it was impossible. The bite when it came stung a little, but not like she expected. And all of a sudden, a warm security washed over her, like she was in the safest place she could be—in Lucas' arms.

A shudder went through his body, and then his warm seed permeated her insides. Lucas held her so tight, it almost hurt, and he muttered her name over and over. Now they were as one person. They were mates.

* * * *

Fear clawed at Nita's stomach. She had chewed off each one of her fingernails and wished for something more to chew on. After Lucas had left her in the care of the other shifters and Zandrea, who had arrived a short while later with Brant, he and his brother took off to find Deandre. When they returned the next morning, neither admitted to what they had done, but Nita had a new sense now that she was mated to Lucas. She could pick up on his feelings, and he was definitely feeling vindicated. There was no doubt in her mind that he and Brant had killed Deandre and covered it up somehow. She had accepted it as what he felt he had to do.

Now, a month and a half later the horror of it all had passed, and she thought she could settle down in safety and calm. The pack had indeed taken away Lucas' position as Alpha and passed it on to another shifter. At least they hadn't tossed him completely out of the pack. But now, Nita had something new to worry about.

She sat curled on his bed running her fingers through her hair and wondering what she was going to do. When the door opened, she jumped. Lucas narrowed beautiful dark eyes on her with a look of curiosity.

"What's up, baby? You've been jumpy lately."

"Nothing," she squeaked.

He shook his head, making a *tsk* sound. "Out with it."

How could she tell him? "I don't—"

"Nita!" he grumbled.

"I'm pregnant," she blurted out. "I'm so sorry. I know we made a commitment to the pack that we wouldn't and I had protection, but I don't know. Oh goodness. I'm sorry, Lucas..."

He covered her mouth with a gentle kiss and then drew back. "Silly woman. I already knew that a couple weeks ago."

She stared. "What?"

He shrugged. "I sense every change in your lovely body."

Annoyance that he didn't say anything hit her. She resisted slapping his smug face. "You could have said something."

"I had to make arrangements."

"What arrangements?" She allowed him to scoop her to his lap and rested her head on his shoulder.

He sighed. "Arrangements to join another pack. It hurts to leave, but it must be done. We will be following Brant and Zandrea this time around, to a pack that lost their Alpha. They're young, and no one was in a position to lead. Besides that, they are more lenient than our pack now. They are open to half human half shifter children. And since Zandrea's expecting, it works out."

"What!" She sat up, but Lucas forced her back to his chest.

"These things happen." He chuckled in her ear. "Almost accidentally."

Nita narrowed her eyes on him, and he offered an innocent grin. Her heart swelled with love for him. She knew it was a big step for him and

Brant to leave their pack, but it was also time. Things changed in life, and they had to change with them or be left behind. All Nita knew was that she wanted to spend all her life with Lucas. At his side, she could face any challenge with confidence.

City Wolf 3

Chapter One

Stacy gripped her glass of white wine between two fingers and the thumb of one hand while crossing her body with her arm and bracing the other hand under her elbow. She resisted slumping against the wall and revealing to one and all how bored she was. Bored? Yeah right. She was lonely, and her feelings were hurt that none of the guys at Zandrea's party had looked her way beyond a glance of appreciation before turning back to their conversations with each other. If she didn't know better, she would have suspected the assholes were gay, but there were other women there beyond her two best friends, and those women had more than one of the guys pushing up on them, trying to get some play. Then here she was, in the corner, alone.

For real, she'd been shocked out of her mind to learn what Zandrea and Nita's boyfriends were wolf shape-shifters. That had bad sci-fi movie written all over it, but it would explain some of the crazy ass stuff that had happened since they had all been dating. Zandrea had told her it was against the rules for humans to know about them, but since Stacy was her girl, she couldn't bear lying to her any more.

So, Zandrea had invited her to her party, but warned her that the place would be jam-packed with other wolf shifters. She had neglected to say every one of them, even the damn women, were physical perfection. Stacy had never considered herself an anecdote. In fact, she thought she was very pretty, with a good body, but she had anger issues and a real attitude problem. Every one of her ex-boyfriends had said the same thing—along with her mother, her teachers when she was still in school, and her boss.

She searched the overcrowded room, straining to pick up bits of conversation around her, admiring the dark suits on some of the guys, and the casual slacks with open collared shirts on the others. Zandrea's house was sweet too. Zandrea had called the room they were in, the party room. The thing looked like it was twice the size of Stacy's entire apartment, and the fireplace, the artwork on the walls, and the furniture just screamed money.

Were they all rich too? *Damn*!

She felt a frown steal over her face, and as hard as she tried to erase it and give off vibes of being available, she couldn't do it. Could they sense what she was feeling, that she had hang-ups with men, that she fought like hell to keep them away from her heart? From the little Zandrea had told her, she was pretty sure the shifters couldn't read her mind, but they did have a keen sense of smell. And real wolves, or the all-animal variety, could sense what a person was feeling by smell. Or was that only when it came to fear?

Hell, they were men, right? Most of them didn't want anything permanent. She didn't either. All she wanted was a little fun, maybe a bed partner for a few months. That wasn't too much to ask. She moved her glass to the side of her body and glanced down at herself. Her dress was smokin' if she did say so herself. The second she'd tried it on, she'd known the dress clung to her body in all the right ways.

With lycra in the deep blue material, it stretched nice over her boobs and hung low enough to show off some cleavage. The length barely reached a half foot past her ass, and she'd caught several of the men sucking in a breath and nudging their friends when they'd spotted her. She had thought the usual look of 'come and get you some' thrown over her shoulder would bring at least one of them to her, but nope. Nothing. What the hell was her problem?

Miserable, she gulped down the last of her wine and then headed over to a server to snag another glass. Maybe if she loosened up enough, she could just walk up on one of the men and take what she wanted.

With her second glass half gone, she surveyed the crowd. One man in particular had been catching her eye all night. He was tall, like they all were, maybe six four or five. His shoulders were so broad, she could see herself either hanging onto them while he worked her, or with her legs slung over them while he... She forced the thought from her mind. First she had to get tall, dark, and sexy-as-hell to look her way.

Feeling her usual boldness returning, she glided in his direction, weaving through the other people in the room, but never taking her eyes off him. He stood in a crowd of his buddies, a drink in his hand and a smile on full lips she wanted to lick and then kiss until her own were numb. His midnight blue eyes sparkled like he was happy with life and everything in it. She wanted them on her, to change that look from simple happiness to all out lust. Damn, she was horny.

She drew closer. He gestured to his friend, shook his head, and then reached up to push back a lock of hair that had fallen on his forehead. Her fingernails tore into her palm. *Don't worry, baby. I'm going to fix that for you soon*, she told him silently.

At last she was in front of him, cutting him off from his friends. She let her breasts brush his chest and tilted her head back to look up at him. His eyes shifted from her face to her boobs, lingered there a while, and then moved back to her face. He grinned.

"Hey," she said, in no hurry to explain herself. After all, her body was saying everything it needed to, and the growing bulge between them was a good answer.

"Hey," he responded.

"Kiss me," she demanded.

One of his dark eyebrows rose. He didn't move, and the smile didn't lessen either. In fact, his eyes seemed to indicate he was laughing at her. All of a sudden, Stacy felt like an idiot. He was going to push her away and talk about her with his friends. But she was always bold. She'd lived her life that way, and she couldn't back down now that she'd come so far.

"Well?" she asked him.

He shrugged. "What the hell."

She had just enough time to wonder what was up with that, like he didn't want to but was humoring her, before his mouth descended on hers. She thought he would give her a soft peck, and it would be over, but somewhere she heard a tinkle of breaking glass, and his arms came up around her. He gripped her waist and lifted her up to his body then ran a hand down over her ass. Stacy clung to him. She had to because when he thrust his tongue between her lips and moaned in greedy hunger, it was all she could do not to fall on the floor from all the strength leaving her body.

She'd had a comb in her hair with jewels on it, to hold back her long hair. He threaded his fingers into her hair and pushed the comb away. Stacy ran her hands into his hair as well, loving the silky feel of it sliding between her fingers. She'd never kissed a white man, and damn if she didn't know what she'd been missing.

The man broke the kiss and ran his mouth down her throat, sucking at her skin and licking her until she shook from head to toe. When he moved to her shoulder and had pushed back the thin strip of material there holding her dress up, someone shouted, "whoa," and yanked him away from Stacy.

Shrill whistles filled the room, and several of the men clapped. Embarrassment stole over her, but she was still on fire. She'd made a connection. Now all she had to do was get this guy's number, and they could finish this in private. Turning her attention away from those looking on, she glanced at the man and smiled. "I'm Stacy."

He grinned in return. She picked up on his easygoing attitude and liked that about him. "I know. Zandrea and Nita's human friend."

Relief flooded her. So he knew what he was getting into, and he knew she was aware of them as well. "Yeah. So you want to go somewhere and... uh...talk?" She smirked at the crowd. "Away from nosey folk?"

He shook his head, and she blinked.

"Huh?"

His smile widened, and he leaned out to whisper in her ear, although she knew from what Zandrea told her, all of them had over the top hearing ability. "Stick with your own kind. I'm not interested."

And with that, his arrogant ass, spun on his heel and walked away, leaving her in the middle of the floor looking like a fool.

Chapter Two

Nash had learned a long time ago that keeping a smile on his face and a joke on his tongue would keep everyone from knowing what was truly on his mind. He was hardly ever, if ever, in a bad mood, and never rude. Well, not much. But just now, he'd told that human woman he wasn't interested, that she should stick to her own kind. He'd felt it like it was a punch to his own gut when her feelings were hurt. Yet, like him, she didn't show it. Anger blazed in her eyes a moment before he turned away. He suspected if he had stayed there another second, she would have told him off with the scathing tongue Lucas had told him she had.

Oh he knew her all right. He'd been right there with all the other guys staring at that sizzling body of hers when she walked in. Every one of them had enjoyed the view, but none of them would go after it because she was human. Least of all him. Lucas had lost his position as Alpha of their pack, and Nash had just gained the position. He was not going to let some chocolate goddess that made him want to rip off her dress and lick her from head to toe, jeopardize that. No way. Not for sex, that was sure.

He cared deeply about the pack. He enjoyed the position as leader. That wasn't going to change any time soon. He would fight to the death to protect his people, and he'd only left the city to come here to Zandrea and Brant's party because he'd missed his friends. They were family, and their lives had gone in separate directions. A rare visit had been in order, so he had accepted the invitation. Who the hell knew Stacy would make him weak with one amazing kiss? Wasn't going to happen a second time.

The elders were calling for him to choose a mate. A woman of his own would keep him out of trouble to some extent as well as satisfy his needs. But when he chose her, she would be wolf. Period. Not a human like Brant and Lucas had chosen. Hell no. Too much trouble.

In the farthest corner away from her, he nursed a drink and kept his eyes on those he was conversing with, pretending that her scent wasn't in his nostrils and the memory of her lips under his wasn't replaying over and over in his mind.

Lucas slapped him on the shoulder, looking like a contented, mated shifter with a new baby boy at home in his nursery and another one on the way. "Hey, what was that about, Nash? Thought you weren't going down that road."

Nash laughed. "Are you nuts, boss? No way. I have no interest in a human woman."

"Didn't look that way to me." Lucas winked. "And drop the boss stuff. You're Alpha now, remember? I'm just a lowly grunt, following my Alpha now."

They both glanced over to Brant standing with his arm around his wife. Brant had always longed for the position, and since they had hooked up with a younger pack who didn't have a leader, the man had become unbearable with the pups looking up to him like he was a god.

"How's that going for you?" Nash asked.

Lucas rolled his eyes. "I've told Nita to convince Zandrea to let herself get pregnant again. We could all use the break. If his head gets any bigger, it will pop. Or I might have to challenge him just to knock him down a peg. I'm still his big brother."

Nash laughed. "By what a couple months? Give *him* a break. Let him have his fun. He'll sober after while. The pups will mature and realize he's just Brant."

"Better be soon," Lucas growled. "Whatever, I'm content at least at home. Nita's having another baby. Did I tell you that?"

"Only three hundred times."

Lucas punched him. "Time for you to get your mate. Maybe you should consider Stacy. She's not bad to look at, and from the kiss, it looked like you two were ready to go at it. In fact if I hadn't yanked you off her, you would have bitten her. You know that's the first step in mating."

Nash waved his hand. "Get real, bud. I'm not taking a human. Forget it. And unlike you and Brant, I will not be driven half crazy in the middle of lust and bite a woman by mistake. When I take my mate—who will be a shifter by the way—I will bite her fully in my right mind having made the conscious decision to do it."

"That's what they all say."

Nash kept his smile in place and forced his eyes not to shift to their darker state. That way he wouldn't give even the slightest sign of Lucas' words irritating the hell out of him. What he wanted to do was grit his teeth and bust something up just to take the edge off his anger. His body might want her. Okay, he admitted that. She was a beautiful woman, and he'd be lying if he said he'd never wondered what it would be like to fuck a black woman. All guys thought about it. But he was not the asshole that used women just to fulfill a fantasy. He was better off leaving it as just that—a fantasy.

Whistles rose around the crowded room, and Nash sniffed the air. His wavering smile widened. He knew that scent anywhere. Laila, female shifter to rival all of their females. He'd met her once back in his city, when Lucas was still Alpha. That had been years ago, and at the time, he'd thought she was more interested in his buddy. But Lucas hadn't recovered his heart from Gloria at the time, so he barely acknowledged Laila's existence.

Nash threaded through the crowd, trying to get past the horny wolves with their tongues hanging out of their heads looking at Laila. He spotted her near the door, her willowy figure encased in a blinding red dress that was so sheer and so form fitting, she should be naked. He found himself growing hard. Laila knew what she was doing. The woman was giving off pheromones by the bucketfuls, and every unmated male in the room was responding to the call, including him.

With an extra forceful elbow to his nearest rival, he drew up in front of her. "Well, well. Look what the cat dragged in," he said with a grin.

She wrinkled a pert nose and pouted up at him, her short, dark curls dancing about her head when she shivered. "Cat? Don't be gross, Nash. This is a party."

He chuckled and stepped closer, pretending to search the area around her. "Where's your mate? Surely you didn't come all the way here alone?" Her territory was sixty miles away from his, which would make it eighty miles from the city Brant and Lucas now lived in with their mates and children.

She waved a delicate hand. Nash had felt she was insanely beautiful but a little too thin. He had always figured she'd been around humans too long and engaged in constant dieting. The last time he'd met her she hadn't eaten anything other than salads and fruit. The mere thought of a meatless diet made him want to mimic her shiver from earlier.

"I dragged a friend of mine down here. He's parking the car. But we're not mates." She rested her hand on his chest and locked her gaze with his. "I heard you were promoted. Congratulations."

"Forget it, fellas," someone called out. "You know what that means. She's Nash's mate now. Laila always did want to land an Alpha."

Laila let out a low growl in the direction the comments had come from. "Shut your mouth! You don't know me."

The unafraid shifters whimpered like puppies and then laughed. Nash wrapped an arm around Laila's thin shoulders. "Don't worry about those losers. They're just jealous. Come and tell me what you've been up to."

While Laila curved her lovely body to his side, they strolled across the room to a sofa. For no apparent reason, Nash's gaze drifted in the direction he had last seen Stacy. A man who was clearly one of them soon strolled over to her with two drinks in hand and a lecherous smile on his face.

Before he could control his emotions, Nash blurted, "Who the fuck is that?"

Laila raised questioning eyes to his and then glanced in the direction he was looking. "Oh, that's just Alphons. You'll love him. He's all Alpha, but he hasn't gotten a post yet. Looks like he's found his next lover. The man's appetite can't be stopped. Oh well, let's talk about us."

Chapter Three

Stacy slipped into her car and kicked off her heels before turning over the engine and roaring out of Zandrea's driveway. By the time she had made it to the street, her cell phone was ringing. She dug it out of her bag and read the caller ID. It was Zandrea.

She tapped the answer button on the gadget attached to her ear. "Yes?"

"Okay, what's wrong?"

"I don't know what you're talking about," Stacy told her.

"Girl, you know you're lying. You forget we've been friends since they invented the microwave?" Stacy burst out laughing when Zandrea did. Her friend went on. "I know your ass didn't skip out on me and drive back to town when I invited you to spend the weekend with us, so that means you're making a midnight run. Is it ice cream or cookies?"

Stacy grumbled. "Both."

Zandrea sucked her teeth. "Ouch, that bad? Come back, and let me go with you. We can disappear for a couple hours and talk. We can even do like we used to sometimes when none of us could find a man and stay out until the sun comes up. I know the perfect place to do it."

Shifting gears, Stacy took the next corner driving too fast. Her wheels gave a satisfying screech. "That's the problem. I made a damn fool of myself with that asshole, Nash. But you can be sure I won't let it happen again. All those guys in there, and I couldn't get my hands on one."

"Are you nuts?" Zandrea tapped the phone on something, and Stacy had to pull the ear piece off to keep from having an eardrum burst. "Girl, you talk about getting your hands on a man? First of all, the way you and Nash were going at it, I thought he was going to rip your dress off right there in the middle of the floor. And trust me, boyfriend was all up in that. Second, that other guy, what was his name? Alphons. Sexy as shit! He looked like he wanted what you were offering too. Nash is stubborn, straight-laced from what Brant tells me. I bet you could have your pick between both of them in no time."

While Zandrea spoke, Stacy had drawn up into a 7-Eleven parking lot and shut off her car. She strolled with purpose to the door and was soon cruising the short aisles for snacks. She had to work hard to keep the extra pounds from creeping up on her, but she was also an emotional eater. And right now, she needed something sweet.

"I'm not all that sure I'm interested in Alphons. He's a little on the creepy side, like he's up to something. I mean, he's hot and all, but I don't know." Stacy shoved the freezer door up and leaned down into the bin to grab a Nutty Buddy. "And as for Nash, he can kiss my ass. I won't even go into what he whispered to me."

Zandrea was quiet.

"What? Your man heard him, right?"

"Yeah, they have ears like you wouldn't believe. Brant heard what he said and told me. Don't let it get to you. Like I said, Nash just doesn't want to lose his position as Alpha like Lucas did. The pack he's in is kind of strict, which is why we had to move. They didn't want us to have mixed kids, half human, half shifter."

"That's bull—"

"Stacy!"

"Well it is." She sighed. "Look, I get it. He doesn't want to lose his job. Hell, my job ain't crap, but I'd fight to keep it too because for real, I've only got myself to depend on. I don't have money like those guys. Whatever. I'm still not forgiving him for humiliating me like that. I don't need him."

"But you want him."

"Drop it, Z," Stacy warned.

She stared down at the ice cream and changed her mind. After opening the freezer again, she dropped the Nutty Buddy inside and leaned down to grab an ice cream sandwich. A groan behind her made her freeze, and then she remembered that her dress was too short to be leaning over that much. She frowned and closed her eyes. With a deep breath, she stood up straight and spun around to face the jerk. Alphons stood there with his arms crossed over a powerful chest and running a tongue over his bottom lip.

Before she could say a word, he closed the space between them and put a hand on either side of her hips, forcing her to sit on the edge of the cold freezer. He rested his lips on the ear opposite the one with her Blue Ray clip on it, and had the nerve to blow in her ear. "You look good enough to eat," he breathed.

She tried to pull back, but there was nowhere to go. "Alphons, this is not the time or the place. How did you know I was here?"

He didn't answer, and she realized he didn't need to. He had picked up her scent and followed it. Annoyance made her want to frown, but she resisted it. If she had any sense at all, she would forget her hurt feelings and just take Alphons to a motel so they could both satisfy their needs. It was what she had said she wanted anyway. No strings, just sex. He didn't have to say so for her to know that's all Alphons wanted from her.

From his curly black hair, and his olive complexion, she knew he was Italian or something near it. If she slept with him, that would be a first as well, and her body did heat up because the man was sexy, but she hesitated. Like she'd told Zandrea, Alphons creeped her out just a little, for no apparent reason.

He drew back and grasped her hands, almost making her drop her ice cream. "Why don't we find the appropriate place?" he suggested. "I know we can have a good time, and"—he sniffed the air—"you're ready for me."

She jerked out of his hold. "Lay off with that crap. I'm new to this shifter stuff, and the sniffing me out thing is creepy, so I'd appreciate it if you bring it down a few notches." She turned toward the front of the store. "Besides, I got a man."

He followed behind her. "No...you don't."

Stacy gritted her teeth but didn't say anything to that. After she had paid for her ice cream and was back out on the street, she remembered she hadn't picked up any cookies. Either way, now she didn't want anything. Tiredness stole over her body, and she put a hand to mouth to stifle a yawn.

"Look, Alphons, I'm tired. It's been great meeting you, but—"

He pushed her against her car with his hands holding her hips in place. When his mouth came down on hers, Stacy automatically let him part her lips so he could push his tongue into her mouth. Like Nash had done, he groaned while he kissed her, like she was delicious to his taste buds. Were all five of their senses heightened?

Alphons ran his hands along her thighs, shoving her dress higher. He ground his hard on between her legs, and she gasped at his boldness. She couldn't help but be turned on. The man felt like a rock, a *big*, unyielding rock. Her thighs spread wider with no conscious thought on her part. All of a sudden, all she wanted was to get him inside her. She was so wet, she was almost whimpering for him to do it right there. The weird part was that she felt like she wasn't in control of herself, like he had bewitched her or some crazy mess like that.

A loud laugh interrupted them. "Damn, guys, get a room!"

Alphons raised his head, and Stacy caught sight of his eyes. They had gone from deep brown to silver. That was too freaky. She shivered, and then they both turned to see who had interrupted. Stacy could have shrunk through the ground. Nash and the woman who had come to the party late like she was the shit stood there watching her and Alphons. Both of them looked amused, Nash like he was laughing his head off at her, which grated on her already thin nerves.

The woman pounced on Alphons, taking his arm in hers and dragging both men toward the store. "What are you doing here, Alphons? I thought you would have had her in a motel by now. You're slipping, my friend."

Stacy stared. Was she for real? So open about what Alphons wanted. She shook her head and spun to face her car, but Nash was suddenly in front of her, blocking her from opening the door. She glanced around him to find that the woman and Alphons had disappeared inside 7-Eleven.

"What the hell do you think you're doing, Stacy?" Nash demanded.

She looked up at him. He wasn't frowning, but he wasn't grinning like he normally was either. Something told her he was angrier than he let on, which he didn't have a right to be after he had rejected her offer. "None of your damn business, that's what."

She yanked at the car door and got it open a few inches before he slammed it again. "You know nothing about wolf shifters. They're too much for a woman like you."

A hand slid to her hip, and she realized her dress was still hiked way too high, but she wasn't going to stand there in front of him and fix it. "Oh no you did not just say a woman like me! I don't know who you think you are, but you're nothing to me. I do what I damn well please, and you can keep your opinions to yourself."

She had been gesturing to him with a finger pointed. He caught hold of her wrist and jerked her forward to bump his chest. Desire licked over her skin, but she crushed it down.

"You're playing with fire."

"Like I'm too stupid to take care of myself, but my friends are just fine?"

His hold tightened, and she resisted a wince, not wanting to give him the satisfaction.

"I can vouch for Lucas and Brant. I don't know Alphons. From what I sense, I don't trust him. I've never seen him around before and therefore have no idea why he's shown up now. There must be a reason, and Laila hasn't been forthcoming about him."

So in other words, Nash didn't want her, and he didn't want any other shifters to want her either. He had been checking up on who Alphons was and where he'd come from. Nita had told her that Nash was a new Alpha, leader of his pack, just like Brant was now. So maybe the position had gone to his head. Maybe he thought he had to control the lives of all shifters and keep them safely away from relationships with humans. Well, he could kiss her black ass.

"You have three seconds to get your hands off of me, Nash. I don't care what you think. If I want to fuck Alphons' brains out on the first night I met him, that's my business. Not yours." She jerked her arm away from him, but moved up so she could stare him in the face. "You get made the Alpha of your group and think you're in charge of everybody. Well, I learned a couple things from my friends, and I know that Alphons isn't in your group, so you have no jurisdiction. As for me, if you think you're going to tell me what to do, you're wrong. I'm not the one."

She thrust her car door toward him causing him to have to jump back so she wouldn't slam it into his hip, and she fought hard not to grin at gaining ground on him.

"Why don't you go in the store and get control of your girl, 'cause it looks like she's ready to give it up to Alphons herself."

When Nash turned to look, Stacy hopped into her car, locked the doors, and turned over the engine. In seconds, she was out on the road. Not until she was pulling into Zandrea's driveway again did she wonder what had happened to her ice cream.

Chapter Four

Frustration raged through Nash's mind and rippled over his muscles, making them contract and ache. No matter how many times he rolled his shoulders and stretched, no matter how many miles he had run in his wolf form, nothing helped. For two days, he had been joking and laughing with his friends, keeping the easygoing persona in place, when all the time, what he wanted was to rip Stacy away from Alphons' side and fill her with his stiff arousal.

Why her, damn it? Why did she have to take away his peace of mind with one kiss, one touch of her body? Why did he have to see her naked beneath him every time he closed his eyes? And even having Laila for the taking didn't help matters. Shifters were highly sexual by nature. They often had several lovers at once. It was no big deal until they were mated, and he was pretty sure that Laila still tossed her long legs over Alphons' shoulders even though he was sniffing around Stacy. Nash didn't care about that.

The problem was Stacy would. She was human. Human women, from what he had seen, did not like sharing their men, and he was pretty sure she would be hurt in the end. The damn woman hadn't listened to a word of his warning. Instead she'd torn into him with her razor sharp tongue.

Later, he had laughed at himself for letting her shut him up so completely. She was bold. He'd give her that. Yet, the knowledge had only fueled his desire for her, and he had started wondering what being her lover would be like. That was a dangerous game. So he had let Laila seduce him. He had let her release her pheromones to make him relax while she went down on him, and later rode him. But although he had released several times, it did nothing to put out the fire Stacy had ignited.

One taste, one good, long, feeding between her legs, and he could move on. Couldn't he? Hearing her cry out, call his name, wouldn't drive him to want more and more. He wouldn't lose himself and find that he had bitten her, halfway to making her his mate, before he knew what was happening. He was nothing like Lucas and Brant. More to the point, he couldn't see himself falling in love with any woman, which he believed was needed for him to take a mate without thinking.

No, when he bit a woman twice, making her his for all time, it would be by conscious decision. Love would have nothing to do with it. She would serve a purpose, meet his sexual needs and bear his children. Nothing more. That's all he could ever let himself feel.

After his second ten mile run, he returned the back way to Brant's house, still in his wolf form. A doggie door had been made into the mud room's entrance, and he took it before changing back to his human form. Naked, he stretched and ran a hand across his sweat-slickened abs. He'd take a shower, have a snack, and find Lucas and Brant. Maybe a game of pool with them would get his mind off Stacy. He could get through the next twenty-four hours before it was time to return home.

He had taken all of two steps when the door to the rest of the house opened, and Stacy walked into the mud room. Nash stopped. When she saw him, her eyes grew round. They grew even bigger still when her gaze lowered to find he was growing hard at her seeing him without his clothes.

"Damn," she muttered.

He forced a cocky grin. "What, you've never seen one this big?"

She rolled her eyes. "Boy, please. Don't flatter yourself."

At first he was irritated at her dismissal, and then he noticed how she had trouble looking away, and she had clenched her hands at her sides. Her sweet little tongue was caught between her teeth. In that instant, Nash forgot his resolution and stalked up to her. He placed a hand against the door behind her, causing it to snap closed, and crowded her so she had to step back against it. He didn't allow his body to touch hers. He wanted her to see what she was missing, what could be inside her right now.

With a raised eyebrow and a smirk on his face, he watched her in silence. The play of emotions over her beautiful face was amusing, or it would have been if he wasn't heating up from his core being this near to her. His voice pitched low, he quipped, "You know you want it, Stacy."

She flattened her hands against the door behind her and turned her head away. Temptation got the better of her, and she turned back to stare. "Hey, I made my offer. You turned me down, remember? I'm not going there again. You missed out."

With a hard shove at his chest, she made enough space between them to turn her back on him. When her hand closed around the doorknob, he laid his on top of it and stroked her soft skin with a thumb. His shaft twitched against her back. When she began to tremble, he knew he had her. He ran a hand around her hip and down across her thigh. She gasped and moaned before clamping her teeth together. Oh no, she wasn't getting away with that.

He caught the hem of her mini dress and lifted it to rest his hand on her warm center. She cried out. "Nash! What the hell do you think you're doing?"

Her words were accusatory, but they lacked heat. He hadn't missed how her breathing had picked up, and her hips had curved so that she pushed her ass toward him. He took the offering and wrapped himself around her small body. Desire leaping out of control, he wrapped an arm across her chest and molded her to him. Yet, he didn't pause for a second in his exploration between her legs.

With a deft finger, he pushed her panties aside and eased a digit up into her wetness. Stacy shook hard. "You so shouldn't do that," she rasped. "I-I-I don't want it."

"Liar," he accused her. "You want it." He rested his mouth against her hair, kissed her once, and then whispered, "You want it so badly, you can't stand it. See how wet you are? Fuck, I could eat you all day long."

"Nash..."

"I'm going to taste you," he insisted.

Before she could protest further, Nash whipped her around and dropped to his knees. He watched for her reaction as he lowered her panties and helped her to step out of them. She clenched her dress between stiff fingers. "Here? We can't—"

He could argue with her, dare her to be wild like the wolves were. He knew it was in her, to have sex in public, even out among the trees like he enjoyed when his inner beast wanted to be free. But that would be delaying his tongue the satisfaction it craved. Instead of explaining it to her roughly, but without hurting her, shoved her legs apart and thrust his tongue toward her dripping cream.

All thought of helping Stacy to relax and enjoy herself at that point left Nash's head. All he wanted was to eat her, to suck and lick every last drop until he'd had his fill. He ran his tongue along her folds, stroked her thighs while he fed, and used his thumbs to part her so he could delve for more. Forgetting himself, he slid a hand behind her and splayed his fingers across her ass. With the strength only his kind had, he took her weight with ease in his palm and lifted her higher to meet his hungry mouth. Shoving one of her thighs higher, he began to kiss along her heated skin, capturing the tangy moisture he found there. While he did, he let his nose tickle her swollen bud, and a tremor started in her muscles.

"Oh goodness, Nash. W-What are you doing to me?" He paused long enough to see her head fall back, and then he licked her with more fervor. She was about to come, and he wanted it so hard, she'd be on her knees pleading with him to give her more.

"Mm," he hummed against her nubbin. "You're so good, Stacy. Come right now. Cream in my mouth, and let me eat more of you, honey."

He heard the tears in her voice. "You don't...deserve. Ah! I'm can't help it!" Her thighs contracted around his head, and soon she pumped her thick, spicy cream into his mouth. He licked her until she cried out his name a second time with a second orgasm, and then he set her down to rise to his feet.

It took a few minutes before her anger returned, and she balled her fingers into a fist and sent it straight into his jaw. "You're an asshole. You know that? A big-headed asshole."

Without another word, she yanked her dress down, yanked the door open, and stomped out of the room. Nash grinned rubbing his jaw. He glanced down to find the wispy panties she'd left him as a souvenir on the floor. Not even a punch in the jaw and her obvious hatred of him could make him regret what he had just done.

Chapter Five

"Oh damn, girl, he did what?" Zandrea demanded.

Stacy rolled her eyes. "Z, if you didn't hear it the first time, I'm not repeating it. I feel so embarrassed. I can't even believe I told y'all. I was like a whore in heat. I practically had my legs wrapped like a vise around his head." Stacy rolled over on her bed and buried her face in her hands. She continued in a muffled tone. "I can't face him. I'm not going down to dinner tonight. I can't do it."

Nita waddled across the room and patted her back. "It's not a big deal, Stacy. You said you've been wanting some. So he gave you a couple orgasms. So what? I mean you two were close to that when you kissed the first time during the party." She laid a hand on her rounded belly. "I know from experience that those guys can't get enough. Shoot, Lucas thinks I'm a baby machine or something, like he has to have as many children, as fast as possible. I even have to beat him off me during that time of the month."

Stacy sat up and stared at her friend in horror. "Ew! That's disgusting. TMI, Miss Thing, TMI!" She sighed. "I guess you're right though. To all of them, what we did wasn't a big deal. For real, I'm not a virgin. We all know that, but I've never gotten freaky in a mud room either, and especially not at someone else's house. It's depraved."

Zandrea burst out laughing. "Oh crap, you're picking up Nita's vocabulary. Quick, get this girl some dick."

"Witch!" Stacy threw a pillow at her friend, but Zandrea jetted to the side like she was a shifter herself. If they hadn't told her the truth about their boyfriends, she would have known something was up by the changes that had taken place in the two of them. And while Stacy had at first thought wolf shifters was a sexy idea, she didn't think she'd take to being turned into one, or whatever was happening to her girls. "All right, I'll go down to dinner, but I'm not talking to that asshole. He used me."

Zandrea held up a finger. "Correction, he seduced you, and got you off. If he was using you, he would have gotten him some while he was at it."

Stacy thought about that, and her friend was right. If Nash had been all about getting his, he would have done more than go down on her. He would have pushed for her to let him between her legs, or asked her to go down on him in return. Not that she'd given him a chance since she slapped the mess out of him. He must think she was an ungrateful wench. She laughed. Poor man probably had gone up to wash the sweat off of his chiseled body and at the same time jacked off to get relief.

If she was any kind of a woman, she would go find him and return the favor, but the problem with that was that he scared her. Nash was different from any of the guys she'd been with in the past. Yeah, the obvious physical difference, but also it was how he drew her. Like when she'd been searching the room looking for a likely man to come on to, her eyes had kept returning to him. And it wasn't like he was the finest man in the room either. They had all been fine, smokin' hot with no flaws she could point out with a microscope. So it had to be all him, who he was.

Not to mention that mouth. Oh man, had he done some things to her body. What he had made her feel should have been illegal in all fifty states. She felt like she had become his slave and all she could do was give him what he wanted. Zandrea had told her they had some kind of ability, but she didn't say what. Could he have used it on her, to make her give into him? All of a sudden, she was angry. If he did use some voodoo on her, she was going to do more than slap him. She was going to kick his ass.

In fact, right now, before they went to dinner might be as good a time as any to find out. She moved to the edge of the bed and dropped her bare feet over the edge. "I'll see y'all later. I have to find out something."

Nita grabbed for her arm. "Where are you going, Stacy? I don't like that look on your face."

"Yeah," Zandrea agreed. "I know that look. It's the same one you wore when you beat down Kevin that time he picked you up for work and grabbed your ass while y'all were headed out the door."

Stacy rolled her eyes. "Yeah, and just like he walked away with a puffy eye, the one I'm looking for is going to have the same thing if I don't like his answers to my questions."

Nita laughed. "Aw, lord, now you know you ain't right, Stacy."

"Nita, stop trying to talk slang!" Stacy and Zandrea told her at the same time.

The mama-to-be poked her lips out and waved her hand at Stacy and

Zandrea. Stacy had to fight to hold onto her anger as she let herself out of her room. Nita wouldn't change. She'd keep trying to be more 'black' as they said, and Stacy and Zandrea would keep cracking up at her attempts.

As soon as she closed the door behind her, she forced her mind back to Nash and reminded herself that she was pissed off at how he treated her. She hadn't missed the fact that he kept her panties either. She'd gone back down there after she was sure he had left, and she didn't find them. After he explained what he did to her, she would demand he give her, her panties. She had a thing for panties, and those he had were a part of a matched set. Hell, they were Victoria's Secret. For what they cost, he was damn sure going to return them.

By the time Stacy reached the first floor, she realized what it was she had been hearing all the way down here. Growling. Someone, or more than one someone, was snarling and growling like an animal. Her heart began to pound, and every muscle in her body locked up so that she couldn't move off the bottom step. She gripped the railing until her fingers ached. Nearby a door opened, and she let out a small squeak, but it was just one of Brant's guests, a seventeen-year-old boy. At least he looked like a seventeen-year-old. When he'd come on to her the day before, he'd said he was fifty-nine. She didn't believe him.

He paused in front of her and held up a hand, his young face crumpled with worry and what she was sure was fear. "You shouldn't come down right now, Stacy. Too dangerous. Why don't you go to your room, and wait until we say it's okay for you humans to come out."

"The hell we will," Zandrea shouted behind Stacy. "What's going on? What's all that growling about? Whatever's going on, they better take it outside. If they rip up my living room, somebody's balls are mine."

Zandrea's attitude snapped Stacy out of her fear. She laughed and moved ahead, brushing by the boy. "Yeah, they better look out. Z don't play messing up her stuff." She followed her friend out to the living room, and they stepped into the room just in time to watch two wolves going at it. The bigger of the two had the smaller by the scruff of his neck, and he yanked him off his feet and threw him through the French doors, splintering wood and shattering glass.

Zandrea screamed, but Stacy knew it was because of the damage to her home and not the possibility of the wolf being hurt. "Brant! What is going on? Why are you letting them destroy our house?"

Her boyfriend walked over and gathered her in his arms to keep her from rushing toward the fight. "It's okay, baby."

"It's not okay!" She wiggled in his arms but wasn't going anywhere.

While they argued, Stacy glanced around at the crowd of men and women present. Most of the guests had gone home after the party, but Brant and Zandrea's closest friends had stayed for the weekend. Stacy found herself searching for Nash among the five or six men standing there, and he wasn't among them. The other man that was missing was Alphons. He and Laila hadn't taken the hint that the rest of the weekend was for family and close friends.

Stacy crossed the room to Laila. The first time she'd laid eyes on the sexy bitch, she didn't like her. She was wild and super thin. All the guys had run up on her when she came in the night of the party, including Nash. Stacy didn't want to admit she felt jealous of the woman, but she didn't like lying to herself even if she did deny her feelings with others. She was jealous all right, and it ate her up to have to ask the wench anything about what was going on.

"So what's up?" she asked through clenched teeth.

Laila didn't spare her more than a glance, but seemed to feel the moment called for drama. She pressed a hand to her chest and sighed noisily. "They're fighting over me. I didn't mean for this to happen, but when you look like I do, men fall at your feet. I admit, I didn't know which of them to choose."

Stacy would have laid hands on the woman right there, and then two fights would be going on. Someone grabbed her arm. She tried to yank her arm free but found it trapped in a steel hold. Glancing back, she found Lucas behind her, anger in his eyes. "Don't," he told her. "We have enough to handle with them." He nodded toward the wolves rolling over each other as their razor sharp teeth sank into thick hides. "Contrary to what you've just been told, they are not fighting over a woman, but over a position."

"A position?"

He nodded. "Alphons has challenged Nash for the position of Alpha, and Nash had no choice but to accept. It's our way, and we knew it was coming sooner or later. I expect Brant will be next."

He glanced over to where Brant was standing watching the fight, with Zandrea clinging to his arm. Brant must have told her the same thing Lucas had just told Stacy. Zandrea must be envisioning some mangy mutt ripping at her man. Stacy wanted nothing to do with that bull crap. Every woman liked a dangerous man, but this was pushing it way too far. They were wild, and from the looks of it, Alphons was doing everything he could to kill Nash. More than once he had lunged at the Alpha's throat with his teeth bared.

Everyone had drifted behind the scuffling animals, and now they were all out in the grass at the back of Zandrea's house. Stacy thought it was a good thing they had bought a secluded mansion with no neighbors close by. The entire property was surrounded with trees. She shivered in the early evening air and dared to take her eyes off the fight to glance up at the sky. The full moon was already high in the sky even though the sun hadn't fully gone down, and she wondered if it affected them. They weren't werewolves, but she didn't know all the rules.

After what seemed like hours, the growls and barks became less frenzied, and the circling with heads low ready to attack had less threat. The smaller of the wolves actually bowed his head to the other one. Stacy blinked. Did that just happen? She had no time to think about it because they both began to change back to their human form, both naked. Everyone behaved as if it was natural, and Stacy had to put a hand up to her chin to force herself to stop swinging her lustful gaze from one man to the other and back again. *Damn!*

She was surprised that no one approached the men though. For real, they had to be cold with the temperature having dropped. The others began drifting back to the house, Brant and Lucas dragging Zandrea and Nita with them. Stacy didn't move, and neither did Laila. At least at first.

Stacy jumped when Laila suddenly cried out "Nash! Are you okay, baby?"

"Laila, don't! You know better," Lucas called out.

She didn't listen, and Stacy watched in shock as Nash growled at Laila. The moment she put her arms up to wrap around his neck, he caught them and squeezed, still growling. She cried out, but Nash wasn't done. He yanked her to him and sank his still pointed teeth in her shoulder. Laila screamed, but she didn't fight him off. Lucas and Brant both barreled past Stacy to rip Laila away from Nash.

"Fuck, fuck, fuck!" Brant kept repeating, and Lucas tackled Nash to the ground.

Stacy tried to clear her whirling thoughts to try to figure out what just happened. After all, the wolves healed fast, and Laila despite how delicate she looked, was one of them. Surely, it wasn't a big deal that the dumb ass had been bitten.

Nita and Zandrea moved up on either side of her, their expressions low. "What?" Stacy demanded. "What the hell is the big deal?"

Zandrea met her eyes. "Sweetie, that's how they take a mate. The male bites his woman twice, and it's forever. She just got the first."

Chapter Six

Stacy was behind the wheel of her car. Driving was what she liked to do when she had to work out the frustrations that were in her life. She loved handling a stick. The power, the control, under her hand, was a real rush. That rush was what she needed and a highway, somewhere the police wouldn't pull her over if she was doing eighty or more.

Nash didn't have a thing to do with her, and she shouldn't let it mess with her head. She had told herself that over and over as she hurried upstairs to change from the cutesy dress she had intended to wear to dinner, and into a pair of low rider jeans and a T-shirt. She'd slipped her feet into sandals, so she could yank them off the minute she was in the car. Driving barefoot was another way to work out her anger.

She was halfway down the driveway, her lights illuminating the pitch black night, when someone stepped out of the trees onto the road. The light reflected in his silver eyes making her heart pick up its beat and her hands shake. She slowed down to pull alongside him and rolled the window down.

He bent to peer into the car. "Need company?"

She hesitated. Usually she liked to be alone in a time like this, but what the hell. She popped the locks. "Get in."

He strolled around the front of the car and slid into the passenger side. Stacy barely waited for him to shut the door before she was off again.

"So where we headed?"

"Does it matter?" Glancing over at him, she was struck with how fast he had healed. When the fight was over and he'd transformed, his face had been riddled with small slashes like Nash had torn him to pieces. He would have been so messed up if he didn't have that ability. Women liked a man's scars, but that would have been ridiculous. "So what was that about, Alphons?"

He shrugged. "Simple. I have one goal in life. That's to be an Alpha. Nothing else matters."

She shifted to a higher gear and directed the car toward the highway. "What about Laila?"

"What about her?"

"Look, don't play me, okay? I'm not stupid. You've been up in my face, but I know you're still hitting her too."

He raised an eyebrow. "And you're innocent?"

"What's that supposed to mean?"

He didn't answer but tapped his nose. She focused on the road, disliking him and regretting ever picking him up. If his attitude had anything to do with why he wasn't leader of his own pack, then she could understand. Alphons didn't care about anyone or anything. She didn't have to know him longer than two seconds or have special powers to pick up on that.

So he had smelled Nash on her. Didn't a shower mean anything? She guessed not, but whatever. He had only come on to her, and they hadn't even progressed past that first kiss. Alphons acted like he was hot to get in her panties, but in all the times he found her wherever she was in the house over the last couple of days, she hadn't lost all reason like she had at the 7-Eleven, and that relieved her big time. Being that out of control was too much. And yet, she had spread 'em wide and fast for Nash.

Her anger coming to a boil again after it had simmered down, she shoved thoughts of Nash out of her mind. He was mated now. Or halfway there. From now on, they wouldn't have anything to do with each other beyond casual interaction when they were around Zandrea and the others at the same time. That's how she wanted it anyway. When she got a man to share her bed for a while, he would be someone she couldn't fall for, someone who couldn't break her heart. That man was not Mr. Big Shot, Nash.

Out of the blue, Alphons reached across the space between them and stroked her cheek. Stacy resisted pulling away. His hand fell lower to rest on her chest, his knuckles grazing her nipple. She bit her lip when the small peak pebbled beneath his touch. She was still horny as hell.

"We could go somewhere to be alone," he suggested.

"I don't know."

"What's there to know, Stacy?" He massaged her breast while she squeezed her legs together. "You're a woman. I'm a man. We're not attached to anyone." At her frown, he continued. "Not seriously anyway. See, there's a motel."

Stacy took control of herself. Too much this past weekend, she felt like these men were jerking her around. She was not that type of woman, and Alphons needed to get that straight right now. "Look, you're fine and all that, Alphons, but I'm just not feeling it. If you jumped in my car hoping we were going to be intimate tonight, you've got another thought coming. I'm sorry."

She had figured her words would piss him off, but instead he grinned. He reminded her of Nash with his incessant smile in every freakin' situation. Alphons moved his hand from her breast to her lips and tapped lightly. The intensity in his eyes made her nervous, and for the first time, she wondered how well Lucas and Brant knew this guy. *Great, Stacy, this is the first time you thought about that? Way to go.*

"Why don't we head back," she suggested. "I'm tired, and—"

Something came over her. She didn't know what it was, but out of nowhere, she longed for Alphons with every fiber of her being. The pull was so powerful, she'd even turned her head away from watching the road to watching Alphons, but he forced her head straight. "Watch the road, Stacy, and then take exit twenty-five. That's a good girl."

Stacy didn't want a thing in the world except to please Alphons. He was her everything. When she pulled off the highway and directed the car to the parking lot he had pointed out, Alphons told her to shut off the engine. She did and then unbuckled herself to climb onto his lap.

Alphons laughed and kissed her. "Now, beautiful woman, you're going to do exactly what I want you to do, aren't you?"

Her lids drooped heavy over her eyes, and she nuzzled into his chest to rest her head on his shoulder. "Of course. Whatever you want, Alphons."

Chapter Seven

Alphons checked on Stacy, still sleeping at his side, and then rolled off the bed. He strolled to the door and stepped outside into the early morning. He couldn't suppress the grin that spread over his face. How he loved being born a wolf shifter. They could release pheromones to the opposite sex and have them eating out of their hand. Of course, Alphons had taken it to new heights with a little genetic manipulation and some friends in dark places. He could push a woman to the point that she not only craved his touch, but she actually longed to obey his every command.

He supposed he should have more ambition for his life than to aim for an Alpha position. After all, he could seduce and enslave the richest, most powerful women in the world, and soon he would be the one with all the money. However, he wasn't limitless in his ability which was why he had tanked last night after manipulating Stacy. Eight hours of sleep had never felt so refreshing. Now he was alert enough to carry out his plan.

After one last stretch and a few more deep breaths, he turned back into the room to wake Stacy. He shook her, and the covers fell back to expose a bare shoulder, reminding him of what Nash had done last night. What an idiot. He'd bitten Laila, and just one more would make her his mate. But that little sexy she-wolf had jumped the gun. She hadn't trusted Alphons to get the job done, to move Nash out of the way of his goal. Sure, he had been humiliated to lose the fight to that ass, but he was not giving up by any means. Laila should know him well enough by now to know he always had a backup plan. And that plan involved the sweet human in front of him.

"Come on, Stacy. Wake up," he snapped, shaking her again.

Her lids rose, and her deep brown eyes focused on him. She was beautiful. He had to give her that. And her body! He grew hard just remembering how she looked under the covers.

Stacy blinked at him and then looked down at the bed. He saw the realization come into her eyes that she was naked. "What the hell?" she screamed, and sat up. A hand raked through her tangled hair. "Did I...Did we...?"

He grinned. "Of course, baby, and it was so good." He leaned down and kissed her cheek. It took everything in him not to burst out laughing at her horror, which he expected was more from her not remembering what had happened than anything else. After all he was a shifter. He knew he looked good, especially to the imperfect human. Damn, he was arrogant, and he loved it.

They didn't fuck, of course, but she didn't need to know that. He had taken her clothes off only so she would be more accepting of him when he wasn't using his control over her. He much preferred a female shifter because he liked sex as hard and wild as it could be. The ability to heal was important, and Stacy wouldn't do him any good if she was torn apart, unable to go after Nash.

That was his real use for her. He had done his homework before he showed up uninvited at Brant's party. He'd known about the third unattached human woman and guessed that because of the successful mating of Brant and Lucas, she could be used to tempt Nash into breaking his pack's rules. Joy had surged through him when one of the guys told him all about how Nash and Stacy had been practically fucking in the middle of the floor. The knowledge had given him an added certainty that his plan would work.

Soon enough Nash would make Stacy his mate, and the elders of his pack would toss him out on his ass. That would leave the field wide open for Alphons. He couldn't wait. Now that he had things in motion, nothing could go wrong. He didn't spend the last few decades learning how to bend people to his will for nothing. This was going to pay and pay big. Only then would he consider making Laila his on a permanent basis.

"Now, we really should get back. We're heading home today. I can ride with you if you want."

"Hell no!" She slung the sheet around her body and rose. "I mean, no thank you. I need the peace to think about some things, get my head right. I'm going to tell you the truth, Alphons, I don't remember a thing about what happened between us, and seriously, if what you said is true, I regret it."

He touched his chest in feigned offense. "You wound my pride."

She rolled her eyes. "Get real. You don't give a crap. You got yours, and that's all that matters." He watched her swaying ass while she walked over to the bathroom door, and then she turned to look at him. "I'm sorry. I'm not a morning person, and it ticks me off that I can't remember. I guess...we can talk in a couple days, okay?"

Just as he thought. She was more open to him thinking they had already been intimate. It was scary sometimes how well he could read people. He nodded. "Sure, baby. Whatever you want."

* * * *

"What is she thinking?" Nash murmured while he watched Stacy unfold her curvy figure from behind the wheel of her car, and that bastard Alphons sliding out of the passenger side. He'd known they were out all night. Zandrea had whined to Brant, and Brant had come to him, as if Stacy was *his* responsibility.

Lucas was unfazed. "She's thinking she's a single woman with the right to sleep with whomever she chooses. What's it to you? You've got more important issues to deal with. Have you forgotten about Laila?"

He gritted his teeth and slammed his fist on the windowsill. The noise caught Stacy's attention, and she glanced over toward the window where he was looking out. His first instinct was to duck out of sight so she wouldn't think he had been watching for her return, which he was. Yet, he resisted hiding. Maybe she would realize that she couldn't make foolish decisions that made her friends worry. Not him, but Zandrea. He tried to see the humor in this situation, enough to make him smile, but failed. "As far as I'm concerned there's nothing to discuss regarding Laila." He closed his eyes a moment, and finally calmed enough to plant a smile on his face. Then he turned around and joined Lucas for a cup of coffee, taking a seat across from his old boss. "I briefly considered taking Laila as my mate, but after what she pulled, I don't think she'd be the right woman."

"You think?" Lucas frowned before taking a sip from his cup. "She's manipulative, and every time she enters a room full of men, she amps up the pheromones. No one likes to fight off that level of sexual pull every second of the day."

Nash managed a laugh. "That's funny, because you act like you're not fighting the pull at all with Nita...*all day*."

"That's different."

Nash shrugged.

"Anyway," Lucas continued. "Laila knows the rules. A wolf just coming out of a fight is still too pumped up on adrenaline to think straight. He should not be touched, because for a brief window, he'd even attack his own mate should he deem her a threat. Laila should not have gone anywhere near you until you calmed down."

"Like she didn't know that?" Nash thought about what Laila had done. All it would take was once more. The humiliating thing was he had already been boasting that he was not like Brant and Lucas. He would never be out of his head enough to bite a woman. He'd never thought it would happen after a fight. All of them had more sense than that. "But then it wasn't lack of sense that drove her. She tricked me."

Lucas grunted. "Yup, and if you're not on your toes, my friend, she's going to do it a second time, and you'll find yourself shackled to her for the rest of your long life. She's sexy as anything, but..."

"But I don't want my right taken away from me. My choice."

Nash picked up on the sound of a door opening and Stacy's voice echoing through the house. He didn't excuse himself from Lucas before he stood up and rushed from the room. Rounding a turn in the hall, he came upon them together, Alphons' hand on Stacy's chin while his face was less than an inch from her soft lips. Nash clenched his fists but forced his expression to remain impassive. He hesitated to walk past and wound up freezing in place, unable to take his eyes off them.

Alphons whispered something to her, and Nash, not wanting to pick up on lust filled words or reminders of what they had enjoyed the night before, made sure he didn't tune in. Stacy nodded at whatever he said and leaned in to kiss his lips. Nash couldn't watch anymore. He turned away and decided at that moment to pack and go home even though Brant had asked him to stay and leave later. He had wanted to discuss one of his pups with Nash and Lucas. Nash was sure Lucas could handle it and give Brant the advice he required. Nash's pack needed him back where he belonged.

While he stuffed clothes in a haphazard way into his suitcase, grumbling under his breath, a knock sounded at his door. He sniffed. She was there. Her sweet voice calling out to him confirmed it. Annoyance at his body's reaction to her made him stomp across the room and yank the door open.

She jumped. "Hey, Nash."

He cocked an eyebrow up at her. "Hey."

She crossed her arms over her chest and leaned her weight into one hip. He let his stare follow those curves until he realized she hadn't said anything more.

"Was there something you needed?"

"Yes." She hesitated.

He reached out for her hand and tugged her inside the room. At least he could take the time to warn her off of Alphons. He didn't know the guy very well, but coming out of nowhere to challenge him when he didn't even know the pack he wanted to be in charge of did not sit well with Nash. A good leader developed a deep bond and a knowledge of his people before he felt he was ready to guide them. Alphons seemed to care about no one but himself.

Stacy's shoulder brushed his chest when she walked by, and he actually lifted a hand to touch her before he caught himself. Clearing his throat, he shut the door. "So?"

"Something's wrong with my car," she rushed out. "I was wondering if you could give me a lift back to town when you go, and I'm going to call triple A to send a tow truck for it. They'll haul it back home to get my mechanic to look at it."

Nash narrowed his eyes at her. He'd never heard anything that sounded more like a lie, and yet, Stacy didn't strike him as the kind of woman who would be sneaky about trapping a man. She was direct. If she wanted something, she would let it be known. "Didn't look like anything was wrong with it when you drove up."

"I know, right? I'm not sure what is going on. Whatever, I need a ride. I know Brant or Lucas would give me a ride, but they live out here. I don't want to make them take me all the way home and then have to drive back. You and I live in the same city. So what's the big deal, Nash? Will you do it? Please?"

Suspicion crawled over his skin. After all she'd only just stepped in the house, and Alphons had been whispering to her. Could he be up to something? Could he have put her up to getting him to take her home? For what purpose? Nash would have thought a man like he seemed to be would have his head swelling to have two beautiful women share his bed. Which one of them wouldn't get off on that? Nash'd had multiple lovers in the past, and they had all known about it.

He scratched the back of his head thinking it over. A reason to tell her no didn't come to mind, and really home wasn't all that far, not the way he liked to drive. Opening it up on the highway was a rush. Also, if he kept the conversation to a monotone, he just might avoid saying something he would regret like "Let's pull over and do what's on both our minds."

Before he could say another word, she had her body pressed to him and her hands running down his sides to his legs. He tensed when she reached around to grab his ass. *Fuck, there goes my resolve.*

"When you asked for a ride, Stacy, I thought you meant in my car."

She smirked up at him and tilted her head to the side, her eyelids low and her eyes full of sensuality. "You know you want it."

"Wanting it and accepting the offer are two different things." He removed her hands from his body and stepped back. "I'll take you home, but I am not getting trapped into anything. Not a second time."

Her hands went to her own hips. "What is that supposed to mean?"

Nash moved past her, grabbed his suitcase from the bed and headed for the door. "It means the only riding we'll be doing is in my Aston Martin."

Chapter Eight

Stacy tapped her fingers on the armrest in Nash's car until she felt like she was going to lose her mind. She didn't even know how she had gotten into this mess. One minute she was set on driving home alone so she could think through her actions this weekend, and the next she was convinced something was wrong with her car, and she needed Nash to take her home. To make things worse, the jerk acted like she had a virus he didn't want to catch. Even when her fingers had accidentally brushed his on the armrest, he'd flinched in disgust. Yet, that damn pleasant look had never left his stupid face.

"What's your problem?" she finally demanded after a long silence.

He spared her a glance before focusing on the road again. "Excuse me?"

"You heard what I said." Stacy leaned out and located the volume on the frickin' elevator music he had playing on the radio and turned it down. "You always have this sunny day look on your face, even when I know you're pissed off."

"Oh you can read minds now?" His eyebrows went up.

"Cut the bull, Nash. You're pissed way off, and you know it." She so wanted to point her fingers in his face, but she didn't dare. "I ask you for a ride, and you act like I'm trying to attack you. Last time I checked, I've never raped a man, so you can knock off the fear."

He laughed, and she thought it was at last genuine. "Trust me. I am not afraid of you."

"Oh yeah, then why are you scared to share more than two words of conversation with me? I'm not Nita. I didn't bother going to college, but I don't consider myself a total idiot either. You high saditty guys think you're better than us common folk. Is that it? You hate it that you're attracted to me?"

"Is that the card you're playing?" he demanded. "That I think I'm better than you? So I can't just not want you. I have to think I'm better not to want you? Whose nose is high in the air? It's not mine."

For some whacked out reason, Stacy felt stimulated. They were arguing, but she was enjoying herself. Usually when she told guys off, or anybody for that matter, she always won the argument and shut them down. Something told her Nash wasn't about to back down. Maybe because he thought that would mean admitting she was right about him. "Oh your nose is definitely out of joint, boyfriend, because I've got your number. Yeah, you like to pretend you're all happy go lucky, but for real, something is eating you up inside. You're just as messed up as the rest of us."

His knuckles went stark white on the steering wheel, and his palms made a squeaking noise, he held on so tight. She was riling him up. That was for sure. But she wasn't backing off either, even if she didn't give it all she had, not knowing how a man like him would respond to her pushing his buttons.

"What, no comeback?" she teased with a half smile.

Nash responded with his own grin, but didn't bait her. Stacy sighed and sat back in her chair. "So you think you'll win the argument by not answering. Is that it?"

"You like to argue."

"So what of it?"

"I like peace," he told her.

"In other words, we're too opposite and can't be together."

He shifted gears, his preference for a stick denying that they were too different. "Was that on the table? Our being together."

"Bite me, Nash."

For just an instant the look on his face told her he wanted to, and she gasped, remembering that he already had bitten a woman, and it damn sure wasn't her. Not that she wanted to be his mate. She didn't want any mate, not to be tied to a man.

"Oh yeah, I forgot. You're already taken anyway."

She couldn't have ruined their playful banter faster if she'd thrown a bucket of cold water on his head. His expression grew dark, and he tightened his hands on the steering wheel. For the next few minutes he didn't say a word or look her way. Stacy wanted to dig at him again to get him to play with her, but she didn't dare. Apparently, he wasn't happy about what had happened.

"So if you didn't want to make her your mate, why did you bite her? Z told me about the whole two bite thing," she admitted.

"Zandrea should keep her mouth shut about my people's business."

She crossed her arms. "Maybe you should be more careful where you put your mouth." She had so not meant that to sound like it did. The words reminded her of Nash's mouth between her legs, licking her until she wanted to melt into a puddle on the floor. She chewed her lip, pressed her legs together, and stared out the window. With any luck, he wouldn't pick up on how turned on she was right about now. His loud sniff told her otherwise, but he didn't address the issue.

"You were out all night with Alphons, and now you're here with me." He glanced at her and then focused on the road again. Irritation that traffic had slowed to a crawl was etched on his face. "What game are you playing, Stacy?"

"Everybody said you never let anything get to you. When Brant and Lucas were panicked over bonding with Zandrea and Nita, you were the one to keep them in check. But I'm not seeing it. Ever since I met you, you've been grumpy. Come on, loosen up and have a little fun, Nash. It won't kill you."

She reached across the space between them and laid a hand on his chest. He jumped so much, one would have thought she had scorched his skin, but feeling bold and determined to get him out of whatever dark place he was in, Stacy didn't draw back. She ran her palm down over his rigid form until her fingers curled around the swollen piece in his pants. A small moan passed her lips.

Nash kept her from stroking him. "Tell me."

Her eyebrows went up. "Tell you what?"

"Tell me why you would jump out of his bed this morning and try to get into mine now. I don't know you very well, but I think you're not the type of woman who sleeps around that much."

She drew away. "You're right. You don't know me." She didn't want to tell him a thing, but for some reason she did open up. "My father abused my mother for years, as far back as I can remember. When I was ten, I pleaded with her to leave him, for us to just go somewhere and forget him. At least then there would be no more late night arguing at the top of their lungs, no more broken dishes or whatever he got his hands on, and especially no more crying. Me and my mother."

When she paused to take in a few calming breaths, he reached out to stroke her cheek. She turned her face into his palm and closed her eyes, but only a moment.

"You know what she said about why she wouldn't leave him?" He shook his head, and she went on. "Because she loved him. She loved him more than her own life, more than my life. Can you imagine a mother saying that shit to her ten year old child? I vowed right then that I wasn't going to let a dumb ass man into my heart."

She thought he would try to convince her that the right man was out there for her like everyone else had said who knew her past, but he didn't. He nodded in understanding and uttered, "Makes sense."

Stacy blinked. "Are you serious?"

He shrugged. "I've made a similar vow for other reasons. Love is overrated. Unfortunately, for my people it's different. I won't love my mate before I bond with her, but I will need her like I need my next breath after we are mated. The good thing about that is that she will have the same radical change in her emotions toward me." He rubbed his chin. "Then again, I could simply marry like regular men and never actually bond. That's an option. Never been done though."

Stacy turned to face him. "What? You're crazy. Your people are unique and interesting. To know someone couldn't ever hurt you or they'd be screwing with themselves is way more than enough to mate. We don't have that luxury. And you're out of your mind if you think a regular marriage will work. What about when she meets another guy and jumps him. What about when this guy gets her pregnant, but she claims it's your baby, and you have to foot the bill for a kid that looks nothing like you, and everybody knows it."

Nash burst out laughing. "Wow, you are cynical. More so than I could ever be." He shook his head. "All of that, huh?"

"Boy, please. That kind of drama and more happens in this world. You just don't know it." She slipped her shoes off and put her feet up on the dash. Out of the corner of her eye she saw the annoyance in Nash's expression, but ignored it. She could so rile him whenever she wanted. It was sad...and funny. Then she sobered. "You know what the scariest part is, Nash?"

"What's that, baby?"

She stiffened. The pleasure that rippled through her at the endearment shouldn't have even happened, and she didn't think he realized what he said, so she didn't make a big deal about it.

"The scary thing is that I've punched guys before, when they pushed me too far. I did it to you. I did it to the guy I work with. I mean he had it coming since he thought he could just grab my ass, but..."

"But you're scared you're following in your father's footsteps?"

"Yeah." She dropped her head on her knees. "If I were a man, I would have really hurt a woman by now, just like him. How sad is that?"

"Stacy."

"What?" She didn't look up.

"Look at me, baby."

She hesitated and then twisted her head to the left to peek at him over her arm.

"You're not him. You'll never be like him because I can see no matter how hard you try to hide it, you have a lot of heart. If you feel like you need to talk to someone about it, you should, to work through it. And if you need a sparring partner"—he winked—"I've been known to hold my own with kick boxing."

"Kick boxing? Ah, man, I've wanted to try that. You know how? You could teach me." She grabbed hold of his arm and bounced. His gaze dropped to her breasts.

His usual grin spread over his full lips. "I might. But for now, let's scratch a small itch, shall we?"

Chapter Nine

What had he been thinking? He knew. When she had started telling him about her past, the pain in her eyes had made him want to pull over and take her into his arms. She had kept her voice low, steel running through the pitch, but he had sensed the betrayal there as well. Stacy had expected her mother to provide a safe environment, and when she didn't, and then admitted that Stacy's life meant nothing, Stacy had crumbled inside. Only her tough exterior, what she showed to the outside world kept her going, he guessed. Maybe they weren't so different.

He knew what heartache was, and he knew he didn't want to experience that level of torment again. Besides love, Nash had never denied the rest of his needs, and that had included sexual needs. He could admit now that he wanted Stacy. And knowing how she guarded her heart, he figured they could have a small affair, not lasting too long where emotions would creep in, but just long enough to enjoy each other's bodies a few times.

So he had suggested the motel. He should wait a few days, let her get Alphons out of her system, but he didn't want to. Ever since he'd tasted her, he craved more, much more. He needed to have himself stuffed inside of her with her legs wrapped around him and her crying out his name as he pounded their pleasure home.

"Stacy!" he growled.

She scrambled out of the car and around it to take his offered hand. He drew her to his side and allowed his palm to skim her round ass. He was used to smacking his lover's ass when the mood struck him, but he hesitated with Stacy. Even though plenty of people engaged in spankings that could take the sexual experience to new heights, he wasn't sure if it would upset her, and the last thing he wanted to do was make her afraid. So he settled on stroking her instead. While they strolled over to the motel office to check in, he traced the crack of her ass and then lower to her entrance there. His shaft tightened. He was going to get some of that as well.

Once they were inside the room, he kicked the door closed and nodded toward the bathroom. "Strip down and go get in the shower. I'll join you there in a minute."

She gave him a look that said who did he think he was bossing her around. He responded with a raised eyebrow, daring her to disobey. After a few moments, she rolled her eyes and followed his order. He chuckled under his breath. Stacy was fiery all right, and he enjoyed teasing her, getting her worked up, whether it was pissing her off or getting her hot. Both gave him added excitement in his life that he hadn't experienced in a while.

While he was removing his clothes, his cell phone rang. He glanced at the caller ID and saw that it was Laila. She had programmed it into his phone before all the craziness began. Letting the call go to voicemail, he waited and watched to see if she left a message. She did. He retrieved it and listened to her smooth recorded voice.

"Nash, call me. We need to talk. I'm...I'm already having symptoms from your bite." After a few beats of silence, she left him several numbers where he could reach her, along with a brief outlining of her schedule over the next week. Then she hung up.

He sighed and powered off his phone before sitting it on the nightstand. Truth be told, he was feeling the changes as well. A pull toward Laila. He wanted to see her. A connection had begun between them because of his bite, and Laila would be experiencing it as well. But there was no fucking way he was going to tempt himself or her that way. She wasn't going to be his mate. Not now, and not ever. If he maintained miles between them for the next fifty years since he didn't intend to break the connection by taking another mate, then that's what he would have to do. Laila would just have to accept that fact. After all, she knew the risk she was taking.

Right now, Nash was going to focus all on Stacy. He checked the doorknob to the bathroom half expecting it to be locked, but Stacy wanted him as much as he wanted her. He hadn't missed her suggestive words earlier in the car, about him being careful where he put his mouth. He had smelled her arousal. She had been wet, and it had driven him nearly out of his mind. The years of hiding his true emotions had been well worth it.

The moment he spotted her long, curvy body, glistening wet and golden brown, he lost any thought that had been tumbling around in his head. All he could focus on was stepping in the shower with her and taking what he wanted, what he craved.

* * * *

Stacy had seen guys lusting over her before. Hell, that dumb ass Kevin had it in his eyes every time he laid eyes on her, but the emotion in Nash's eyes made her weak with want and scared her at the same time. When he opened his mouth, she expected to find sharp teeth that would tear her to pieces, but his teeth were normal. The tips of his fingers grazed her nipples, and she couldn't imagine what his mate would feel because this sensation had her wanting to let him boss her whenever he wanted to.

He plucked and tugged her nipples until she whined, trying to get closer to him. That was impossible because she'd already lined her body with his huge, muscular one. The man's form was made for her pleasure. She actually titled her head up to take a lick at the water beading on his shoulder. She shuddered.

"Stacy, what have you done?" His voice was ragged, like he had been running miles without stopping, and all moisture had left it.

"What do you mean?"

He gripped her arms, staring down at her. "How can you...? How can I...?" He seemed unable to complete a sentence. The next thing she knew his tongue was down her throat, and he had lifted her up in his arms. Stacy encircled his waist with her legs almost crying when the tip of his shaft pressed her soaking wet entrance.

Nash broke the kiss. "I need to be in you. Say yes, Stacy. I've got to have it now. I can't wait for foreplay. I promise I will please you."

"Yes, yes, please, yes!"

He was in her. Oh man, it hurt so good. He was too big and more than enough. She spread her legs wider and tried to get them higher. He bumped her against the shower wall, and with the lukewarm water streaming over them, he pounded deep inside her. His rhythm was fast and hard. Stacy screamed his name, dug her nails into his shoulders and tried her best to angle her body so she could take more of him. Let him not stop. Let him never stop!

Nash held her beneath her ass with one hand and grasped one of her ankles so he could lift her leg higher. Her head lulled to the side, her mouth dropped open, and her eyelids drooped closed.

"You're so strong, Nash," she muttered. "What a turn-on. Make me come, please."

"As often as you want, baby. Hold on." He drove harder and faster. The friction, the tension, and Nash calling out encouragement to her made her inner muscles begin to bunch, pushing her closer to an orgasm. Nash released her leg and moved both hands behind her, forcing her body forward so that his would brush her small engorged bud. She fell against him but he never stopped pushing into her. "Come on, my sexy little, goddess, give me your sweetness," he grumbled. "I know you like what I'm doing to you, don't you?"

He ran his teeth over her neck. She couldn't think straight. He licked her wet skin, and she shivered. All the strength left her body. She couldn't do it. She couldn't finish it. But Nash kept guiding her up and down his thick, long shaft, pushing her to ride him, demanding her climax to obey him.

And then it came, it came with power to take over her mind. She wanted to cry out, but the words didn't move past her throat. A soft gasp was all she could manage when an orgasm slammed through her core, powerful enough to take control of her body. While it pulsated over her, Nash used his middle finger to massage her ass. He pierced the tight hole just a bit, and she came again, this time screaming his name.

Gasping for breath, she collapsed on his shoulder, and Nash jerked himself out of her. She whined. "What are you doing? You didn't come."

He turned her so her back was to him. "Tell me you've had it here." He rested his hand on her ass."

She nodded and didn't have to say another word before he soaped her rear with gentle fingers. In the next instant, like he could not contain himself, he entered her from behind. Stacy went up on her toes, shocked at how she ached but amazed that Nash still made her body sing after she'd come twice.

He crushed her body to him with one hand and rested the other on the wall ahead of her. He panted, and the noises in his throat made her shiver. "Please," he rasped out, "keep very still and stay quiet. I-I have to make sure I don't hurt you, and it's hard because I need to come bad. I should have brought a condom in here. You're squeezing me so tightly, Stacy. You ass is so good, baby."

His slow, agonizing strokes didn't make it easy on her to keep still. She chewed on her lip, kept herself on her toes with her hips arched. Nash's huge body was curved over hers, plastered them skin to skin. He nuzzled her neck and again ran his teeth over her flesh before he followed it with his tongue. Stacy could not figure out what he was thinking beyond his physical desires, but she had never felt so wanted, so cherished in the same instant that a man was getting his pleasure from her body.

Nash glided his palm down lower until he rested it between her legs. Gently, he tugged at her bud, massaged it with the pad of his thumb and then threaded fingers inside her. The moment Stacy slammed into a third orgasm, Nash let go of his own. His hot seed filled her ass, and he picked up his pace until he pounded her from behind. His curses of pleasure filled her ears while he worked her body over. By the time, he was done, she didn't have the energy to wash herself, let alone climb out of the shower.

With gentle touches, Nash washed them both, and after drying her body at the side of the tub, he carried her into the bedroom to tuck her into the queen size bed. Stacy yawned, watching Nash through half closed eyes as he prepared to join her. By the time, he had turned all the lights off and slid beneath the thin sheet which was all she had allowed him to cover her with, her body was coming alive again.

Chapter Ten

It took three days for Nash to crawl out of bed with Stacy. By then, she was so sore, she stumbled when she stood up, and he'd hurried to catch her before she hit the floor. He should feel guilty for working her over so much, but he didn't. She'd come way more than he did, and he had thoroughly enjoyed himself, exploring her delectable body. Even while he knew he needed to get back to the pack, he didn't want to leave her. The emotion was so strong, earlier he had searched her small body for evidence that he had bitten her, but he found none. That had made him sigh with relief.

The two of them were just sex starved. That was all. And they were a perfect fit for intimacy. Not that it took much for him to enjoy sex, but with Stacy, it was hard for him to think past her luscious breasts, her sweet lips, and the curve of her hips.

"Stop it," he growled at himself. If they didn't get back on the road now, they never would, and he'd be ousted from his position as Alpha. For a moment he considered if that's what Stacy was working toward all along, but then he dismissed the thought. She had nothing to gain from it.

He stretched his aching muscles and grabbed his cell to power it up. Fifteen messages waited for him. "Damn."

Ten were from Laila, and one was from Lucas telling him that one of the elders had phoned him about a small crisis that needed to be resolved back in the city. He sighed as he listened to the three from the elder. Teenage pups having run-ins with humans. Yeah, he had to get back, now.

By three that afternoon, he was in his apartment, relieved to be home and out of Stacy's presence. Already his mind was clearing of her intoxicating scent, and he could think straight about making a decision not to see her again. The last few days had been perfect. He wouldn't deny that, but shirking his responsibilities was not something he could allow in his life. Stacy was a rare breed of woman, no matter how he looked at it. She was too much for him.

He ran a hand over his chin while he stared unseeing at the junk mail he had brought in with him. "That's a hard pill to swallow. That a woman is too much for me." Ah, well, it couldn't be helped. She'd understand. He would call her in a few days and tell her it had been fun, but that was it.

Nash showered, changed clothes, and jumped back into his car to head over to Brant's mother's house. For the life of him, he couldn't figure out why their favorite meeting place was the bar beneath her house. The place was in the heart of the city, not the best part of town either. Elders, he supposed. Brant and Lucas' father was the first generation of shifters to come into money. Good investments and so forth had set him up, and those under him had followed. Nash had money himself, but he didn't splurge on anything other than his car. His apartment was modest. He had always told himself he would get something bigger, something outside of the city when he found a mate. Thoughts of both Stacy and Laila passed through his mind, but he suppressed them.

He pulled up to the curb, parked, and hopped out of the car before clicking a button to activate his alarm system. After one of the younger ones let him in, he headed straight for the lower level. A scent of alcohol tickled his nose. He had no idea why they drank so much. The stuff didn't affect them long. Then again, maybe that was why. Everyone wanted the buzz to last, but the body nipped it quickly. So they drank more.

The elder who had contacted him stood up from a small table in the corner when Nash entered the bar area. Nash nodded his head in respect. "Sir."

Sabelli snapped his fingers to the woman at the bar. "Gloria, a drink for Nash, please. What will it be, Nash?"

His eyes widened, and he turned to spot Gloria stomping over with a napkin and a small bowl of nuts in her hand. Her wide beautiful eyes dared him to make fun of her, and he pressed his lips together to keep from laughing. Gloria had been the woman to almost destroy Lucas a few years ago when she had broken his heart. How low had she come in the world to be working here?

"Don't even start with your smart ass remarks, Nash. I own this place now. I bought it off Brant's mother a couple days ago. I'm settling down." She held up her left hand, displaying a plain gold band with a small diamond ring alongside it. "I'm mated and married now."

Nash tapped a finger on the table top. "Shouldn't I have known this since I am Alpha? What happened to me blessing your union?"

She remained silent. Nash turned to Sabelli, and the old man had the nerve to look guilty. Suspicion rose in Nash, but he forced a grin on his face and rose to hug Gloria. "Congratulations, I'm sure the guy considers himself very lucky. If you don't mind, I'll have a light beer."

Gloria nodded and spun away to get his order. Nash sat and waited in silence for an explanation.

Sabelli scratched at the scraggly beard on his chin and didn't meet Nash's eyes. "Look, Nash, Gloria's husband happens to be my grandson. I approved and blessed the marriage in your absence. You know how she can be once she gets something in her mind. She doesn't like to wait, and at first I wondered if she'd be too much for Shep, but well..." He indicated the man with eyes clouded over as he watched Gloria work. "He loves her, and surprisingly enough she loves him."

Nash wasn't impressed. Mating did that to them. Whatever feelings they started out with quickly became distorted into obsession. That was something he could do without. Aside from that, Shep looked whipped if you asked him. Gloria was still the sexy seductress who flirted with every man who entered the bar, but her eyes turned to Shep often enough for Nash to be convinced she did it only to challenge his love for her. Gloria was weakened now that she loved and needed Shep.

"Okay, I get that," Nash told Sabelli. Makes sense. However, there's something else you're not telling me."

Sabelli seemed to toss caution to the wind and blurted out what was on his mind. "I've heard rumors that the reason you stayed down there at Brant's, neglecting your duties here is because you are having an affair with a human. Is that true?"

What the fuck? He'd just left Stacy that morning, and already rumors were spreading? Nash leaned back in his chair, and grinned at the man across from him. "When I took the position as Alpha, I vowed not to take a human as my mate, never to procreate with a human, and to defend my people with my life if necessary. As far as I know, I've not missed on any of these things. So who the hell I fuck is none of your damn business." The pleasant expression never left his face throughout this tirade.

He stood up and dug out money from his pocket to pay for his beer. Then he started for the door before calling over his shoulder, "I'll take the pups for a ride to straighten them out. The next time you decide to keep information from me regarding my pack, you will find your ass looking for a new one yourself."

Out on the street again, he unlocked his car and commanded the two young shifters to get inside before he slammed the door closed and pulled his cell phone out. No better time than the present to cut all ties with Stacy. He might have been flip in there talking to Sabelli, but the inquiry had lit a fire under him. After he broke with her and dealt with the guys in his car, he would find out who the hell was passing information on his doings, and he'd deal with him next.

He dialed Stacy's number. After two rings, she answered. "Hey, you." Her voice was pitched low and husky. His dick hardened, and a longing rose inside him so strong, he had to brace himself against the side of the car. Lust. That's all it was. Not affection, and it damn sure wasn't love.

He shut his eyes, dragged in a few breaths, and cleared his throat. "Hey. I was just calling to say it was good. Very good between us. But my obligations are great right now. I don't have time for anything...or rather any*one* in my life. We both knew it was just physical and temporary. So let's call it quits here. Okay? I know you understand." He paused a millisecond for her to respond, and when she didn't he went on. "So...good-bye."

He snapped his phone closed. Behind the wheel of his car and roaring down the road with gritted teeth, he prepared to rip into the two shifters in his back seat. They would be punished partly for what they did risking the exposure of the shifters' existence, and partially for the suffocating pressure Nash was feeling in his chest after how he had roughly and cruelly dumped Stacy. Later, there would be plenty of time for the torment he suspected would result in his own mind when he was alone in the dark.

Chapter Eleven

"Stacy, come out to dinner with me. Just the two of us," Kevin asked for maybe the billionth time on their way back to the car rental agency. "I can show you a good time."

"If you knew the mood I was in right now, Kevin, you wouldn't ask."

He pouted. She ground her teeth. Men who pouted were not sexy. That was a woman's thing in her book, and she hated how that fool Kevin thought she'd be convinced to do anything for his ass when he pouted at her.

"Is it because of that phone call you just got?"

"Shut up!"

"Come on. You can talk to me. We've been coworkers for years, and I'd like to think friends for almost as long." He laid a hand on her arm, and without thinking she grabbed it and jammed his fingers back. He howled, and Stacy let go. She almost lost control of the car pulling to the side of the road. She threw the car in park and jumped out. Before she came to herself, she had run a good ways down the road with Kevin yelling for her to come back.

Oh no, oh no, oh no. She was like *him.* She was like her father. She hadn't even thought just now. She had reacted. Nash had said she could work out the anger with him—and the fears too—because she had admitted to it sometime during the night when she had been laying in his arms. The problem was she had been the one doing all the opening up, and he hadn't shared jack with her. How could she have missed that? How could she not have noticed that he had lain there, stroking her arms, encouraging her, comforting her, but never opened his heart? Of course not. Didn't he say right from the beginning that he didn't believe in love?

Or had that been what she said? She should have known she was fooling herself from the start. Nash had caught hold of her the moment he touched her. And he had sealed it, in just three days. Tears filled her eyes and spilled down her cheeks. It had all been one-sided, proven by the fact that he kicked her to the curb—over the phone!

Kevin came running up waving his hand in the air. "Hey, why'd you run off? Look, my hand's fine. You smacking me around is nothing new. Why the overreaction now?" He leaned in close to her with a lecherous grin on his face. "Wanna make it up to me?"

Stacy just stared at him. Was Kevin what they called an enabler? A few years ago, she'd read everything she could get her hands on about abusers and the people they always got away with hurting. Stacy had thought then that no one like that was in her life. Zandrea would have definitely kicked her ass if she laid a hand on her, and even Nita would have forgotten all her education and beat Stacy down. That left Kevin who Stacy had been stuck with most of the time when they drove from place to place delivering and picking up rental cars together. She loved driving and had never let Kevin's goofy tail get to her too much, but sometimes he pushed her too far, or something in her life set her off, and then this. She remembered the times she had punched him, but she'd thought it was just her defending herself against a coworker who got a little grab-happy sometimes. Yet, maybe it was more.

No, she didn't want to believe it. Believing that would make her... Her cell phone rang in her pocket, and she was disgusted that she hoped it was Nash calling back to say he was sorry for what he had said. She'd tell him where he could stuff the apology and have the last word. But it wasn't him. While shuffling back to her car knowing her next step was to find a therapist to talk to, she answered the call.

"Hello?"

"Stacy."

She stopped walking just in front of the car and waved Kevin away. She watched in silence as he grumbled his way to the passenger side and slipped in before slamming the door closed.

"What do you want, Alphons?"

He tsked. "Is that any way to talk to the man who cares most about you, baby? I thought we had something going? Remember, you said you'd call. I haven't heard from you, and I threw my pride out the window and decided to call you instead."

She frowned. "Cut the crap, Alphons."

His voice grew more serious. "You've disappointed me, Stacy."

"What the hell are you talking about?"

"I've heard rumors. That you've been sleeping with Nash. From what

I've heard, I expected you to tell me there was no chance for you and me because you and he had mated."

"What?" she shouted. She swung away from the car, hoping no police would happen along to find out why she was parked on the side of the road without car trouble. Shortly after she'd gotten home, her mechanic had phoned to say her car was fine as usual, since Stacy made sure she had it checked regularly. She had no idea why she'd thought something was wrong and had had it towed. To find out that someone was running their mouth behind her back about her business was worse. "I don't know who's been all up in my business, but I don't appreciate it. And as for you, I can sleep with who I want to. You and I have not made a commitment to each other. Like I said, I don't even remember what happened between us. Look, I've got to go. I'm not in the mood for this crap."

"Stacy, be quiet!"

She opened her mouth to tell him what he could kiss, but something came over her. Dizziness hit her so hard, she sank to her knees. Somewhere nearby, she heard a car door open, and Kevin was there beside her asking if she was okay. She tried to answer, but couldn't. The phone slipped from her fingers, and then everything went black.

Kevin yelled in the distance. "Stacy! Stacy, answer me."

* * * *

Stacy opened her eyes to a pounding headache in a darkened room. She attempted to sit up but found her hands bound above her head and her ankles tied to something, with her legs spread. She shifted her body and realized she was on a bed. "Where am I? Hello? Can anyone hear me?"

There was no answer. She yanked against her bonds but only managed to hurt her wrists and ankles. For a minute she thought about giving in to the fear welling up inside her, but she stomped it down. Holding her breath, she struggled to pick up any noises whatsoever beyond the room, but it was as if whatever house she was being held in was empty. There was no telling how long the person who had tied her up had been gone, or when they were coming back. If she was going to get out of this, she was going to have to do it herself.

Discovering that her feet were bare—the ass had even taken her socks off along with her sneakers—she used her toes to feel the space below her and found the baseboard. The piece was made of wood. Stacy remembered thinking how strong the leg muscles were that a person could kick a door in if the adrenaline was high enough. If the fear that had her almost shaking could be considered adrenaline, she was going with it.

A couple deep breaths, a prayer, and a few stretches, and she began to kick at the wood below her feet. After the first blow, she stopped to see if someone would come bursting in, but the house remained quiet. Blow after blow seemed to do nothing at all. Stacy started cussing up a storm. "Give, damn it! I'm not sticking around here to get my ass killed. Give!"

A deafening crack filled the room. She whooped and longed to take a breather, but she couldn't risk it. A few more kicks, and the baseboard snapped away from the posts at each end. Stacy jerked her tired and achy legs up over the posts, and the rope slipped off to hang limp from her ankles.

Her throat was dry. She'd give herself no more than a minute, and then she would work on her wrists, which would be trickier.

* * * *

Nash pulled into the parking lot outside of his apartment and stepped out of the car. He slammed the car door shut and started toward the building. He would grab some paperwork he had meant to look over for a new investment and then take it with him to the restaurant where he planned to have dinner. Not that he had much of an appetite tonight, but he knew better than to ignore fueling his body. What he should do was get out of the city and run until he dropped. That might release some of the tension that had settled like a fifty pound rock between his shoulder blades. If not, then at least it would exhaust him enough to sleep through the night.

He reached his door and slipped his key into the lock. Pausing, he waited for her to greet him. He'd picked up her scent well before she had settled some feet away, leaning against the wall.

"Hello, Nash, baby. Miss me?"

"Laila." He turned the lock and opened the door. She followed him inside, and he shut the door behind her.

"Well?" she demanded. "Did you?"

He shrugged. "I bit you once. That makes me miss you."

She shrieked in frustration. "You don't have to say it like that. It takes away all the enjoyment of knowing you want me."

"And you tricking me takes the enjoyment out of choosing my mate. That makes us even, so get over it."

Her tone turned to pleading. She pouted and strolled over to him to rest a hand on his chest. "Come on, baby, be nice. You know it's inevitable. If I promise to behave myself, we can have a lot of fun tonight. Don'tcha think?" She rubbed her breasts against him, and while Nash enjoyed the sensation, he couldn't help but compare her to Stacy. As sexy as Laila was, she came out lacking.

He grunted. No, he had to forget Stacy. Half forcing himself, he laid a hand on Laila's lower back and jerked her closer. She squealed and grinned up at him. Her soft lips parted in invitation to him, and he lowered his head toward hers. Her warm breath met him before her lips touched his. Excitement coursed over his body. He brought the other arm up to cup the back of her head, and he tangled his fingers in her hair. With a vengeance, he kissed her, shoving his tongue into her mouth, and crushing her beneath him. The low howl in her throat matched the one forming in his.

I want Stacy.

He blinked and drew back to stare down into Laila's face. "I..."

"What?" She tried to pull him in again, but he resisted. When he would have turned away, she grabbed his shirt and jerked him around. He'd forgotten how strong a female of his kind was. Stacy, though bold and headstrong, was small and delicate, and he had relished carrying her from the shower after he had washed her. Longing gripped his chest.

Laila seemed to guess at his thoughts. "You're thinking about her, aren't you? You know you can't have her, Nash. Not her and the Alpha position. I know your buddies mated with them, but it will never work in the long term. You know that."

He grumbled. "I know that, damn it. I don't need you reminding me."

She put her hands on her hips. "Apparently, you do need me to remind you because you're standing here thinking about her when you could be fucking me." She moved back a step and ripped the front of her blouse open. She wasn't wearing a bra. Her erect breasts bounced into view, giving him a painful hard-on. He sighed and raised a hand to stroke what she offered him, but he stopped just short of connecting with her warm flesh when his front door banged open and smashed against the wall.

Nash swung around. "What the hell?"

Brant stood in the doorway with Lucas right behind him. Brant scowled seeing what he was doing. "You idiot! I've been calling you for the last four hours."

Nash shrugged. "I turned off my phone and drove all over creation. So what? I needed to clear my head. What's the big deal with smashing my locks just because I wouldn't answer your call? And coming all the way out here was a bit much, don't ya think?" Nash presented his usual smirk to his friends.

Brant stormed across the room and dug a thumb into the soft spot just inside Nash's collar bone. He howled and tried to shove Brant away, but his friend held on. "Fool, you're here with this"—he gestured to Laila and flared his nostrils like he smelled something bad—"when Stacy is God knows where."

Nash stopped struggling against Brant's hold. "What do you mean by that?"

Lucas elbowed past Brant and held up a digital camera. "This." Before Nash could ask for an explanation, Lucas pressed a button, and the tiny device began to play a short clip. No picture was visible, but the sound was crystal clear. The recording was of Stacy yelling and pleading for Kevin to stop hurting her. The unmistakable sound of a whip cracking against skin followed by Stacy's screams of pain ripped the sanity right out of Nash's head.

One roar, one guttural cry of bloody vengeance tore from his throat, and he was fully in his wolf form, charging out of the door.

Chapter Twelve

Nash's nose didn't rise far from the ground for a good forty-five minutes while he hunted. He threw in all of his strength and experience running and chasing down his prey from years of being the beast that he was. He'd find her. He'd find that bastard that dared to put his hands on Stacy, and when he did, Nash was going to tear every inch Kevin's skin from his body. No one had the right to hurt her. Stacy might not be his mate, but he'd be damned if he was going to stand by and let her be abused.

For a moment he had considered why Kevin would do such a thing. From what he knew of Stacy's coworker, he had assumed that the man was in love with Stacy. At least that was the conclusion he had come to when Stacy had told him about the man during that three days they spent together. That is, when they weren't wrapped around each other's bodies.

Remembering their time together, regret rolled over him. Each time he had opened his mouth to share with her about his past and why he didn't believe in love, he'd only shut it again and let her do all the talking. He'd seen the frustration in her eyes at his not opening up like she had been doing, but at the same time, he'd seen how being able to talk to him had a healing affect for her. The relieving of some of the pain in her heart had seemed to have a scent, and he'd picked up on it. At least that's what he'd told himself, because only when a wolf shifter mated could he be so attuned to his partner. There was no other way that he could know Stacy so deeply without biting her.

Lucas darted up beside him, followed by Brant. Both were in their animal form. "You picking up Kevin's scent?" Lucas called out to him while they dodged screaming humans and avoided being hit by cars.

"Yes," Nash bit out. "I know his scent. It was strong at her place when I took her home, and the only other male scent there. We're close. When I get to him, don't stand in my way, Lucas."

His former boss growled. "Don't do anything stupid, Nash. You're an Alpha now. You have to think of your pack above all else. No one must know about our existence. And we never attack humans."

Nash sprinted faster. "He will die. Don't tell me you wouldn't do the same for your mate."

Lucas was silent for a moment. Finally he answered. "I won't kid you. I'd mutilate the bastard if he so much as laid a pinky on Nita. However, you're forgetting that Stacy is not your mate. You haven't bitten her, and unless my eyes deceived me just a while ago, you were about to fuck another woman."

Nash launched himself at Lucas, unable to see him as anything but someone standing in his way of getting to Stacy. Lucas side-stepped him, and Nash missed in his attack. He circled around and came at Lucas again, but his friend slammed a paw across the side of his head and sent him flying into a car tire. Lucas pounced and pinned him down. Nash fought hard and would have gotten loose if Brant didn't come down hard on his chest with sharp teeth bared.

"I'm not your enemy, Nash," Lucas snapped. "Find her and figure out what the hell you want at that time."

Brant began to bark like a regular dog, and Nash glanced around to see several humans staring in their direction. *Fuck.* Some of them might be wondering if they were losing their minds having heard wolves talking with human voices. Nash barked as well, and Lucas followed. Relief slid into the people's expressions as if they were glad it had all been a trick of their imaginations after a long day at the office. They moved away, still leery of the wild animals.

Lucas and Brant climbed off of Nash's chest, and he stood up to sniff the air around them. Kevin was close, and where Kevin was, he would find Stacy. Fifty feet from the location of their fight, they paused in unison at an alley, and Nash didn't hesitate to take the dark entrance. Head low, ears pricked up to catch any sounds, he padded on quiet paws down the narrow passageway.

Brant behind him began to growl. Nash had smelled it too. Blood. Lots of it. When his paw came down in something thick and wet, he knew he'd found what he was looking for. Even in the darkness, he could make out the man's form as if it was twilight. Kevin's sightless eyes stared back at him from the concrete.

"What the hell is going on here?" Lucas demanded.

Nash shook his head. "I don't know, but one thing is for sure. Kevin was murdered by a wolf, and there's no fresh scent of Stacy's anywhere around here. Where is she? Where the hell is Stacy!"

* * * *

Stacy landed on the floor, curled in a ball. She swallowed repeatedly to keep from throwing up at the sharp pain in her wrist. She'd gotten out of the bonds, but in the process had hurt her wrist. She prayed it wasn't sprained, or worse, fractured. Her throat dry, and her heart pounding, she pushed with the other hand up off the floor and then felt around in the dark. This was no time to pause to catch her breath or to feel sorry for herself. Whoever had taken her could come back any second. She had to keep moving.

While she fumbled one tiny step at a time, she tried to recall the last thing that had happened to her before she woke up tied to the bed. The side of the highway. She'd pulled over because she had been freaking out over hurting Kevin…again. And then she had started feeling dizzy, like she couldn't keep her eyes open. Had Kevin slipped her something to make her sleep and then brought her here? Would he do such a low thing? She didn't give him any play like he wanted, so would he go this far? Impossible. She'd known Kevin for years. He might stoop to tricking her or getting a free feel of her ass sometimes, but kidnapping just didn't fit his personality. That boy would be too scared So who then? Who would do such a thing?

Then it hit her. Alphons. She had been talking to him on the phone at the time, and for that matter, she couldn't remember them sleeping together at that motel either. It fit. And then shock and terror took control of her hard. Her fingers had just closed around the bedroom doorknob when the possibility that Alphons might have drugged and raped her hit her mind.

Tears poured down her cheeks, and the nausea she'd fought off minutes ago, returned with a vengeance. Her legs grew weak. She shook her head and covered her mouth while she swayed side-to-side, struggling to remain on her feet. All this time, with Zandrea and Nita's experiences with the shifters, Stacy had thought it was sexy. She'd been happy for her friends but jealous too because she wanted a man. Someone for when loneliness hit or an urge needed to be dealt with. But they were…they were…dangerous. They were animals who took what they wanted, when they wanted it.

Stacy remembered how Lucas was when he first met Nita back at the club. He'd been all over her, and Stacy had to practically beat him off and argue until she was hoarse to make him leave Nita alone. Yet, in the end he'd gotten her. So now what? Alphons wanted her, and she didn't have any say in the matter? What about Nash? No, he didn't want her, and that was for the best. She didn't want anything more to do with any of them. Not Alphons, not Nash, and not even Lucas and Brant. It was a good thing that her friends lived in a different city now. That was best for all of them.

A thunderous crash sounded on the other side of the door. Stacy screamed, turned, and ran across the room blind. She tripped over something and fell flat on her face. Before she could regain her feet, the bedroom door opened, and feet shuffled across the floor. Hands grabbed at her, and she shut her eyes and began to kick and scream. That asshole Alphons wasn't getting any more of her body if she had to dig his eyes out or die fighting him off.

"Stacy!" Nash cried out. "Baby, it's okay. It's me. Calm down. I'm here to take you home."

He tried to take her into his arms, but she kicked harder and swung her fists at him. Pain ricocheted through her sore wrist, but she ignored it. "Don't touch me, animal," she shouted. "Get you filthy hands off me. I hate you. I hate all of you. Don't touch me ever again!"

Chapter Thirteen

Nash sat on the couch in Stacy's apartment, dressed in a pair of slacks, bare feet, and his shirt hanging open. He had slipped into clothes only for the sake of Zandrea and Nita, but he would take them off again soon, so he could hunt down Alphons and end his life.

"What are you going to do?" Lucas said.

"You don't need to ask."

Lucas perched on the edge of the couch and folded his arms over his chest. "I'll go with you when you go. I know you wanted to be sure she was okay. It couldn't have been easy putting her out like that so you could bring her home. You did the right thing."

"Don't patronize me," Nash growled. "I know I had to use a pressure point to get her to sleep so she wouldn't hurt herself. I know she doesn't trust any shifter after all of this. What I don't get is why the bastard faked the beating. He didn't lay a hand on her that we can see, but he went and killed Kevin. What is he up to?"

Zandrea came out of the back room, anger simmering in her dark brown eyes. She almost exuded the aggression of the wolf. More and more she was like them. If he didn't know any better, he'd say she was becoming a wolf shifter. She crossed the room and stopped in front of Nash. Before he could blink, she slapped him hard across the face. "You son of a bitch! Why did you let this happen to her? Why didn't you protect her?"

Nash stood up, crowding her. He was angry, but he wasn't about to hurt her. Brant nearby, still went on the defensive. Nash moved out of reach of Zandrea's hand. "For your information it's not my responsibility to protect her. She's not my mate."

Zandrea shrieked and would have come after him if Brant hadn't caught her around the waist and held her against his body. "I want him found and killed," Zandrea screamed. "Stacy said he raped her. She doesn't remember anything about sleeping with him, but he says they did after the party at a motel. How could she not remember? What did he do to her? Do you hear me, Nash? You'd better *make it* your responsibility and find Alphons and kill him for what he did to Stacy!"

Nash had gone still, as well as his friends. Stacy couldn't remember being intimate with Alphons? He recalled his time with her in detail, how tight she'd been, how perfect. He remembered thinking that even though she wasn't a virgin, she felt like one, and he couldn't believe how good it was being inside her. If Alphons had spent the entire night having sex with her—and being a wolf shifter, he would have—then Stacy would have been sore as hell and definitely *not* tight.

He exchanged glances with Brant and Lucas, and both his friends nodded. Nash crossed the room and entered the bedroom. Behind him, Zandrea was still ranting, and he guessed, still fighting to get free of her mate so she could slap him again. She couldn't cause any real damage, but then he wasn't in the mood for her attitude either. He knew what he needed to do. He knew that even though Stacy wasn't his mate, he'd kill for her in a heartbeat. Beyond that, he would do what he could to protect her.

When he entered the room, he found her lying across the bed, her face buried in a pillow. Nash picked up small sniffling sounds coming from her while Nita rubbed her back.

Nita glanced up when she heard him and gave him the same accusing look. Why did they both blame him as if this was somehow his fault? He felt the same way, but they didn't have a right to. His lips compressed, he could barely push words past them to ask her to leave him alone with Stacy.

"Why should I?" Nita snapped. "She doesn't trust shifters, and if I wasn't mated to Lucas, I wouldn't either. All it's produced is trouble, and poor Stacy doesn't deserve this. What do you want, Nash?"

He neared the bed knowing his face was impassive, not giving a clue to the emotions churning inside him. "That's between Stacy and I. Leave."

"You bas—"

"Honey, come here," Lucas called from the doorway.

Nita gave Nash another harsh look, but without hesitation, she walked to obey her mate, and the two left the room, closing the door behind them. With a sigh, Nash moved to take up the warm spot beside Stacy that Nita had left. He reached a hand out to touch her but changed his mind and drew back. Putting space between them was safer, so he shifted to a chair at the side of the bed.

"Stacy, turn over and talk to me, please."

"You know what you can do for me, Nash," she responded in a muffled voice.

"I want to talk about you sleeping with Alphons."

She sat up. "You cannot be serious! Damn, you men are all the same. Always in competition with each other. Don't want anyone to one up you? Are you worried about me preferring him over you? Well don't worry about it because you dumped me over the phone, remember? Besides, I'm never getting involved with your kind ever again. Got that? Ever!"

He had sat quietly while she ranted, but then he stuck a hand out and grabbed one of her tight fists agitating the blanket around her waist. She had been trembling uncontrollably when he had brought her home, even fully dressed and unconscious. Seeing her that way had torn at him in ways he did not want to explore.

Before he could make contact with her hand, she drew back, and fear filled her eyes. Nash's throat closed with anguish at making her afraid. "Don't," he whispered. "I would never hurt you, Stacy. I promise you that."

She looked away. "Don't make promises you can't keep."

"I don't believe Alphons ever had sex with you."

"What are you talking about?" She would have stood up, but he pushed her back down and jerked his hands from her shoulders when she shuddered. However, she didn't try to rise again. He had to be satisfied with that.

"When we were first together, the experience was..." He did not want to admit how good it was, that he couldn't get the memory out of his head. "You were almost like a virgin, tight...There is no way you had sex with a shifter before me and was not worn out afterward. Remember how you were after you and I were together for one day?"

She gasped. Her eyes widened, and then hope entered the deep chocolate pools. "Do you really think so?"

He nodded. "I do."

She chewed her lip thinking about it, and it was all he could do not to run his tongue over that soft flesh and taste her until he was drunk from her sweetness. How could have told her he wouldn't see her anymore? How could he think he could live with that? Every atom of his being ached to possess her and make her his. He closed his eyes. *No!* He would never take a mate. Not even Stacy.

"But why?"

Her words jerked him out of reverie, and he was grateful for it. "I'm not sure, but I suspect it's because he wants my position. He wanted me to make you my mate, and Alphons strikes me as the kind of wolf that loves it so rough, he would tear his lover. You could never be with me if he damaged your body. Being human, you wouldn't heal so easily."

She shivered. "Are you for real? That's depraved! How could he like hurting his partner?"

Nash shrugged. "It's the animal in us." He narrowed his eyes on her. "The animal in *all* of us shifters."

Some of the usual boldness came back to her expression, and she rolled her eyes at him. "Uh huh, you think I don't know what you're trying to say, Nash? Don't even worry about it. I have never chased after a man, and it's for damn sure, I'm not chasing after you." She stood up and dropped the cover to walk over to the window. Nash had trouble keeping his eyes off her ass. After a few moments, he didn't try but enjoyed the view.

"I wasn't playing when I said I don't want anything to do with any of you. The fact that Alphons never touched me doesn't change that." He thought he caught a small sob before she went on. "He didn't want me, and neither do you. I'm just some kind of tool for shifter games. Whatever. I'm a strong woman, and I can take care of myself. If you didn't come after me, I would have found a way back home on my own."

Nash rose and strode over to stand behind her. He couldn't do it. He couldn't let her think he didn't want her. Thinking that she wasn't desirable had hurt her deeply. He could almost feel the emotions ripping through her. He rested his hands on her shoulders and leaned down to nuzzle her neck, grateful that she didn't flinch or try to move away. "Silly woman, you are the most beautiful creature I've ever laid eyes on. My body comes alive just hearing your voice, and my shaft tightens painfully when I touch you."

He moved in close so their bodies were molded together. "Tell me, does this feel like I don't want you?"

This time she shivered and arched her back so that her ass pushed into his hard-on. He suppressed a howl of need but grinded into her.

"Stacy, I want to be buried so deep inside you that I can't find my way out. I want you to scream my name as I make you come again and again. Do you understand that?" His voice had grown harsh with his control nearly unhinged.

"Y-Yes."

"Don't ever think I don't want you." He turned her in his arms and dragged her tight to his chest. He spoke against her soft lips. "Just because I have decided not to make you my mate does not mean I don't desire you or that I can't get enough of this luscious body. It's incomparable, without a doubt."

A tear rolled down her cheek, and he wiped it away.

"Baby, don't be afraid. I promise. I'll find him and kill him for hurting you."

She didn't meet his eyes but stared straight ahead, her plump lips curved in determination. "I know you will, and I'm not scared anymore. But I want to know one thing, Nash. And I mean it, don't you lie to me."

He stiffened, sensing what she was going to ask. "What's that?"

"Why don't you want a mate? Why don't you believe in love?"

Chapter Fourteen

She watched his eyes drift away, like he was both remembering something from his past and avoiding talking about what his issues were. His hands slid down from her hips to land at his sides, and he turned away. Stacy suppressed a whimper. Just like she told him, she wasn't begging for his attention even though it hurt for him to turn away from her. She thought if she confronted him on the fact that he hadn't shared anything about his past with her, that would make him talk, but apparently not.

"Okay, fine. Whatever, Nash. You can kiss my ass." She moved to walk by him, but he caught her and held her in place. She didn't say a word, buted wait for him to speak.

"I had a mate."

She gasped. "For real? Where is she?"

His face was like stone. "Dead."

Stacy couldn't believe the jealousy that rose up inside her. He still loved this woman, and it was wrong for her to hate that, but she did. She was sorry she had asked and felt like crap for pushing him when it still hurt him so much. "I'm sorry. Just pretend I didn't—"

"She was human." At her expression, he smiled. "Yeah, hard to believe, isn't it? And cruel that fate would hand me another human woman who makes my blood boil?"

Warmth washed over her. So the man wasn't immune to her. She had to admit she liked the sound of that, but he didn't seem like he was going to give in to those feelings any time soon. She wondered if Alphons had suspected as much, had known Nash was stubborn as hell and that it would take him kidnapping Stacy to push Nash to make her his mate as a way to protect her. Stupid. He hadn't counted on Nash not falling in love with her.

Nash could have her body to satisfy his lust, but only love would drive him to make her his mate. Even *she* knew that. Alphons thought he was all that, but he hadn't planned on Nash being this hardcore, or that whatever pain he was still experiencing over his former mate wasn't letting him go so quickly. Figuring it out made Stacy want to cry all over again because it didn't give her any hope either. She had run her mouth talking about she was done with them, but the fact of the matter was, she loved Nash. Fool that she was, she loved his stubborn ass with all her heart.

After some time, Nash went on. "Funny as it might seem, I think I would have handled it all better if she had been killed. I could have moved on and found another mate after some time. But being human and not having our healing ability, Sondra contracted a human disease."

Stacy sank to the bed with a hand over her mouth. She swallowed and then reached to pull him close beside her so she could hold him. He didn't resist, and she kissed his cheek and rubbed his back. "Cancer?"

He nodded. "Pancreatic cancer. I watched her grow weaker with each passing day, and I cared for her until the end. It took everything inside me to let her go and not go with her when she passed. From then on, I decided a smile was all I would ever show to the world. No one would know how losing Sondra had destroyed me. I am still fractured, and nothing could fix that. No *one* could fix that."

Stacy blinked. She dropped her hands to her sides, realizing that he was emphasizing yet again that his heart wasn't open to her. How many times did she need him to rub it in, that she wasn't going to be the one? "I'm sorry. I-I hope you'll find happiness in some small way in your life, Nash. I really do." She moved over a little, putting a foot of space between them.

"You mistake me."

She frowned at him. "What are you talking about?"

He reached out to stroke her cheek. She ached to let herself sway into his touch and resisted closing her eyes to bask in the way it felt to be so close to him. Nash was silent for a moment, and then he heaved a sigh as if he'd come to a decision.

"I'm not going to make you my mate, but if you want, we can be married in the human sense."

"Say what?" She would have moved her face from his hand, but he trapped her in place with both hands.

"I'm asking you to marry me, Stacy."

"In the most unromantic way imaginable! The hell!"

He dropped his hands to her waist and hauled her onto his lap facing him. A hand snaked around her so she couldn't get away. Nash found her lips with his and kissed her until she stopped struggling. She couldn't help herself. Just tasting him was so satisfying and so unsatisfying at the same time. One kiss made her want to do whatever he wanted and to go on kissing him for the rest of her life.

At last he raised his head, and he guided hers to his shoulder. "Physically, we're perfect together. I'm not going to deny that I want you all the time. I'm as much into you as a human man would be, and as much as I can be without biting you. Can't that be enough for us, Stacy? Can't you accept me as your husband and have my children?"

It was all she could do not to cry. "But I want to be loved."

"You said you didn't believe in love anymore than I do. You said after your father…"

She shook her head. "Don't."

"Stacy," he almost pleaded, making her half believe that he loved her somewhere deep in his heart where he didn't recognize it. "Don't deny us the small happiness we could have together for the sake of an antiquated term like 'love'."

"Antiquated?"

He didn't respond. She grumbled. What was she going to say? One minute the man had dumped her. The next he wanted to marry her. Even Zandrea and Nita weren't married yet, and they were popping babies left and right. Brant and Lucas didn't really believe it was necessary as they considered the mating all the bonding that was needed. Funny, an actual marriage offer made Stacy feel cheated somehow.

Then she remembered Alphons. "What about your position? Zandrea said you can't be with a human and keep your job."

Nash smiled. In her emotional state, Stacy wasn't sure if it was genuine or one of his practiced fake ones. "I'll work it out."

"How?"

"Don't worry about it. What's your answer?"

"Damn it, Nash. Give me time to think about this. You don't spring this kind of thing on a woman five minutes after you meet her, especially when you haven't even told her you love her."

He seemed about to explain, but she placed a finger over his lips.

"Don't even. I don't want to hear it again. I know how you feel. You've made it crystal clear. I need time. Can I get that at least?"

He kissed her and lifted her up to sit her on the bed. Another kiss, and he stood up straight in front of her. "Okay, take all the time you need. After my business is done, can I come back here tonight?"

She wanted to tell his ass no, but couldn't resist him. "Yes, I guess. There's an extra key on the hook over the kitchen phone. Used to be Z's. Take that to let yourself in if it's late."

"All right. I'll see you tonight."

"Nash?"

"Hmm?"

"Be safe. Please. I..." She swallowed back the tears.

"I'll be back. I promise."

* * * *

It was after two in the morning when he came back. Stacy lay in bed waiting for him to join her, but he went straight to the bathroom. The moonlight glistened off his pale skin. He was naked, and she knew wherever he'd gone, he'd been in his wolf form. She wondered if he'd found Alphons and if he killed him. She wondered how he would take what she had to say to him. The shower came on, and she shut her eyes, sniffing up the last tears she would ever again let herself cry over Nash.

When he stepped out of the bathroom, she stiffened and waited for him to come to bed. He dried his body and tossed the towel to a chair before climbing up from the bottom of the bed. Hovering over her, he took hold of the sheet spread over her naked body and dragged it downward.

"I know you're awake, baby," he whispered.

"How do you know?"

She guessed that he was grinning in the darkness. "By the sound of your breathing. I also sense your fear. You have nothing to fear from me, Stacy. I promised that I wouldn't hurt you, and I won't. Our time together will be just as good—no better—than it was that first three days."

"Confident, aren't we?" She smirked.

"I'm sure we can please each other."

He pulled her legs apart and gently settled between them. Stacy moaned at the sensation of having him hard against her core but not slipping inside even though she was soaking wet. Instead, he surprised her by threading his fingers with hers at her sides, and he kissed the tip of her nose with a tenderness she had never seen in him. The ache in her chest threatened to choke her, and she was finding the vow not to cry hard to keep.

Nash pushed farther between her legs. His hard shaft pierced her moist center. Stacy gripped his arms, gasping for breath. "Nash," she almost sobbed.

"You're…You're going to leave me, aren't you?" he answered. Before she could say a single word, he pushed into her. She cried out at the intense pleasure, the perfection of being one with him, even if it was destined to be on a physical level only. Nash pumped deep inside her and pulled back. He glided in again, and she felt herself slipping. Muscles in her core clenched in response to his invasion. The man was everything, absolutely everything. How could they not be mated the way this felt, the way she wanted to die for him, die without him.

She grasped her knees and hauled them higher so that if possible she could get him deeper still. Let him possess her, take over and make her scream his name. Let her come until she fainted and couldn't take another second. She even longed to be sore because that meant he'd given her everything he had if not his heart.

Nash pulled free of her body and turned her to her belly. He followed her down to the bed, trapping her beneath his strong length, and he entered her again while he brought his arms around to crush her to him.

"Tell me the truth," he begged while he drove forward. "Tell me, Stacy."

"I love you," she cried out. He drove harder and faster. She whimpered in response. "I need you so much, but I can't. I just can't…"

"Stacy."

She was going to come right now. Hard and so good. "Yes! Please, Nash. Please!"

He filled her, hot and so good she shook all over. His mouth branded her his forever even if they were apart. She cried, and he must have tasted her tears, but he didn't say a word. For the rest of the night, they made love, until Stacy couldn't go on. She collapsed in his arms and fell into a restless sleep.

Chapter Fifteen

"Who is she, boss?" one of Nash's men asked him. He didn't consider these guys friends. They were subordinates in his pack. He was still Alpha, and they did what he said at all times, but he had not allowed anyone to get close to him. He never would again.

"Who is who?" he responded, knowing who Josh was asking about.

Josh nodded toward the sexy African American woman nursing a drink at the bar while she watched couples dance. Nash had known the second she entered the club and hadn't removed his eyes from her since then. He wanted to tell Josh that she was no one, but he didn't want to insult Stacy by saying the words. He wanted to tell Josh to mind his damn business, but he couldn't manage that either. In fact, for a long time now, he couldn't even slap on a smile to hide his feelings. All he could do was remain silent to keep from biting off everyone's head.

After a few moments of deep breathing, he stood up from the stool he occupied. "She's my daughter's mother."

Josh's eyes grew round. "What the hell? I didn't know you had kids."

"Correction. Not *kids*. I have one daughter. Perfect just like her mother. If the elders knew, I'd lose everything, but what do I have? Huh?" He looked at Josh who stood there with a blank expression on his face. "Nothing," Nash told him. "I have absolutely nothing."

Nash strolled across the club's floor, weaving around swaying bodies and avoiding a few advances from women. He came to a stop in front of Stacy and her fiancé, a human who Nash had checked out thoroughly to make sure he was both strong enough to protect her and good for her. The man had passed every test Nash had thrown his way without knowing what Nash was. At last, with reluctance, Nash had accepted him for Stacy, knowing he had no other choice in the matter. Stacy was stubborn. She had put up with his interference only because of their daughter, but she'd laid down the law right from the start. Now Stacy was getting married in three days, and there wasn't anything Nash could do about it.

While he stood over her, she watched him with wide, beautiful eyes that drew him in. "Dance with me," he commanded.

Her fiancé frowned. "Hey, buddy, we put up with you because of Stacy's daughter, but don't push it."

"*Our* daughter," Nash snapped, indicating Stacy and himself. "Mine and hers." He raised an eyebrow at her, and she dropped her palm in his before they stepped onto the dance floor. Nash pulled her close, but she resisted allowing him to crush her small figure to his. His entire body ached to have her under him, longed to be buried to the hilt inside her.

"Don't even go there, Nash. Every few weeks, you get all possessive and interfere with my relationship, and it's not going to work anymore. I'm getting married in three days, and I'm sure you haven't forgotten that."

He sneered. "How could I?"

"Where's the nice guy I used to know? You're all grouchy and mean all the time now."

"He's dead. You killed him."

She gasped and would have jerked out of his arms if he didn't tighten his hold. He was hard as a rock, and with her now molded to his body, he knew she felt it.

"Asshole! Let me go, Nash. It's over, remember? I'm getting married."

"Don't remind me. If you think for one second he'll replace me—"

"Come off of it," she snapped. "You don't give a shit about our daughter, so don't even go down that road again. I'm tired of hearing it, Nash. The same old bull all men spout when they don't want the responsibility, but they don't want any other man taking responsibility either."

"I support the both of you."

She tried for the hundredth time to put distance between them with her hands pressed to his chest, but he wouldn't let go, and she gave up. "Yeah, you give me a check every month. I gave in to your bullying and didn't work for two years, but that's over now. After the wedding, I'm getting another job."

He ignored her declaration of getting a job. She wasn't tossing his daughter in some stupid daycare whether she liked it or not. He was going about all this wrong, but he couldn't think straight. Everything pissed him off, Stacy, her fiancé, his pack. Even Lucas and Brant were riding his ass lately.

The music changed to a faster pace, but Nash's only response was to flip Stacy around so that he could cup her body from behind with his. He wrapped his arms around her, holding her close while he buried his nose in her hair. From the corner of his eye, he caught sight of her fiancé weaving his way through the dancers with a pinched look on his face. Nash narrowed his eyes in Josh's direction, and his subordinate moved without hesitation to head off the jealous lover.

"Why didn't you choose me?" he demanded of Stacy. "If you were going to get married anyway, you could have been with the man you love and not some loser. Because you can't convince me that you've stopped caring about me and that you love him."

She grumbled, struggling against him. "Do you hear yourself? You're so sure of my love for you, but you're blind to what you feel for me."

"What's that supposed to mean?"

She forced enough space between them to put her head back so she could look in his eyes. "You love me, Nash. And that's what hurts me more than anything. You don't care that you love me. You don't care that I love you. You just refuse to risk coming to that point again when you have to lose me. And you would lose me. I can't outlive you not being a shifter. Yes, I would begin to change like Zandrea and Nita are changing, but there's no guarantee that will include age and healing ability. In life no one has those assurances. But all that doesn't mean anything because you're too stupid to realize you're living through that pain of loss right now instead of years from now when we've had a life together."

Nash was stunned. So much so, he forgot to hold onto her, to keep her flat against his chest. She wiggled free and faced him.

"If you won't accept me, Nash, then let me go. Holding on hurts too, and you promised you wouldn't hurt me."

When he didn't respond, she turned and walked away. He reached out to grab for her but pulled back just before his fingers made contact. She was right. He couldn't hold on any longer. He had to let her go.

* * * *

Nash stood like a statue against the wall during Stacy and her husband's reception. He held a cup of punch he didn't remember getting. The only reason he had come was to pick up his daughter. He should have taken her and left so he wouldn't have to see how happy Stacy was and remind himself that she was about to go away on her honeymoon.

By now, he was pretty sure that the elders knew about his little girl, but they hadn't said anything. Probably because he didn't mate with Stacy and because she was marrying a human. They were ready to sweep it under the carpet as long as Nash didn't claim his daughter before the shifter public. They would have a rude awakening, because Nash had every intension of doing just that. It was too late for Stacy, but he would not lose his sweet daughter, not for anyone.

Lucas moved up beside him. "What are you doing, Nash?"

"Nothing."

His friend shook his head. "You're staring at her. You're the fool who let her get away. Now it's too late. Stop tormenting yourself. What you should be focusing on is doubling your efforts to find Alphons. It's been years, and I can't believe he's fallen off the face of the earth."

Nash never took his eyes away from Stacy. She was so damn beautiful in that bright yellow dress that hugged her soft curves. The shade complemented her creamy brown skin to perfection. He longed to run his hands over her hips and to kiss her lips. Instead, that bastard would get that pleasure, the sheer privilege of stripping her out of her clothing until he got to feast his eyes on what should be Nash's.

A growl ripped from his throat. "He's here again."

Lucas gasped. "You're serious?"

"Yes, I got word a couple days ago that he's been spotted in the area. He screwed up when he killed that human who was trying to defend Stacy. Now, he's wanted for murder by the humans and the shifters. He'll never gain an Alpha position. So my guess is he wants revenge even though it's his own fault. He'll make his move, and I'll be ready."

Nash watched Stacy pose with her husband behind her. The two of them stood smiling for the camera while holding the cake knife. His gut turned, and he had just spun away, intending to leave, when the sound of glass shattering filled the reception hall. Nash picked up on the scent right away. He was about to change, when Lucas caught his arm.

"No, there are humans here. We have to do this as we are."

As if in slow motion, Nash watched Alphons come through the window, swipe a clawed hand across Stacy's husband's throat, and then grab Stacy. All thought of protecting their secret fled Nash's mind as he changed, ripping from his shirt, slacks, and shoes, and ran after them.

"Lucas, protect my daughter," he called over his shoulder. In full wolf form, Nash leaped over the body of Stacy's dead husband to follow Alphons and Stacy out the window. This time the bastard wouldn't get away. Nash would kill him, and Stacy would never leave his side again.

Chapter Sixteen

Stacy did a little biting of her own and chomped down hard on Alphons' cheek while he ran with her. He howled, and when he was distracted, she elbowed him in the stomach and ripped out a chunk of his hair.

"Damn it, woman, are you nuts?" he yelled.

"Get your hands off of me, Alphons. I know what you did. I'm not going to end up like Kevin." She tried to take advantage of his loosened hold and get away, but he wasn't going for it. His fingers digging into her arms, he lifted her like she weighed nothing and tossed her upside down over his shoulder.

He doubled his speed, and when Stacy looked back to see where they were going, her heart sank at the sight of the car at the end of the alley they ran down. Nash would never catch them even in his wolf form.

"Don't be stupid, Alphons. Nash will kill you. Put me down now, and you can get away."

He laughed. "Nash, huh? Funny you didn't say a word about your husband. He'd dead, you know."

Guilt hit her hard. Zandrea and Nita had warned her not to do it, not to get married. Both of them knew she didn't love her husband, even as good to her as he was. Back on that club dance floor in Nash's arms, her body had sang, like it had missed its mate and recognized him as Nash, not the man she had said I do to just a couple hours ago. And now, just because she had been selfish, thinking to protect her heart from further damage from Nash's rejection, an innocent man was dead.

Her throat thickened, and she began to cry.

"Oh, now you cry. Save the tears, baby. You'll need them for later. Let Nash come. I want him to watch while I kill his mate. I'm not going to kill him though. No, losing a second mate in his life will be enough to drive him out of his mind."

Stacy gasped. "You knew? About his mate?"

"I do my homework."

They were coming up on the car. This was her last chance to get free before they were too far from Nash. "Anyway, I'm not his mate. Nash never bit me. He bit Laila. In fact, I'm surprised he hasn't taken her completely by now."

If she thought she would bait Alphons talking about Laila since the man seemed never to have let her go, she was wrong. Alphons only laughed and stopped at the car. He tossed her on the ground like a sack of potatoes, and shoved a foot in her stomach to hold her down while he opened the car door. She cried out.

A growl behind them made Alphons swing around with a gun in his hand. Stacy had no idea where it had come from, but he didn't pause for a second. He squeezed off two rounds, and the animal's howl in pain reached her ears in the dim lighting in the night. Stacy knew it was Nash. She cried harder, but she wasn't going to be the weak thing that couldn't defend herself.

With one hand she reached up toward Alphons' crotch, and with the other she grasped his ankle. At the same time she squeezed the mess out of his goods, she sank her teeth in his calve. Alphons screamed. He brought the gun down on her head, but she wouldn't let go. Even when her vision blurred and her head started spinning, she squeezed and bit harder.

Alphons went over onto his back slamming to the ground. Stacy didn't give an inch. She crawled up his body and began to pound at him as hard as she could, her fists flying everywhere since she had no idea how to fight or control them. She thought the gun went spinning away, but she couldn't be sure. Hands came up from behind her, and she twisted to attack whoever it was, but her arms were sealed to her sides.

"It's okay, Stacy. We've got him." It was Brant.

She wiggled to get free. "Where's Nash?"

Brant released her in time for her to turn around and see the wolf she knew was Nash get up from the ground, and with a burst of energy rip Alphons out of the man's hands who was holding onto him. Before she could see the finishing blow, Brant covered her face and forced her head to his chest. Shivering from head to toe, the reality of what she'd just experience finally sank in, and she didn't fight him.

After what seemed like an eternity, more hands were grabbing for her, and Brant let her go. She looked up to find Nash tugging her into his arms. He was naked in his human form, and someone she didn't recognize came up to drop a blanket around him. In the distance, police sirens blared.

"This might be a dark street, people, but it is the city. We need to move. Now," Brant instructed.

Soon, Stacy was on tucked on Nash's lap in the back seat of someone's car. She was relieved to spot her little girl pass the car being held in Lucas' arms. Her baby adored her Uncle Lucas and was not worried about Mommy or Daddy, especially with cake in her hands. On a shaky sigh, Stacy turned back to Nash. He had not taken his eyes off her the entire time.

"Oh no, you were shot, Nash. We have to get to the hospital." She tried to search his body under the blanket.

He shook his head, his face grim. "Don't worry about that. I'll be fine when Lucas takes a look at it." He paused staring at her.

"What is it, Nash?" She wondered if he was thinking of her husband, and guilt washed over her again realizing that she had dismissed him from her mind yet again. She'd have to stay up half the night, she was sure, talking to the police, explaining things. Oh no, she shouldn't have left the scene. What would the human guests say?

As if he guessed her thoughts, Brant glanced in the rearview mirror at her. "Don't worry, Stacy. Lucas will take care of the humans, and we're used to cleaning up messes. I'm sorry about your husband, but I have the feeling it's for the best."

She didn't answer, but Brant's words did settle her mind about how they were going to explain it all. Fear gripped her for what she was getting herself into dealing with the shifters, but in spite of it, she clutched the blanket around Nash and leaned closer to him.

"I'm sorry, Stacy," he whispered in a hoarse voice. She thought he was crying, but when she looked at him, his eyes had gone so dark they looked black.

"Nash?"

"I'm sorry, that I cannot allow you to be apart from me again." With those cryptic words, he came down on her shoulder, and his sharp teeth cut into her skin. Stacy cried out, but didn't pull away. Nash's arms tightened. He moved back an inch and came down again. A second bite. She was his!

Tears flooded her eyes, and she sobbed on his chest while he licked away the small trickle of blood from her wound.

"Stacy?"

She shook all over, and her teeth chattered as she clung to him. "Yes?"

"I love you with all my heart."

About the Author

Tressie Lockwood has always loved books, and she enjoys writing about heroines who are overcoming the trials of life. She writes straight from her heart, reaching out to those who find it hard to be completely themselves no matter what anyone else thinks. She hopes her readers will enjoy her short stories. Visit Tressie on the web at www.tresslock.webs.com.

Also available from Sugar and Spice Press:

Sensual Bites
by Dahlia Rose

Dahlia Rose, bestselling author of "Velvet Leather and Roses" and "Caribbean Blue," brings you love and passion like no other in *Sensual Bites*. A compilation of some of her short stories, including her featured novella "The Lover's Diary" and "Of Gods and One Woman" which heralded a 4.5 review rating from Enchanted Reviews. From a fireman teaching his friend that love lost can be regained again, to a ghost who could only reach out to one man to save her from the abyss, each story in this book will make your heart ache for the possibilities of magic and the sweet desire of falling in love. Dream of happily ever after with Dahlia Rose. Find it in each page of this remarkable book.

Color Blind
by Jordyn Tracey

Loving Jiro - Kiara meets a sexy Japanese man, who at the community center where she teaches art. While Jiro promises if Kiara comes to him, he will never hurt her, he is also used to man-woman relationships from his culture, and Kiara doesn't understand the rules. On top of that, he is a cold-blooded assassin, and refuses to change. How can Kiara love a man as unyielding as Jiro coming from the abusive relationship she leaves behind?

Lakota - Tawni's Native American boyfriend is a male model. He's sexy, rich and devoted to her, but all they do is fight. When Tawni begins dreaming of Lakota with the personality that matches her fantasies, she feels so guilty. To make matters more interesting, Tawni's dream lover calls her his wife, and pleads with her to forgive him for calling her back from the dead! Is it all a dream or is something else going here?

Find these works and more at www.sugarandspicepress.net.

Made in the USA
Lexington, KY
25 July 2011